Breaking Routine

MELISSA TEREZE

Lori,
There is always a second chance for a happy ending!

First Edition January 2021
Published by GPC Publishing

ISBN: 978-1-915242-04-4

Cover Design: May Dawney
Editor: Charlie Knight

Find out more at: www.melissaterezeauthor.com
Follow me on Twitter: @MelissaTereze
Follow me on Instagram: @melissatereze_author

ALSO BY MELISSA TEREZE

Another Love Series

The Arrangement (Book One)

The Call (Book Two)

The Ashforth Series

Playing For Her Heart (Book One)

Holding Her Heart (Book Two)

Other Novels

Mrs Middleton

In Her Arms

Before You Go

Forever Yours

The Heat of Summer

Forget Me Not

More Than A Feeling

Where We Belong: Love Returns

Naked

Co-writes

Teach Me

Titles under L.M Croft (Erotica)

Pieces of Me

Here's to a better 2021…

CHAPTER ONE

HARPER GREY HAD ABSOLUTELY NO IDEA WHAT SHE WAS DOING. IT was a Friday afternoon early January, and she could barely see the road through her windscreen for the relentless rain. Her mum had told her the M6 wouldn't be busy just yet; how wrong she'd been.

Harper just wanted to make it to her destination. Her new home. She wasn't supposed to be making this journey alone; Callie, her supposedly loving and committed partner, should have been with her. But no, Callie was preoccupied with the woman from work. The one she'd been sleeping with.

The radio presenter on *Smooth FM* introduced the next song, Patrick Swayze's *She's Like the Wind*. Harper barked a laugh; this journey couldn't be any more agonising. "She was more like a bloody hurricane, Patrick."

Rather than wallow, Harper changed the station, bopping her head when Little Mix's *Shout out to My Ex* blasted through her speakers. This was definitely more like it.

Her satnav alerted her that she was due to pull off at the next junction; at least the rain wouldn't be so bad off the motorway. She never had been fond of surface water while she was driving 70 m.p.h. with lorries either side of her.

Harper relaxed into her seat, slowing and remaining in the inside lane until she reached her junction. She should be excited—she now owned her first home—but Callie and her infidelity had really put a downer on celebrations. Harper's belongings were already at the new house, the furniture being delivered at the end of next week. So long as she could get her office set up in the spare room, she could live without a couch for another week. Now, she just had to sort through what she owned and what Callie had brought by two weeks ago.

Four years together, an engagement, and Callie decided to sleep with the new intern at the office. Apparently, love was "different" these days. That was Callie's excuse when Harper found the iMessages on their shared iPad.

Instead of owning her actions, Callie told Harper that their relationship was stale, and getting cosy with someone else was supposed to reignite her feelings for Harper. The total opposite had happened. Harper was glad Callie's 'experiment' hadn't produced the expected results. She couldn't abide a cheat, and Callie's excuse for doing so was piss-poor in Harper's book. Harper had never so much as looked at another woman, but Callie? Well, she had an entirely different outlook.

She would *never* take Callie back, but Harper would sort through her things and hand over what was necessary. She didn't intend to hold a grudge; it wouldn't solve anything, and at least this way, she wasn't tied to Callie. The house was solely in Harper's name, and now the reason for that made sense.

She had expected Callie to want her name on the deeds to the house. They'd rented together for 18 months beforehand, so when Harper found the most beautiful home she'd ever seen, it made sense to put their money into something that would one day be theirs. Callie initially jumped at the idea, setting up a viewing just a few days later, and then they made a weekend of it in the town they would hopefully move to. But when they decided to put an offer in several weeks later, Callie started to back out, claiming that work was suddenly kicking her arse. Callie told Harper to buy it if she wanted to, but that she couldn't commit. In one breath, Callie was fearful of losing her job, but in the next, she was looking at a promotion. None of it had made sense to Harper at the time, but to make life easier *and* to ensure they didn't lose out on the house, Harper agreed to be the sole buyer, her parents helping her out with the deposit. She figured they could add Callie to the documents at a later date. How wrong she'd been.

So, here she was, moving 90 miles away from her hometown, not a soul in sight that she knew. But in time, she would find her place. The beauty of working from home meant she could do that from anywhere. And The Lakes was her destination of choice.

You've got this. A new start.

❄

Harper cut the engine on her small, gravelled driveway, just a streetlight across the road illuminating the path to her front door. The house still looked quaint, her eyes drawn to the freshly painted white sash windows. It had been the windows alone that convinced her to put in an offer, the idyllic surroundings only furthering her desire to live in this town.

At the bottom of the hill lay a huge lake. At the top of the hill, a town with coffee houses, gift shops, and a range of restaurants to choose from. That had been what appealed to Callie, but Harper was just happy to live in a place that resembled a postcard from when she was a kid. The Lakes had been the destination when it came to summer holidays over the years, and this year, once the weather picked up, Harper was determined to try her hand at paddleboarding—if she could ever build up the courage.

Then there was the option to follow the various hiking trails with waterfalls and tracks along the way that she could get lost in. Once she turned away from the screen each day, she wanted nature. She wanted fresh air, snowfall in the winter. And from her bedroom window, she could see exactly that. Snow covered hills and mountains, misty mornings as it rose from the lake. Yes, she would likely end up with frostbite given the fact that she wasn't prepared for the elements here, but she would learn…and she would love it.

She exited her car and grabbed her holdall from the boot. This was her final trip here with everything she owned, but since the darkness had already blanketed the town, she would wait until morning to collect the rest from her car. Right now, she wanted a hot shower and a restful sleep. Something she hadn't had in a few weeks.

Whenever she lay her head on her pillow, Callie came to her mind. During the day, it wasn't so bad, but once Harper had time to think, her mind started to wander. Where had she gone wrong? Had she not been a good enough girlfriend and, ultimately, fiancée? Did she not love Callie fully and with everything that she was? Harper knew she had, she would have given up the world for Callie, but something had gotten mixed up along the way.

Callie had strayed, breaking Harper's heart in the process.

And now, she was starting over.

Harper could stand around thinking about what should have been, or she could get herself inside and light the open wood burning fire. Callie wasn't here, she never would be, so thinking about their relationship was wasted. Harper just wanted to move forward and concentrate on herself.

She took her keys from the inside pocket of her coat, grinning with excitement as she slid it into the lock. She made a mental note to have an outside light installed; it was a little too dark on her property for Harper's liking. As she glanced over her shoulder, she realised she had nothing to worry about around here. There wasn't another person in sight.

Harper pushed her shoulder against the door. The lock would need a few squirts of WD40 at some point over the weekend; she didn't want to force it every time she came home from walking in the hills. But with an old place like this, something original, she expected it to need some extra TLC over the winter months. But the summer would surely make up for it.

As she stepped through the door and pressed the light switch in the hall, Harper frowned. Why didn't she have any electricity? She moved further into the living room, the carpet squelching beneath her Vans. Her heart stumbled for a moment. This couldn't be happening.

She took her phone from her pocket, using the torch feature to get a look at what she could. She'd apparently had a leak of some kind, one that had spewed all over the place. She pressed a hand to the carpet on the stairs; thankfully that was dry, so her belongings hadn't been damaged. But downstairs was ruined, and she had no idea why.

"I can't see a bastard thing in here!" Harper didn't want to, but she really could cry right then. What was she supposed to do with no electricity? She certainly had no intentions of tackling the fuse box herself. Not when there had been a substantial leak. She may be stupid in some aspects of her life, but she knew better than to mess with electricity around water.

She had to think. She couldn't stay here tonight, but she also couldn't sleep in her car. Frostbite would be the least of her concerns if someone found her the following morning, dead and frozen in her driver's seat. Dramatic, yes, but Harper really could do without all this tonight.

She pulled up the internet on her phone, sighing when she realised she had no service. The Wi-Fi wasn't going live until tomorrow, but with no electricity, that wouldn't matter.

Harper secured the house and lifted her hold-all from the driveway. There were several B&Bs up the hill, one just a block away. Her only hope this evening was that one of them had space for her. She decided to try the one she'd stayed at twice during trips here with Callie, a gay friendly one they'd found on the Cumbria Pride website. She hadn't thought to specifically seek out somewhere that accepted them, but it was a small town, and neither Harper nor Callie knew whether they would be welcome at a little family run bed and breakfast. But at this B&B, they had been welcomed and really looked after.

Harper trudged up the hill, the ice-cold wind cutting through the skin on her face as she ascended the steep incline. If she hadn't felt so tired from her journey, she would have gone further and headed into the town, but she really didn't have the energy. When she left the motorway, she'd sat in traffic for over forty minutes. And then the rain had been relentless again, leaving her with no option but to drive significantly slower than she would have liked.

This was just a mess.

Relieved when she reached the bed and breakfast she'd stayed at just a few weeks ago, Harper pressed the doorbell, hoping and praying they could fit her in. She remembered the couple who owned it, quiet but very helpful. Jude and…Cait, she thought.

Nothing.

No answer.

As Harper turned to walk back down the small stone path, the outside light flickered on, and Cait's face came into view behind the old wooden door with a huge glass panel sitting in the middle of it.

"Can I help you?" A woman with a soft tone landed in front of her, dark bouncy curls falling into place below the shoulder. They'd met twice before; Cait likely wouldn't remember, but Harper did. She recalled how captivating her eyes had been, inviting and mellow.

Harper shivered, hiking her hold-all further up onto her shoulder. "H-hi. I was wondering if you have a spare room for the night?"

"Oh." Cait paused, stepping out onto the path and looking around. "Where have you come from?"

"Just the next block. I was supposed to be moving into Park Lodge today."

"You're the new owner?"

Harper offered a lopsided smile. "Unfortunately, yes." She

shivered again, causing Cait to take her by the elbow and guide her into the warmth of the B&B. "Oh, wow. That heat feels so nice."

"I only have a single room suite available tonight."

"That's fine. I'll take it. How much?"

"Don't worry about that right now. Go through into the lounge and warm yourself up." Cait's dark eyes softened as she took Harper's hold-all from her shoulder. "Go on. I'll bring you a hot drink. Tea or coffee?"

"Coffee, please." Harper rubbed her hands together, the tips of her fingers icy cold. She really needed to acclimatise to this place, but tonight, she just needed a thick duvet and some rubbish TV. She would probably fall asleep within ten minutes of climbing into bed anyway.

Cait returned a few minutes later, holding a tray with a cafetière and two cups. A porcelain milk jug sat beside them with a jar of brown sugar cubes.

"I know I'm really pushing my luck here, but do you by any chance know an electrician and a plumber?"

"What for?" Cait asked, setting the tray down between them as they took seats on opposite couches.

"When I got to my house tonight, I found I have no electricity. And there's been a leak."

"Oh, no. That's awful." Cait offered a sympathetic smile, pouring two coffees. Harper focused on Cait's delicate hands, her manicured nails. Simplistic, that's how Cait appeared. And friendly. "I have a handyman on my books, if that's any use to you. He's qualified for both your problems. I can give him a call in the morning."

"That would *really* be a massive help. I'd really appreciate it." Harper knew she was asking a lot, but she didn't know where else to turn.

"I'll call him, and we'll get you sorted out. Don't worry."

"You're Cait, right?"

"I…am." She frowned, her brown eyes rich and soft, just like chocolate.

"Sorry. I've stayed here twice in the last few months. I was here with my girlfriend in room five for the weekend about a month ago."

"I knew I recognised you. I was wracking my brains in the kitchen trying to figure out how."

She recognised me? Harper punched that thought from her mind. Cait had a husband.

"We were here while we finalised the details on the house."

"She's not with you tonight?"

Harper sighed. "No. We broke up. But it's fine, I'm still doing this. That house is far too beautiful to give up."

"Park Lodge is something else. We considered buying it and opening another B&B, but it deserved a real chance at a happy ending. I didn't want to go in there and destroy the interior with walls and en suites."

"Well, thank you. I'm glad you didn't." Harper smiled, taking a cup of coffee from the tray. "And thanks for fitting me in. I considered sleeping in my car, but the weather is awful."

"I won't have you sleeping in a car. Not when I have a perfectly good room upstairs for you. With breakfast in the morning."

Harper blushed when Cait smiled in her direction. She had no idea why. "Oh, don't worry about me. I just need a place to crash for the night."

"Your house will need to dry out. I'll book you in for a couple of weeks, and if anything changes, you just let me know. And since you've been here before, I'll discount your stay."

"That's really kind of you."

"You're about to become our neighbour. And around here, we help one another out."

"Well, thanks."

"Come on. I'll show you to your room, and you can get settled in. The rest can wait for another day."

Warmth spread through Harper as she followed Cait up the stairs. The B&B was cosy, homely, but she really wished she were settling into her own place this evening. But Cait was right, staying here was the best option. "Oh, I'm Harper, by the way."

Cait beamed as she stopped halfway up the stairs and turned around. "It's really nice to meet you, Harper."

CHAPTER TWO

Cait pulled her woolly hat from her head, stepping through the door of the B&B with a wad of newspapers under her arm. Guests didn't always pick them up, the internet seemed to be preferred these days, but she liked to have the option available. Jude would read them if nobody else did.

She removed the snip from the back of the door; the B&B wasn't open to the public just yet. Cait and Jude had become an unintentional tourist information centre over the years, but Cait had come to enjoy pointing people in the right direction. If it meant tourists could "stumble" upon an unexpected trail, it made it all worthwhile.

The sound of footsteps on the landing caught Cait's attention as she added the newspapers to the rack in the lounge, the local station playing on the radio on the windowsill. She poked her head around the door, a flash of rich auburn hair in her line of sight. *Wow, she's pretty.* Harper was slightly taller than Cait, perhaps an inch or two, but that was the perfect height, you know? The ideal ratio for hugs…or the likes of.

"Hey, mornin'," Harper said, zipping her hoodie up as she reached the hallway. "Could I scrounge a cup of coffee before I see what the damage is at home?"

Cait reached for a piece of laminated card. "Here. Pick breakfast, too."

"Cait, it's really okay."

Cait didn't know why Harper felt as though she was putting her out. It was her job to be on hand. "Please."

"I'll just have some toast." Harper perused the menu. "Oh, my God. Eggy bread?"

Cait offered a full smile. "My favourite. Not many order it, but my parents used to make it every Sunday when I was a kid. It reminds me of better times. Happier times."

Harper blew out a breath. "I could really use a reminder of better times."

Cait noted the pain behind Harper's vivid blue eyes. "If you can't remember them, you create them. And living here is very good for starting over."

"I'll take your word for it." Harper handed over the menu. "And a helping of eggy bread…if there's any going begging."

"Absolutely. Follow me."

❄

"I THOUGHT she didn't want breakfast?" Jude frowned, disposing of a scrap of bacon from a guest's plate. "This is why we tell guests we need breakfast orders by 7 the night before."

"It's a few slices of bread and a couple of eggs."

"So?"

Cait spun around, sighing. "So, since you're in a mood *again*, you can put some extra bacon on the grill for me, too."

"She hasn't even paid for her room yet."

"Jude," Cait warned, pointing a spatula at him.

"Don't *Jude* me! She will probably take off without paying."

"Of course. And I'll have to chase her an entire block to get it from her. Do you have any idea how ridiculous *and* miserable you sound?"

"I just…I think you forget that this is a business."

Cait's eyebrows shot up with surprise. Had Jude really said that? "Since I'm the one who hasn't been out with friends for six months or dated in years, it's hard *to* forget."

"Sorry," Jude said, opening a fresh packet of bacon. "Why don't you arrange a girl's night out for next weekend, and I'll be on call?"

"Really?" Cait's entire body buzzed. She'd missed so many nights out lately. Tourism and staycations had her working seven days a week. By the time she got upstairs each evening, she didn't have the energy to even watch TV let alone head into town. It was the same routine every night. Shower, then bed. "I'll call around. See who can make it."

"You deserve a night off."

And she did. Jude had never been as on the ball as she was when it came to the B&B. Cait had to be sure everything was how it was supposed to be, but Jude? He buggered off down the pub with his mates on a Friday night. Saturday too if he could get away with it. Then there were football games, golf, and anything else he could use as an excuse to not work.

"So, do you have any bacon ready?" Cait plated up two lots of eggy bread, offering Jude a flutter of her eyelashes as she spied crispy bacon ready and waiting to the side of the grill.

"That…was mine."

"And what do we always say?"

Jude clenched his jaw, his nostrils flaring. "It's all about the guest experience."

"Amen, brother." Cait took a pair of clean tongs from the dishwasher, helping herself to the bacon Jude was keeping for himself. "Now, I'm sitting down with our new guest for breakfast while trying to keep her sane and not worrying about her house issues."

"Sure you are."

Cait froze, turning back to face Jude. "What's that supposed to mean?"

"Nothing. You just seem really giddy this morning. You know, since our guest arrived."

"Don't be ridiculous." Cait would admit that she found Harper interesting, those blue eyes had pulled her in the moment she stepped outside the B&B last night. But sitting down to breakfast with Harper really didn't mean anything. Cait wasn't that stupid. Harper was way out of her league.

Jude eyed Cait. "You can't say she's not easy on the eye. And you said she was here with her girlfriend last time, so we both know she bats for your team."

"Bats for my team? It's not 1998, Jude. Nobody says that anymore."

"Deflecting." He waved a spatula in the air, laughing. "Just... don't go out there fluttering your eyelashes like you did to me. I don't want to have to come looking for you to find you in a compromising position. No thanks."

"Charming."

Cait's belly fluttered. Did Jude offering to stay home and on call next week mean that he wanted her to get out there and look for someone she could spend her time with? *What time?* Cait laughed, shaking her head. She didn't know what "time to herself" was anymore. She hadn't done for as long as she could remember.

Harper sat at a table in the corner of the breakfast room, her eyes glued to her phone. Cait didn't know whether she should turn around and leave Harper in peace, or whether she should do her job and provide breakfast.

Have I been giddy? No, she hadn't. She had merely been herself. Something Jude didn't see often because he was never around for breakfast. The only reason he was here this morning was because the young lad Cait employed had broken down on the way into the town. It also explained his mood. God forbid he should help out with the business he part owned.

Cait cleared her throat, stepping up to the table Harper sat at.

"Eggy bread. And I've thrown some bacon on too for good measure."

"Yes. My kinda woman." Harper's eyes widened, and she held up her hands. "Sorry, I didn't mean…you know. I just love bacon."

Cait understood. She wasn't sure she'd ever be *anyone's* kinda woman. But she could live in hope.

"You love bacon. Got it." Cait studied Harper, satisfied that she wouldn't be rejected if she joined her for breakfast. "Would you mind if I shared this table with you?"

"No, of course not. Take a seat. At least when I call my mum to tell her everything has gone pear-shaped at the house, I can also reassure her that the people here are lovely and haven't left me to fend for myself."

"I called my handyman before I left this morning. He's getting here for midday."

"Wow. That was quick."

"Well, I'm sure you want to get into your new home and get everything set up. It's a beautiful house."

"Yeah." Harper slumped her shoulders. "It feels like it's not going to work out for me. The place is far too big for one person, but I can't bring myself to let it go. I really want it to work here."

"Do you have a job lined up?"

"I work from home. Graphic design."

"Oh, well that makes life easier for you while you're here, I suppose. If you need any extra space while you're staying with us, just let me know, and as soon as a bigger room is available, I'll swap you."

"Cait, you don't have to do that." Harper reached her hand forward, stopping mid-air before it rested on Cait's. And then she pulled it back completely, clearing her throat. "Sorry."

"I want to. Things are beginning to slow down here, so I expect a few empty rooms for a number of weeks now. The Christmas and New Year period are settling down, and the weather isn't great, so that means I can have five minutes to myself…and spare rooms."

Harper glanced around the breakfast room, frowning. "I haven't seen your husband this morning. Is he not working today? It seems kinda busy for you to be on your own."

"My…husband?"

"Yeah. The guy who is always around here. Jude. We met him last time."

"Christ, if Jude was my husband, I'd have lost the will to live by now."

Harper wasn't the first to assume Cait was married to Jude, but Cait was slightly disappointed that Harper's gaydar wasn't going off around her. Perhaps she should work on that.

Harper blushed. "Sorry. That's what I get for assuming and being nosey."

"Jude is my brother. We've co-owned for 5 years, but I think he forgets that fact a lot of the time."

Harper offered a lopsided smile, sympathy in her blue eyes. "Let's you get on with everything here?"

"Yes, but he's great. When he's around."

"Well," Harper paused, picking up her cutlery and tucking into the eggy bread, "I think you've done a great job. This place is so cosy and welcoming. I was dreading being turned away last night."

"I'm happy you enjoyed it enough to consider us this time around." When people came back, it meant a lot to Cait. There was no shortage of B&B's on the main road that ran from the town to the lake; she knew competition was rife.

"We found you on the Cumbria Pride website. Callie wanted somewhere that we could be ourselves, so thanks for having a gay friendly B&B."

"It's important." Cait followed Harper's lead, enjoying her breakfast without interruption from guests. "Before we took on this B&B, I was on a short break elsewhere with an ex of mine. And while we didn't feel completely alienated, we did get those looks. You know…are they together, aren't they? Are they best friends? Did we want separate rooms?"

"God, I hate that." Harper shook her head, moaning in delight as she demolished her breakfast. If she was surprised by Cait's 'coming out', she certainly didn't show it. "This is so good, by the way." She helped herself to the coffee in the cafetiere already on the table, offering Cait a cup. Cait smiled and nodded. "Why do people do that? I mean, I love to people-watch, but I don't sit there wondering if they're going to bed with one another at the end of the day."

"I don't know. I suppose some people are just inquisitive."

"Nosey, you mean?"

Cait laughed, lifting her coffee cup. "Or that. Yes."

Harper lowered her fork, leaning in closer to Cait and lowering her voice as she said, "So, where are all the lesbians?"

Cait snorted. "Not here." She really had wondered over the years if anyone significant would come into her life, but at 41, she was still single, still looking, and still depressed at the thought of never growing old with someone. "But don't take my word for it. My life revolves around this place, so it's not often I get the chance to even look around."

"I think you need to give yourself a day off," Harper said, smiling as she relaxed back. "You never know what's out there. This time next year you could have just spent Christmas with the love of your life."

"Mm. I think I'll settle for some friendly company. It doesn't bring as much drama with it."

Harper took her phone from the table, pushing her seat away and getting to her feet. "You could be on to something there. I was willing to share a house with a woman who'd been cheating on me for several months. Single may just be the answer to a happier life."

Cait's heart sunk. Was being in a relationship these days so bad? Harper believed so, but she had just been through a breakup. Cait was ready to explore. She was also ready to put her foot down with Jude. If she were ever going to have a life outside of the B&B, he would have to step up and take ownership of something. Anything.

"Thank you for breakfast, but I need to get to the house. Can I come and find you when I get back later to sort out payment for the room?"

Cait smiled. "Of course."

CHAPTER THREE

"OKAY, LOVE. ALL FIXED." DARREN, THE HANDYMAN, CAME FROM the kitchen. "You had a burst pipe. I'll come back in a couple of days to fix the electrics. It's pretty damp down here."

"I thought it would be a pipe, but I haven't been here, so I don't know how it happened."

"Did you have the heating set to come on? It was the radiator in the kitchen."

"No, not that I'm aware of."

Harper leant against the windowsill, folding her arms across her chest. They'd had a new thermostat installed the last time they were here, but Callie had set it so that the pipes remained at 5 degrees at all times when the heating was off. It was a new feature to prevent burst pipes during cold snaps and lack of use. Harper had turned the heating on for a few hours a couple of days ago via the app on her phone, but she hadn't played with any of the settings.

"Huh. That's odd."

"Well, it's fixed now so that's the main thing," Harper said, running a hand down her face. "What's the damage? And do you prefer cash or transfer?"

"That's already taken care of." Darren opened the front door, his toolbox in one hand. "But Cait loves the Mediterranean restaurant on the lake if you wanted to thank her. She won't take any money from you, so that's the next best thing."

Harper offered an appreciative smile. Cait likely wouldn't want to go to dinner with her, she was a busy woman, but it was something she could consider. She'd certainly been good company this morning during breakfast. "Good to know. I'll look into booking a table."

"She'll look after you around here. She's a bloody saint."

"Yes, she is. I'd have been lost without her last night."

"I'm sure she'll need a hand with something at some point. We all work together around here to keep one another happy."

"It's a nice area. It's just a shame this happened."

"You'll be fine. Cait spoke very highly of you this morning. And you've been here before, so give it a little time and you'll know plenty of friendly faces."

"Well, uh…thanks." Harper avoided the frown she was almost wearing; Darren didn't need to know she was confused about anything he'd just said. Cait spoke highly of her? Why? "I'll book that table. And thanks for your help, too. You're not a carpet fitter by any chance, are you?"

"Ask Cait to give me a call once you've ordered a new one. I'll fit it for you."

"Oh, I was actually joking, but that would be really helpful." Harper felt another weight lift as Darren smiled over his shoulder, waving as he made his way up the hill.

She really did have to thank Cait, but she wasn't sure a meal on the lake would cut it. If it hadn't been for the wonderful B&B owner or her approachable nature, Harper really would be up shit creek without a paddle.

Harper took the stairs two at a time, rushing into her bedroom. She'd brought her laptop up here when she arrived this morning, not wanting to place it down somewhere that was soaked. And downstairs, she didn't have many options when it came to a dry spot. She could set up home on top of the kitchen units, but something told her that wasn't ideal right now.

She hooked her laptop up to the hotspot on her phone and brought up local florists in the area. Flowers always made someone smile, right? Harper wouldn't know; Callie rarely did anything remotely romantic.

Whoa. No romance going on here.

Harper suddenly stopped what she was doing. Would Cait think she was trying to get her into bed now that she knew she wasn't married to the guy she worked with? Surely not. Flowers were sent by people for all kinds of reasons. Births, deaths, special occasions. And this *was* a special occasion because Cait had really pulled Harper out of the shit this morning. And yeah, Cait was gorgeous, too.

Harper sat for a moment, chewing her lip. *It's just a thank you.* Or was it something more, deep down in Harper's subconscious? She had caught herself staring once or twice this morning. Hell, she'd almost held Cait's hand.

Way too good for you. She shook her head and snorted. "Get real and get a grip."

She ordered an arrangement to be delivered this afternoon, leaving a note attached that read: *You're a saint.* Yes, they may have been Darren's words, but they were spot on when it came to describing Cait. Now, Harper just had to call her ex before she tackled the dripping wet carpet downstairs.

She tapped in a familiar number, waiting for the call to connect.

"Harper?"

"Hey, can you talk for a few minutes?" Harper flopped onto the edge of her bed, a headache fast approaching.

"If you're quick, yes. I have to get to work."

Harper turned her watch towards her. "It's almost 2 in the afternoon. Shouldn't you be there already?"

"Late night..."

Yep. Harper didn't need to know that. But she was sure Callie was grinning on the other end of the phone.

"Well, uh…I just wanted to let you know that it'll be a few more days before I can sort out your stuff. I've had a few issues since I got here last ni—" Harper frowned, spying a bra on the floor under a bucket seat she'd placed under the window. She'd had the seat reupholstered a few months ago, whacky colours and patterns now adorning it. She really loved it, but she didn't love what was underneath it. "You've been here!"

"Of course I've been there. Several times with you." Callie scoffed, the sound of her heels clicking in the background.

"No, no, no. You've been here with *her*."

Callie fell silent, her heels too.

"When?"

"Harper—"

"No, I want to know when!" Harper got to her feet, taking the bra from the floor. It definitely didn't belong to Callie unless she'd had a drastic breast reduction that Harper didn't know about. "Y-You've been here with her and I want to know when, and why!"

"L-last weekend," Callie said, her voice barely audible.

Harper turned around, pulling back the covers on the bed. She'd thought she was doing the right thing by setting up the bedroom when they came by last time so at least they would have had somewhere to crash as soon as they moved in. And, until now, her bedroom had been her sanctuary.

"And you've had her in my fucking bed!"

"Oh, calm down. I just wanted to show her around. We couldn't book a weekend away anywhere, so I thought the house was the next best thing."

"The house? The house that *I* own. The house that *you* lost out on the chance to live in because you've been fucking her behind my back. That house?"

"We only stayed one night. I thought I'd be pushing it if I stayed any longer."

"Oh, well that makes it all okay then, I suppose." Harper's

eyes burned, tears threatening to spill out at any moment. It was one thing to be cheated on by the woman you were engaged to but to find out that she'd brought her new girlfriend to the house that was supposed to be for both of you…that really fucking stung. Way down deep in her stomach. Callie had already broken her heart; this was the final punch in the gut.

"Look, I'll come up next weekend and sort my own things. You don't have to do it."

"No, I don't. But I will. And I'll do it right now, so you better move your fucking arse and get up here to collect them."

"Harper, calm down. Leave them in the spare room."

Harper was sick to death of Callie having it all her way. She was more than done with it all. "Nope, doesn't work for me. They'll be in the garden by the end of the day. And it's forecasted to rain, so I'd leave now if I were you."

"I can't get there now. I have to work."

"Not my problem." And then it hit Harper. "Did you put the heating on while you were here?"

"Of course I did. It was freezing."

"So, not only have you fucked that woman in my bed, you've caused a leak."

"What?"

"The heating. You knocked the setting off to stop the pipes from freezing. I got here last night to find they'd burst downstairs."

"Shit."

"Yeah, shit." Harper clenched her jaw, pinching the bridge of her nose. "Drop the keys you have at my mums. I don't want you in this house ever again. Your shit will be in the garden. Bring that bitch with you. You'll need the help."

"Harp—"

Harper cut the call, bile rising in her throat. She rushed into the en suite bathroom, emptying the contents of her stomach into the toilet. *Wow.* The pain she felt was intense, but it was the anxiety of knowing another woman had been in her bed that really tipped Harper over the edge. She'd been quite content with remaining amicable with Callie, there was no use in being hostile and bitchy, but Callie really had just changed that entirely. If she wanted to treat Harper as though she was something she'd just stepped in, Harper could play that game too. She wouldn't allow Callie to have the last laugh. Not in this lifetime.

Making herself look a little more presentable, Harper rushed out of the bathroom and grabbed her laptop from the bed. She couldn't do anything about her puffy eyes, but she could hold her head high knowing she would never treat someone she loved as though she didn't matter. Cheating was one thing but to bring that same woman to the house of the woman you'd cheated on… that was low.

Checking she had the keys to her room at the B&B, she grabbed her set of keys for the house and rushed out onto the driveway. She had so much to do, carpets to rip up and replace, plus gathering Callie's belongings, but the thought of staying in the house a moment longer had Harper wanting to heave into the nearest toilet again.

She hurried up the hill towards the B&B, her calves burning as she crossed the small road as fast as she could. The cold air felt good against her flushed skin, but she needed to be inside in the warmth of Cait's B&B. She felt safe there. *Cait makes me feel safe, not the building.*

"Hi." Cait met Harper at the door, a beaming smile on her soft features. "Darren says you're all sorted at home."

"I, uh…yeah. Burst pipe." Harper sidestepped Cait, her shoulders sagging as she reached the staircase. Just one flight, and she would be locked away. "Thanks again," she mumbled over her shoulder, taking the stairs two at a time. *Don't be so rude. She's done a lot for you already.* "I'm sorry." Harper sighed as she turned around on the stairs. "But I need to take care of some things. Have a nice day."

Cait simply nodded, that pretty smile on her mouth.

Harper heard Jude's voice in the hallway; he didn't sound

happy, but Cait could run rings around her brother. She seemed like the kind of woman who had everything under control. So Harper slipped inside her room, closed the door, and sunk to the floor against it.

God, I must have really fucked up in a previous life.

The sound of sudden heavy footsteps came closer on the landing, a pounding on the door sending Harper's heart rate through the roof. She quickly got to her feet, wiping a stray tear from her jaw, and opened the door. Jude stood on the other side. "Oh, hi."

"Payment or you have to leave."

Harper frowned. The vein throbbing at the side of Jude's forehead didn't look too healthy. "Okay, um..."

"This isn't a hostel." He folded his arms across his chest. "Payment. Or out."

Harper bit back a sob; she really wished people would stop yelling. At her and around her.

"Can I just find my wallet?" Harper's voice trembled. "It's here somewhere."

"Ah, that's a good one. Lost it, have you?"

Why did Jude think Harper was dishonest? She'd never lied or cheated her way out of anything in life. She wasn't about to start doing so at the age of 30. She had money, plenty actually; her life just seemed to be up the wall since she arrived. Whatever was going on, she certainly hadn't tried to get out of paying.

"No. It's in this room."

Before Harper had time to think, Cait was standing behind her brother. God, this was humiliating. "What the hell is going on?"

"I'm waiting for our guest to pay for the room."

"I've told you I'll sort it out this evening. What's your problem?"

"My problem is that I'm not happy with her staying here until she pays up. You wouldn't do this for any other guest, and she's no different."

"Jude..." Cait, even in her anger, had the softest of voices. She was nothing like her brother.

Harper found her wallet, grabbing it from beneath the hold-all that sat at the foot of the bed. She removed her bank card, her hands shaking as she handed it over to Jude. "H-here."

Jude snatched it from her, shoving it into the end of the wireless card machine he held.

"You know, you don't have to be so aggressive," Harper said, wiping her cheeks once again. "I'm not here for a free ride. And I certainly haven't done anything to warrant you treating me like I've done something wrong."

"Mm." Jude pursed his lips. "How many nights will you be staying? So I can take payment now."

"Just last night. I'll get my stuff together now and get out of your way." She really didn't want to leave the B&B right now, but she couldn't help but feel unwelcome. *Very* unwelcome.

Jude snarled. "As you wish."

❄

CAIT STOOD outside Harper's room, the door closed as she stared dumbfounded. Jude had a lot to answer for, but Cait couldn't bring her feet to move. She could hear Harper sobbing behind the door, but Cait knew it wasn't her place to console her. They didn't know one another; it would be overstepping.

Cait rushed across the landing, almost losing her footing as she caught the toe of her boot on the carpet. She could hear Jude up in the office, the printer whirring to life, but she couldn't even look at him. Unless she planned to throttle him, she really shouldn't go up those stairs. But her feet kept moving in the direction of her brother.

He sat at the desk, the spot Cait usually sat at because he was never around, his eyes focused solely on the computer screen.

"What was that?"

Jude eyed Cait, scoffing. "Well, someone has to run this place. Since you just give guests free rooms whenever it suits you."

"I wasn't giving her a free room, and even if I was, it's got nothing to do with you."

"This is my business, too!"

"Oh, is it? All of a sudden, you're taking centre role?"

Jude straightened his back. "I am. Yes."

"Great. That means I can have a life outside of this place." Cait pushed off the doorframe. "I'm taking the rest of the day off. Tonight too, and I'll work the afternoon tomorrow. You can take care of breakfast."

"What?" Jude's eyes widened. "I have plans tonight."

"Wrong. *I* have plans." Cait stepped into the office, clearing her throat. "And don't ever speak to a guest like that again. The way you've just treated Harper was disgusting."

"She wasn't willing to pay."

"She was. I'm the one who told her there was no rush for payment. She showed up last night and asked me for a price. And she said she'd come to find me this afternoon to pay for her room. But you go in there like a bat out of hell and treat her like a squatter. How fucking dare you, Jude!"

Jude lifted his hand. "Go away."

"Go away? That's all you have to say after the way you just behaved? You know you're in the wrong; you're an embarrassment!"

Cait shot down the stairs, running directly into Harper as she left her room. Their bodies collided with an oomph; Harper startled as she looked up at Cait gripping her upper arms. But it was the tingle throughout Cait's body that she focused on. The warmth of Harper against her as they held one another, time suspended as it slowed around them.

"Sorry," Harper whispered, quickly unravelling herself from Cait. "Thanks for the room. Bye, Cait."

"Don't go." Cait reached out, closing her hand around soft fingers.

"I'm going home. It's fine. I need to get the carpets up anyway."

Cait realised she'd held Harper's hand for too long. But Harper didn't seem to be in a rush to remind her of that. Instead, Harper looked back at her with those heavenly deep blue eyes. "But you have nothing there. How are you supposed to sit down with dinner tonight?" She let go reluctantly.

"I'll go to the chip shop later." Harper took the stairs slowly, Cait following behind.

Robert, the local florist, waited in the hallway, a huge arrangement of flowers in his grip. "Well, if it isn't the lovely Cait. I have a delivery for you. Which makes a nice change. I can't recall the last time some lucky bugger had the chance to send *you* flowers."

"For me?" Cait asked, frowning.

"For you. Ordered today." Rob thrust the arrangement towards her, offering the screen of his phone so she could sign her name. "How are you? Keeping well?"

"Great," Cait lied. "Sandra?"

"Sandra is well. She's holding down the fort while I bring these to you. I should get back."

"Thanks, Rob. See you around." Cait brought the flowers up to her nose, smiling as she inhaled the fresh scent. She'd never seen an arrangement quite like it; they were truly beautiful. And so colourful. "Wow." She plucked the card from them, and her forehead creased.

You're a saint!

Who the hell would send her flowers with a note like that? As she turned to rush out after Rob—this had to be a mistake—Harper caught her wrist. That single touch ignited something inside Cait. A new sensation she didn't recall ever feeling before. "They're from me, if that's what you were wondering."

"Oh." Cait's insides fizzed. Harper was delightful. Which made this all the more awkward, and, in some ways, painful. After how Jude had just spoken to Harper, Cait was struggling to look her in the eye. Cait didn't want her to leave. She wanted Harper to remain here where she could see her daily…multiple times. But Cait understood how Harper must be feeling. Jude was obnoxious.

"Just a thank you for your help last night and this morning." Harper hauled her bag up on her shoulder, her laptop under her arm, and stepped outside. "See you around, Cait."

CHAPTER FOUR

THE LAST OF THE LIGHT REALLY HAD DISAPPEARED FOR THE DAY, leaving Harper sitting in a darkened bedroom, her back to her bed. She couldn't bring herself to get in it. Her laptop was showing she had 30% battery left, her phone wouldn't survive the night, and she was surrounded by the few candles she'd packed and thankfully brought up with her bedroom furniture. Her fingertips ached; it really was cold this evening.

This move, so far, was a complete disaster.

Harper had changed her mind when she arrived at the house around two hours ago, deciding that she would text Callie and ask her to come for her things another day. She wouldn't have it sorted through in time, and the less trips her ex made here, the better.

She'd also managed to evade her mother's calls and questions this afternoon. Harper had texted and explained that she was busy settling in, something her mum thankfully believed. If she'd heard her mum's voice, Harper would have broken down and that would have been the end of the world for them both. Katherine would have been on her way to her daughter's house without a second thought. And while Harper would love to see her mum right now, she was already feeling homesick enough.

She closed her laptop; she would need the last of the battery this evening to surf the internet. She was already bored to tears with no electricity or living room, but it would all come good in the end. It had to.

She'd considered calling around the other B&Bs for a room for the night, but Harper knew how close everyone was around here. Jude had likely already called them and told them all to turn away the red haired, blue eyed squatter who was prowling the area. And right now, Harper couldn't deal with that rejection. She felt embarrassed enough.

She wanted to see Cait, to explain she wasn't anything her brother thought, but Harper was truly devastated. The last thing she needed was the town to think she was here to cause trouble. And if Cait *did* believe anything Jude thought, Harper would be truly devastated. Because in some ways, Harper wanted Cait to see what she was capable of. To be impressed with the woman she was.

Callie wasn't impressed with anything. You're out of your mind if you think someone like Cait could be. Failure!

A light knock on the door had Harper wary. If it was Callie, she would curl into a ball and die. And if it was Callie with whatever her name was, that would just tip this entire day onto its head.

She used the torch on her phone to make her way out onto the landing, peering around the corner and looking down the stairs. She could see a head of dark hair and a bobble hat, but she couldn't make out any features.

Harper descended the stairs, her knees weakening as she reached for the lock on the door. The body on the step turned around; it was Cait. Thank God. She could deal with Cait, but she couldn't deal with her ex. Emotion wasn't on the agenda tonight.

"Hi, sorry. I didn't know who it was."

"Well, maybe if you put some lights on..."

Harper smiled weakly. "I don't have any. Darren is coming

back in a couple of days to do the electrics. He said it was too wet at the minute."

"So, you're sitting in a dark house with no electricity?"

Harper shrugged. "I found some candles."

"And what about food? Drink? The ability to shower?"

Harper loved the concern Cait possessed for her, but she didn't need to trouble herself with those worries. Everything would iron itself out soon.

"I haven't ventured out yet. I can't see what clothes I'm picking out, and it's really cold tonight."

Cait stepped closer to the door, removing her hat. "Can I come in?"

"You'll have to come upstairs. I'm huddled away on the floor in my bedroom." Harper stepped aside, the warmth from Cait's body welcome this evening. "I'd offer you a drink, but well…"

"Harper, about before." Cait turned, devastation in her brown eyes. "Jude was way out of line. I'm so sorry."

"He doesn't like me, I don't think. But you've been lovely, so you don't need to apologise. Especially not on behalf of someone else."

"I've taken the night off work. He got the shock of his life and had to cancel his plans, but I've just left for the evening, and I honestly have no idea where to go."

"Maybe you could visit some friends?"

Cait lowered her eyes, toying with the hat in her hands. "I was thinking of walking down to the lake and getting some dinner. I've called around a few of the girls but it's too short notice. Next week I have plans with them if Jude doesn't do a disappearing act because I walked out this evening."

"For a business partner, he's kinda shit."

Cait nodded as she lifted her head. "He is. But that's not why I'm here."

"Okay." Harper truly had no idea why Cait *was* here. It wasn't exactly warm and inviting.

"Would you like to come into town and have dinner with me?"

Harper immediately wanted to say yes. It would be considerably warmer wherever she went. But Cait surely had better things to do than sit eating dinner with her.

"Come on. I finally have a night off for the first time in…six months. And I'd love it if you joined me."

"Six months?"

Wow. Jude really was a dick.

But then Harper felt a swell of appreciation that Cait had even considered her to spend the evening with. She could get some good food inside her and then sleep this god-awful day away. What was left of it anyway. And she could get to know Cait better. What else could she ask for?

"So, will you join me?" Cait looked like a nervous wreck. But Harper could use the company. And since Cait had escaped the B&B tonight, with neither of them having anything to do, Harper struggled to turn down her offer.

"Yes. Absolutely."

Though it was dark, Harper noticed a blush spreading up Cait's neck. *It's the lighting…or the lack of!* It was ridiculous to even think of Cait in that way. Yes, she was sweet and very pleasant company, but Harper wasn't looking, and Cait was in no way interested. Why would she be? Cait was entirely different to Harper, and though she was generous and friendly, Cait probably saw everything Callie had seen in Harper. Precisely nothing.

Single. That's how it should be.

"Okay, well, I'll just wait here while you do what you need to do." Cait broke Harper from her thoughts, her eyes shining from the sliver of light present in the space. "I'd say I'll take a seat, but…"

"Come upstairs. I just need to grab some shoes and blow out the candles."

Cait's smile widened. "Can I? I haven't seen the upstairs in here yet."

"You really did want this place, didn't you?"

Cait chewed her lip, shoving her bobble hat in her coat pocket. "I did. Jude suggested another B&B, like I told you, but I wanted to buy this place for myself."

"Oh."

"But it's gone to the right person. I know you'll look after it." Cait touched Harper's arm lightly, sending a sensation throughout her body. "And, if I really miss it, I'll just call in for a cuppa."

"Well, you're always welcome here."

❄

CAIT LOVED THIS. The spontaneity she suddenly felt she possessed. Jude and his outburst earlier today had been the final straw for her, but she didn't have the luxury of leaving the B&B like Harper did. No, Cait had to return there tonight, and if she wanted to avoid any sort of fallout, she would have to creep past Jude's level of the house.

It's been so long since I crept.

And it was true. Cait hadn't had the chance to come home late from a night out since last summer. But she knew the potential coming into this industry, and most of the time, she wouldn't change it for the world. While Jude was quite content going out with friends to the same place at the same time every week, Cait had always strived for more. Evening walks along the lake, a random boat trip even though she'd grown up around here and knew the lake like the back of her hand. Just…something more than sitting around the B&B, expecting a call from a resident downstairs.

That was the extent of an "unexpected" night for Cait. Would a guest need something? At 41, she wanted more than that. She wanted to leave the B&B behind at night and live life. Not exist in her beautiful guest house. And that's all she was doing. Existing.

"I'm glad we decided not to go to a restaurant," Harper said, licking the salt and vinegar from her fingers. "And this is the best fish & chips I've ever had."

"I'm glad I impressed you." Those words held a little more than they should have. Because while Cait had gone to Harper's to invite her out for a few hours, she *did* want to impress her.

Harper linked her arm through Cait's, shoving her hand back into her bag of chips. "Seriously, this place is gorgeous at night. I mean, it's gorgeous in the day too, but night is when it really captures me."

"It's a very captivating place. Why do you think I've never left?" Cait relaxed her shoulders, enjoying having Harper on her arm. Even if it didn't mean to Harper what it did to Cait. *You're out of your mind. You've known her for a day!*

"I don't think I could leave a place like this, even if I wanted to." Harper sighed, her breath visible in the air. "And the air is so crisp. So fresh. I bet you don't get sick out here like we do in the built-up areas."

"I suppose not. I can't say I've ever really thought about anywhere else. This is my bubble. My happy place."

Cait stopped outside a small shop halfway up the hill, blowing out a deep breath as her calves burned. For all the years she'd been here, the main hill up to the B&B still took the wind out of her. "Wait here; I'll be right back."

"Sure." Harper leant against the slate garden wall of the house next door, crossing her legs at the ankles. "Not going anywhere."

Cait watched her for a moment, taken aback by just how comfortable she felt around Harper. And then she caught those devastating eyes, her pulse quickening ever so slightly.

She rushed into the shop, taking two four packs of beer from the fridge. "Evening, Bert. Business doing okay?"

"Jam-packed, Cait. Those tourists don't stop."

"No, they don't."

Bert cleared his throat. "Saw you going into Park Lodge earlier. Did you decide to buy?"

"Oh, no." Cait handed over a ten-pound note, taking the carrier from Bert. "We have a new neighbour. Harper."

"Interesting."

"She's a graphic designer, and she's staying at the B&B for a while. Had a leak before she moved in."

Cait made a mental note to enquire about the leak. Darren hadn't said much about it, but he must have given Harper an idea of how it happened.

"Graphic designer. In this town? Ludicrous!"

"I'm sure she'll be in at some point," Cait said, giving Bert a knowing look. "And when she does, please make her feel welcome."

Cait threw her hand over her shoulder as she left the shop, stepping onto the street to find Harper scoffing down the last of her fish.

"Enjoying that?"

"Absolutely." Harper eyed the bag. "Buy anything nice?"

"Fancy a bit more spontaneity?" Cait narrowed her eyes, expecting to be shot down by Harper. She'd already spent a few hours with her, and she probably wanted to get home.

"Depends. If it's beer, you can count me in."

"Would you look at that! I know you so well already."

Harper grinned, pushing off the wall and taking the bag from Cait. "Let me carry that. You've already bought dinner."

They linked arms once again, taking the last of the incline up the hill.

"So, where to? You're not going to drag me to some creepy graveyard, are you? I know I passed one on the way into town yesterday."

"Nope, no graveyards. I may know my way around here, but I draw the line at creepy stuff."

"Okay, well, we can go back to mine if you wanted to…"

Under other circumstances Cait would have loved to, but it was far too cold to sit around in a house with no heating or electricity tonight.

"Actually, I was thinking maybe we could go back to the B&B." She felt Harper tense beside her, clearly not keen on the idea. "Don't worry; I'm not asking you to take a room. We can go up to my place."

Harper stopped on the edge of the pavement. "Jude doesn't like me. I don't think he really wants me hanging around you guys."

"Oh, you think I live with him?" Cait barked a laugh. That really would be torture. "No. He has his own level. I have mine. The house is huge; you won't believe the size of it as you go up to the next level."

Harper chewed her lip, scrunching her chip wrapper in her hands. "I mean, some heat would be nice."

"Why don't you grab what you need from your place, and then we'll go back to mine, drink some beer, and talk about absolutely nothing?"

"I could get on board with that." Harper's eyes sparkled as the streetlight caught them, taking Cait's breath away for the millionth time tonight.

Cait cleared her throat. "Besides, you still haven't told me how the leak came about."

Harper held up a hand. "Let's not go there. I don't have the mental strength for that this evening."

Cait nodded, noting Harper's discomfort. Talk of the house could be saved for another day, because after this evening, Cait was determined to take time away from work more often. And if she had the chance, it would be in Harper's company.

Steady, now. Don't make a fool of yourself.

CHAPTER FIVE

Harper made herself comfortable on Cait's couch, her eyes wandering around the living room she'd somehow landed herself in this evening. She was supposed to be at home, alone and miserable, but Cait had once again come through for her—something she would always be grateful for.

They'd snuck past Jude's level of the house, giggling like schoolgirls as Cait stumbled up the stairs. The more they tried to stay quiet, the noisier they seemed to be. But Cait had assured Harper that Jude wouldn't have anything to say. After all, this was Cait's private space, not the B&B.

"You know, I can put you in that bigger room I mentioned if you want me to." Cait handed a beer to Harper over the back of the couch, her coat and hat discarded, fluffy socks now in place of her shoes. "You really do need electricity."

"No. I'm not getting between you and Jude. I don't know why he has such an issue with me, but he does, and that's that."

"I don't know what's going on with him. He seems really short tempered lately and for the strangest reasons."

Harper lifted a shoulder. "Maybe I just have one of those faces."

"You have a beautiful face." Cait didn't bat an eyelid as she said that, but Harper did. "And he's just a miserable bastard."

"Well, thanks." Heat crept across Harper's chest, spreading up her neck. "But I suspect I'm not many people's cup of tea lately. My fiancée left me, and Jude really doesn't like me. I must be doing something wrong."

"Nonsense."

"It may sound that way to you, but I'm obviously doing something. I really thought me and Callie would be together forever."

"Do you still love her?" Cait sat opposite Harper, a slight sympathetic smile playing on her mouth. "I know she hurt you, but that love doesn't just disappear."

"I did. But after this morning, the thought of ever seeing her again makes me so angry."

"That doesn't mean you don't love her anymore." Cait rested her elbows on her knees, clasping her hands under her chin. "Maybe you just need time."

"Time for what?" Harper asked. "I got to the house this morning to discover she'd brought her new girlfriend to my house and shagged her in my bed."

Cait winced, her eyes fluttering closed. "I'm so sorry. That must have been awful."

"And then I came back here to have Jude pounding on the door."

"I thought something had happened when you got back here this afternoon. You seemed a little…off. But then I realised that I don't know you, so it really wasn't my business to feel offended that you didn't stop to chat."

"I needed to be alone. She also caused the leak downstairs. Not intentionally, I don't think, but still."

"Harper," Cait said, getting to her feet, and rounding the table separating them. She dropped down beside Harper. "Look, I know we've only known each other for, what, 48 hours? But I want you to know that I'm here if you ever need to talk or vent or if you just need a friend."

Harper welled up. Cait was definitely someone she wanted as a friend. "And the same goes for you."

"Oh, I'm just in a never-ending routine now."

"So, break the routine." Harper smiled, taking Cait's hand. "Break it and do what you want to do."

"It's not that simple when you run a B&B. I wish it could be, but it's a full-time job. Day and night."

"You seem like you've had fun tonight."

"I have. So much. And it may have only been a walk into town for fish and chips and then back here to drink beer with you, but it's been so long since I *could* do that."

"Don't just exist, Cait. You're really great and amazing company, but you deserve a night off. You'll burn yourself out and come to resent this place otherwise."

"I really don't want to resent it. I love the B&B, but it's my entire life. Perhaps I should have realised that coming into this."

"Everything seems like a good idea at the time." Harper knew that all too well. She was beginning to wonder if she should have seen the signs with Callie. But then again, there really weren't any signs. "I could have been living on the next block to you with a woman who was cheating on me. Because I just wanted to see the good side of things."

"I'm really sorry she did that to you."

"Me too. But now I can move forward, and like you said, this place is great for doing that."

Cait looked around the room, the soft glow of the lamp in the corner giving the space a beautiful, cosy, ambience. "It really is."

"And I have you, right?"

"You do have me." Cait squeezed Harper's hand. "I'm just a knock on the door away. Or a call, whichever."

"I'm going to need someone to show me around this place."

"I'm your girl. Anything you need to know, and anywhere you want to explore…just ask."

"Well, I can't really explore alone." Harper grinned. "So, you'd better break that routine sooner or later. You wouldn't want the guilt of knowing I'd fallen and broken my leg only to be eaten by some mysterious creature."

"That hasn't happened too often lately. We had a spate of mysterious creature eating deaths in 2017, but it settled down."

Harper laughed from deep within her belly. She could get used to this. Someone on her level. Someone who made her smile, her insides warm and swirly. "You're good company."

"Makes a change for me, all of this. I'm usually up here at night talking to the four walls."

"I know you said you had plans next weekend, but I heard a rumour that you love the Mediterranean on the lake..."

"I do. The food is to die for."

Harper chanced her luck "Let me take you to dinner on Friday night. I'll make the reservation; you just have to show up."

Cait lowered her eyes, sighing. "I'd love to, but Friday is actually the night I have plans with friends."

Damn. That stung. Saturday was a no-go; she had a conference call in the evening with a new client she was working for.

"Never mind. Maybe some other time. It'll be good for you to get out with your friends, and I'm sure I have a crap tonne of stuff to do at home."

"Sorry."

"Don't be daft," Harper said, brushing off her disappointment. "You have a life here; I don't. It's no biggie."

"I could book you on with our table for Friday. You can meet my friends."

"No, I shouldn't. It was a silly thing to suggest in the first place. I have far too much to be getting on with. And you can't hold my hand forever."

"I'd love to take you up on the offer another time." Cait's eyes smiled; this woman was genuine. No doubt about it. "You just give me a date and time, and I'll make sure I'm free."

Harper decided to play it cool. She may feel a connection with Cait, one she hadn't quite explored or had the time to think about yet, but Harper was fresh out of a relationship. She wasn't in any sort of position to woo a woman yet.

"Sure, yeah." She relaxed into her seat, sipping her beer. "So, tell me…best place to check out around here."

"I guess it depends what you're looking for. If it's a potential love life, I really can't help you. I wouldn't have a clue where to go."

"Right. We really need to find you a lady, Cait. You're in your prime. I may be hopeless with relationships, but I can be a great wing woman."

Cait furrowed her brow. "You're the one who needs to get back on the horse."

"All the horses bolted. I'm happy to be single. But you, I mean…you could really make someone happy."

"You don't know the first thing about me. I could be a complete bitch."

Harper's eyebrows rose. "You really expect me to believe for one second that you could be a bitch? Nope. I'm a very good judge of character, and you're going to have women lining up for you. I'll make it happen."

What the hell was Harper doing? Willingly helping Cait look for a significant other. Surely that would only come back to bite her in the arse when she realised that Cait was off the market. Harper may not be ready for a relationship, but that didn't mean it would always be the case. And when that day did come, Cait would be engaged or moving in with the love of her life.

Harper wasn't stupid, she knew she was looking at Cait this evening in ways she shouldn't be, but did Cait feel even a hint of that? Probably not, so it really didn't matter if she found her a date or not.

"I can't commit to a relationship, but thanks for offering to be my lookout."

"You can commit. Because you're going to break that routine, right?"

"Mm." Cait kicked her feet up onto the coffee table, relaxing beside Harper. "According to you, yes."

"And you should know…" Harper leaned towards Cait's ear. She hadn't expected the subtle perfume Cait wore to have her mind spinning, but it definitely was. "I'm usually always right."

CHAPTER SIX

Cait took the stairs gingerly, fully aware that she was way out of line this morning. Jude had handled breakfast alone while she had a lie-in. The first in many years. As guilty as she felt, Cait really was better for it. She'd never made it a habit to climb into bed late, and that hadn't happened last night either, but just some time to unwind was definitely what she'd needed. Now, it was back to work.

Harper stayed over last night, taking Cait's couch when the idea of sleeping in a cold house didn't appeal to her having sat in the warmth all night. When Cait woke this morning, Harper had already left. She was sure Jude would have probably bumped into Harper on her way out, and now she could only hope that he hadn't had words with her. It really wasn't his business who Cait had over, even if it rarely happened.

The sound of fingers on a keyboard caught her attention, her guilt coming back tenfold as she peered into the office. Jude sat with his eyes glued to the screen, the scent of fresh coffee from downstairs wafting towards her. "Hey."

Jude swivelled in his chair. "Morning. Nice of you to join me."

"Sorry. But I did tell you I wasn't working this morning." Cait wouldn't show Jude how awful she felt; he would only play on it. "How was breakfast?"

"Fine. Tom made it in this morning, so I took over on the meet and greet. Pauline took the continental station."

"Great. So, what plans do you have today?"

"Me?" Jude asked. "None. Just work."

"It's okay, I can take over. I have some invoices to get through and a new order for the supplier."

"Supplier has been contacted," Jude said, turning his attention back to the screen. "And I'll handle the invoices."

"Jude, it's fine. Take the afternoon off."

Jude removed his reading glasses, settling them down on the desk. He pushed his chair away from the desk and got to his feet. "I owe you an apology."

"For what?"

"My behaviour lately. I just feel…stuck."

"You and me both." Cait offered her brother an understanding smile. "But if we change some things up, agree to who works what, we can both have a life outside of here."

"That's awfully sudden of you. Why the change of heart? You love this place."

"And I always will, but that doesn't mean I have to work myself into the ground." *Cait* was working herself into the ground. Jude, not so much. "I'd like to see what's on offer around the town."

"I don't follow…"

"I'm 41, Jude, and I have no significant other. I'd like to at least try to date again. The B&B is a success, and I don't think having a day off once or twice a week is going to make it sink, do you?"

Jude nodded. "Understandable."

"So, can we work together to make it work for *us*?"

"Is this about Harper?" Jude leant back, resting on the edge of the desk. He folded his arms across his chest, but Cait didn't feel intimidated. She rarely did. "I saw her leaving this morning."

"It's not necessarily about her, no. But since she arrived, I don't know. I feel…different. And she's encouraged me to date. Maybe I should do that."

"Date…Harper?"

Oh, wouldn't that be sublime. Harper was catching Cait's attention more and more lately. In fact, she'd been disappointed to find her gone this morning. But Harper was finding her feet here, and Cait wouldn't do anything to jeopardise that. While she loved every second they spent together, Cait wasn't sure Harper was interested. And that way okay.

"No, I don't think so."

Jude frowned. "Why? It's clear you two get on really well."

"That doesn't mean she wants to date me, Jude." Cait rolled her eyes, leaning against the doorframe. "I'm just helping her out. She has nobody around here, and, emotionally, I think she's struggling."

"Emotionally?"

"She's had a terrible time since she got out of that car the other night. The house isn't how she left it, her ex-girlfriend has been cheating, and then she found out yesterday that the ex brought her new girlfriend to the house *and* slept with her in Harper's bed."

"Wow. That's really shitty."

"And I don't know, I think she just needs someone to be there for her. Darren has fixed the leak, but she still has no electricity. It's just not gone to plan for her. And having no support on hand must be hard for her."

"Now I feel terrible…"

"She stayed over last night. I called by to see if she wanted to grab some dinner, and she was sitting in there with candles."

"The Johnstone's have just checked out of the king suite this morning…" Jude said, chewing his lip.

"I'm not sure she wants to come back here to stay." Cait wasn't intentionally making her brother feel bad, but she also wouldn't lie to him. Jude had really hurt Harper yesterday; he should know that. "I think everything will settle down soon. And if not, she's welcome to stay with me."

"Bet she is." Jude winked.

"Please don't do that." Cait wrapped her arms around herself. Harper had asked her to dinner last night, and she'd declined. She knew it didn't mean what she hoped it would, but she still felt terrible for letting Harper down. "She's in no position to think about a relationship, and in many ways, neither am I."

"But you've just said—"

Cait held up her hand. "I know what I said. But with Harper… no. She's outgoing and playful, and I'm just me. I wouldn't put either of us through that. She needs someone who can be there more than I could ever be. I may want a day off now and then, but it wouldn't be enough."

"Look, if you're serious about meeting someone, it's going to take more than a day off once a week, Cait. And if you need me to step up, I can. I will."

"Maybe I'll just see how things go. I'm meeting the girls next Friday, though, so can you hold the fort here?"

"Absolutely."

"Thanks." Cait puffed out her cheeks. "So, where do you want me?"

"Out of here. Take the rest of the weekend off. I'll call you if I really need you, but we only have one check in today."

Cait's eyebrows rose with surprise. Jude had never willingly told her to take time off. She shouldn't leave him alone, but Harper was calling her name. "You're sure?"

"I'm sure. Maybe drop in on Harper and run that king suite by her. She may just take you up on the offer."

Cait would do that. Even if she'd prefer Harper to stay with her, she understood that Harper would need her own space. Especially if she had to work.

Cait stepped forward and hugged her brother, offering him a thankful squeeze. "I'm going to make some sandwiches and drop by the house, okay?"

"You're a really good friend."

❄

"MUM, I didn't tell you because I knew you would react like this. I don't need to move back home, I'm fine."

"Harper, sweetheart..." Katherine let out a long breath. "You can't be safe living there if you have no electricity."

Harper flicked the switch on the fuse box, grinning when the living room light flickered on. "Wrong. I do have electricity."

"But you've just said you didn't."

Harper rolled her eyes, taking a seat on the stairs. "Just checked it. It's working fine. I don't think the electricity was related to the leak. It's that bloody kettle you gave me. I told you it used to blow the electrics at home."

"That's right. Blame me."

"It wouldn't have been the end of the world if I had to buy a new one."

Harper loved her mum, they got on so well, but sometimes she was insufferable. Instead of letting Harper find her feet here, she was demanding her daughter pull out of the sale and return home. Harper couldn't live at home again. She'd spent time renting before this move, and the thought of going back home to her mum left her feeling as though she failed. Going back wasn't an option. From today, she was only moving forward.

"Anyway, I should go. I need to find the nearest tip so I can get rid of this carpet. I can't leave it in the garden; the neighbours will talk."

Cait instantly floated into Harper's mind. Wonderful, sweet, and pretty Cait.

"Have you met the neighbours yet?"

"Only one. Cait. She owns the B&B on the next block."

"Ah. The lady who gave you a room for the night," Katherine said. "Remind me to bring her a nice bottle of wine the next time I visit you."

"I'm sure she'd love that." As Harper turned, looking out of the window, Cait was opening the garden gate. Harper rushed to the front door and opened it, motioning for Cait to come in. "Mum, I have to go and get some boxes sorted out, okay?"

"I'll call you tomorrow, love."

"Yeah, okay. Bye, Mum."

Harper cut the call, smiling as she shoved her phone in her pocket. Cait held a wrapped package, her cheeks flushed from the cold.

"I thought I'd come by and see if you needed a hand with anything here. Jude's working again today, so I made sandwiches for us and brought a flask of coffee."

"You're something else," Harper said, her stomach growling. "I was about to hike the hill to find some food."

"Well, no need now." Cait moved into the living room, balancing the sandwiches on a box by the TV stand. "You finally got the carpet up."

"Wasn't hard. I just need to find somewhere or someone to take it."

"Darren has a van. I'm sure he'll get rid of it for you."

Harper nodded. "Okay, but he really needs to let me pay him for all of this. I feel like a charity case. He's already offered to fit the new one for me."

Cait frowned as she looked up at the light fixture in the living room. "I thought you didn't have any electricity."

"That was a ploy. I wouldn't have been able to stay at yours last night if I told you the truth."

Cait's eyebrows rose, one hand on her hip. "And here I am, defending you to Jude!"

"I'm joking." Harper winked, taking the sandwiches and moving towards the stairs. "Come on. I'll tell you all about it."

"Upstairs?"

Harper turned back, already unwrapping the sandwiches. "Unless you want to stand in the living room all afternoon, yes."

"Fair enough."

❄

CAIT KICKED OFF HER BOOTS, making herself comfortable on Harper's bed. Now that she had full daylight, Cait could see the type of woman Harper was. Bedroom furniture, in Cait's opinion, told a lot about a person. And so far, Cait liked what she saw.

Harper clearly loved her friends and family, told by an array of photographs on pin boards, in frames, and on canvases attached to the wall. Candles seemed to be another love of Harper's, all intricately placed in particular spots around her room. But the bedspread was what caught Cait's attention. Bright, paisley, and floral-patterned cotton felt soft beneath her hands; a mass of pillows and throw cushions also sat complexly in place.

This wasn't what she'd expected, Harper was a little...boyish in her appearance. But Cait loved everything she saw. And she loved knowing that Harper welcomed her here.

"So, the electricity?" Cait asked, chomping on a ham sandwich that Harper handed over. "Are you sure it should be on right now?"

"It was a fuse that had blown, not the water damage."

"Oh."

"But I didn't know that until I ripped the carpet up earlier and realised that there was no watermark up the skirting board. The sockets don't look as though they've had water anywhere near them, and I remembered I'd left the kettle plugged in. Mum gave it to me; she was determined to save me a few quid."

"That's nice."

Harper flopped down beside Cait. "It would be if she hadn't given me something that clearly has a fault on it."

"I'm sure she meant well." Cait wondered if Harper and her mother were similar. Cait, herself, had been close to her mother growing up, but the B&B had taken over her life in that department too. "Is she coming to visit?"

"Oh, yeah. I'm just trying to delay her arrival. It would be nice to have a few days alone without her fussing around me."

Cait simply nodded. Harper was independent, there was no doubt about that, but Cait knew that if she was in Harper's position, she'd have her mother on speed dial.

"So, I was thinking about you while I was taking the carpet up..."

Cait's heart thrummed. Harper had been thinking about her. "Okay..."

"Have you decided when you're going to break the routine yet?"

"Actually, I have. Jude has offered to take on more of a role around the B&B so I can have some days off. Which is great, but I don't know how long that offer will last for."

"So, you're all systems go?" Harper asked, taking another sandwich from the wrapper. "Because I had some questions."

Cait paused. What questions? And *why* did Harper have questions? "Questions?"

"Worst date you've ever had?" Harper relaxed back onto her bed, sitting her sandwich on her stomach. "Everyone has had a bad date, so what's your worst?"

"God, there's been a few." Cait laughed, she really hadn't been that lucky when it came to dating. "But the worst one had to be with Gemma. I mean, she was nice, and I'm sure she'd make someone very happy, but she was a bit...dizzy."

"She did something embarrassing, didn't she?" Harper listened intently, her eyes never straying from Cait's. "Come on, I wanna know."

"Okay, so you know those signs they put up when they have temporary traffic lights on the road?"

"The ones that say, 'wait here when red light shows'?"

Cait burst out laughing. She still giggled when she thought about it years later. "Yes. Those ones."

"She didn't trip over it, did she?"

"No. We were walking back from dinner, and we came across some temporary lights. I thought nothing of it, so I was just strolling along without a care in the world. Gemma suddenly grabbed my hand and dragged me back to the sign."

Harper frowned. "Why?"

"The temporary lights were on red."

Harper face palmed herself. "Oh my God. Please don't say what I think you're going to say…"

"She made me stand at the sign and wait until the light turned green again."

Harper cringed, her face red as she held back her own laughter. "Aww. Bless her."

"Harper, I didn't have the heart to tell her it was only cars that had to stop. And I know I should have, it's probably happened since, but she really thought she was doing the right thing by waiting."

"But at least she made you laugh. That must count for something."

Cait had to agree. It really had amused her for many years. "You're right. But it still didn't result in anything."

"Best date you've ever had?"

Cait chewed her lip. While she loved spending time with Harper, she wasn't fond of these questions. They only made her feel rubbish about her life. "I don't recall one."

"What? None?"

"Nope." Cait focused on her hands in her lap. Maybe she could direct the questions back to Harper. Surely her life had been more exciting. "You?"

"I've had some great dates. I'm very easy to be around, I think, so that helps."

"Maybe I should have dated you then." Cait instantly regretted saying that. She hadn't meant it to sound so…desperate. "Sorry, I was joking."

"That's a shame. I would have totally shown you what a nice date was."

Cait's belly swirled with that familiar feeling she had around Harper. Was this just her nature, or was she flirting with Cait? It had been so long, Cait honestly couldn't put her finger on the answer.

But what she did know was that she enjoyed this feeling. She wanted it to continue.

"Ever been in love?"

Cait knew the answer to that with one hundred percent certainty. "Nope."

"I wouldn't worry. It's not all it's cracked up to be." Harper reached over the bed, discarding her sandwich in the bin by her desk. When Harper scooted closer to her, Cait lost her breath. "I mean, look at me. Had the woman of my dreams, got engaged, bought a house…but here I am, single."

"I can't imagine how that must feel."

"At first, it felt really shit. But then I came to realise that it just wasn't meant to be. And I know what she did was wrong, but I have to forgive her at some point. If I stay angry and bitter, I'll just be suffering again. It won't change anything. I'll still be single… but angry and bitter, too."

Cait turned her head, focusing on Harper's sparkling blue eyes. She reached out, tucking some stray auburn hair behind Harper's ear, and smiled. "You didn't deserve what she did to you. You're wonderful."

Harper's cheeks reddened. "T-thanks."

"And I know it's none of my business, but I'm glad you moved here alone. If you hadn't, I probably wouldn't have ended up sitting here with you."

"Why *are* you sitting here with me?"

"Because I feel good when I'm with you. I feel positive and excited, and you make me want to stop dedicating my life to work."

Harper visibly swallowed hard. "Not what I expected."

"What did you expect?"

"That maybe you'd say I was mediocre company, but I was good for preventing unimaginable boredom."

"Take a little more credit, Harper. You're a joy to be around."

Cait's thumb feathered Harper's cheek. "But if you want to forgive your ex, that's your decision."

"I don't want to hate her. And I know I did yesterday, I was awful when I spoke to her, but that's not me. I'll miss her in some ways, but I'm ready to forget about her. She doesn't want me, and I've accepted that."

God, she's so heartbreakingly beautiful.

Cait sighed, lowering her hand. "Maybe something better will come along."

Harper's eyes glistened, those soft frown lines between her eyebrows adding to just how naturally beautiful she was. Cait wanted to lean in and kiss Harper, but she wouldn't. She *couldn't*. Harper was not on the market. She'd said as much since they met.

Harper's soft but hoarse voice came to life. "I think something much better is going to come along."

Cait felt the sincerity in Harper's words, the burn in her stare. "What are you doing tonight?"

"Nothing. Again."

"Right, well, I want you to be ready for 7. We're going down to the lake. Wrap up warm."

CHAPTER SEVEN

Harper took the few steps towards the lake, the silence of the night calming her. Cait had a habit of producing feelings Harper hadn't experienced before, her intriguing nature pulling Harper into a world where everything was perfectly fine despite all that Harper was dealing with. And when Cait was around, it *was* fine. It was great, even.

This afternoon had been different for Harper. When Cait showed up, she was feeling good, but by the end of their deep conversation, she felt even better. There was something between them, something Harper tried to ignore, but how could she do that when Cait brought her to the most beautiful of places?

Harper's eyes followed the moonlight as it shone off the lake, the water painfully still. There was no lap of slight waves, no people, just Harper and Cait walking towards a small platform that ventured out over the water. It was beautiful. If things were different, she might even say…romantic.

"I can certainly see the appeal of this place," Harper said, side glancing at Cait. "It's somewhere to think. To feel. To just be."

"That's why I brought you here," Cait said, her eyes shining. "You seemed like you needed some peace and quiet before."

"I think I need more than peace and quiet. I need...God, I don't know what I need."

"You need people around you."

Harper had never really been a fan of people. They always judged or brought drama with them and that hadn't been Harper's cup of tea for as long as she could remember. But some people, on the odd occasion, had the ability to take her by surprise.

Cait was absolutely one of those people.

"I think I just need to be around you."

Cait cast her gaze on the floor, the smallest of smiles curling on her mouth as she scuffed her feet across the wooden jetty. "I think I need to be around you, too."

"We just clicked, didn't we?" Harper adjusted her wool hat, silently begging Cait to give her something more. A hint of how she was feeling. "Or is that just me who thinks that?"

"No, you're not the only one." Cait rubbed her hands together, her icy breath floating away into the winter night. When she looked up, her eyes studied Harper's face. "I'd like to think that we could get to know one another a little better."

"As friends?"

Cait's features changed; they weren't as soft. "Yes, if that's what you want."

"I'd love to hang out with you, Cait. So long as I'm not getting in the way of anything, I'd really love that."

Cait nodded, suddenly fidgeting with her gloves. "Well, did you want to grab some hot chocolate and sit here a while?"

"Definitely. That sounds like a lovely evening."

"There's a little hut a few minutes away. They do hot Belgian waffles and other things, too. Maybe we could share one?"

Harper smiled, linking her arm through Cait's. She instinctively pulled her closer, keeping one another warm, but really it was Cait's perfume that Harper wanted to breathe in. If she ever came across it again, it would always remind her of Cait.

"Hey," Harper said, leaning in a little closer. "Thanks for inviting me here tonight."

"This is nice," Cait said. "It probably doesn't seem like much to you, but now that Jude's stepped up, being out and about feels like an entirely different life to me. I mean, I'm going out to dinner with friends on Friday, and I'm here with you now…I'd say things are looking up for me."

"Well, if you're having dinner with friends, things are definitely looking up."

"I beg to differ." Cait's eyes focused on the main street as they walked away from the lake. "I'd rather be here with you. You're less intense than my friends."

"I like to be the less intense friend." Harper grinned. "If I'm not intense, I don't cause drama."

"No, you bring happiness and joy. Laughter too. I don't think I've laughed so much as when we're hanging out. And it's nice. It's normal. It's what I should have been doing for so many years."

"It's all about breaking that routine, Cait. The B&B isn't going to die because you went out to dinner with friends. And it won't die because you're walking along the lake this evening." Harper's insides swirled with delight as Cait tightened her grip on her arm. "I mean, how often do guests contact you in the evening? Most must be out having dinner and drinks or relaxing in their rooms after a day of hiking."

"Yeah, it's not many."

"Exactly."

"But I don't know how to put myself out there. I want to, believe me I do, but I don't know where to begin. I haven't had a serious relationship in…wow, I don't know how long. But even back then when I didn't have a business to run, I cocked it up."

"You need to find the right person. Someone who is willing to understand the commitments you have to the B&B. And if it's someone local, I'm sure they'll understand."

"Maybe. I don't know."

"Or maybe you need someone who isn't high maintenance. You know?"

"No, I don't know." Cait narrowed her eyes as she side glanced at Harper. A chill ran through Harper's body; she'd never tire of that feeling.

"Just…someone who doesn't need your attention 24/7."

"But isn't that the point of dating? Never wanting to be without one another."

"Depends how far away you live from one another. If it's close, it can all be worked out. Some people will understand. I know I would."

Cait's smile subsided. Had Harper said too much?

"I'm just speaking hypothetically, of course. I don't expect you to want to date me. I mean, why would you?"

"Many reasons," Cait mumbled, but Harper heard her perfectly. "I know what you mean."

"You'll find who you want when you least expect it."

"Well, I found you and I didn't expect it."

Harper cleared her throat. "As amazing as you are, I've just ended a relationship. I'd never want you to think of yourself as a rebound. And I worry that it's exactly what it'd be."

Harper felt Cait's shoulders slump as they approached the Belgian waffle hut. "I was speaking hypothetically, obviously."

Harper knew that was a lie. She felt it in the change of Cait's body language. But she would let it go for the time being. She needed to fix herself before she even thought about another woman. "Yeah…me too."

❄

CAIT FELT her stomach somersault as she settled on a bench beside Harper. She held a Belgian waffle coated with Nutella and banana with whipped cream to finish while Harper guarded their hot chocolate. Being here like this with another woman felt surreal to Cait, but she'd already said too much on their walk to the hut. Neither had the balls to discuss it further, so Cait would let it go. She'd rather enjoy this evening with Harper than ruin it by doing something she shouldn't.

Even though Cait found herself wanting to plant her own on Harper's kissable lips.

"How's the chocolate?"

Harper licked her lips, her eyes bright as the moonlight caught them. "Perfect. Want to try yours?"

"Yes." Cait's lips parted slightly as Harper handed her drink over, the intense need to make her feelings known now overwhelming. "T-thanks."

"Let me take the waffle while you sip your drink. You'll be all fingers and thumbs otherwise."

Cait was already all fingers and thumbs around Harper; that was becoming increasingly clear lately. And when she was alone with this woman, she couldn't think straight. But Harper wasn't looking. Cait had to accept that.

Why am I interested in the one who isn't?

Cait sipped her hot chocolate, just thankful to have a friend outside of the B&B. And because it had been so long since she'd looked at another woman, it shouldn't be hard to keep her feelings at bay. It was what she did best any other time.

Harper's rich auburn hair dropped down her shoulders, a cream coloured bobble hat keeping her ears warm. "Is that your natural colour?"

Harper smiled. "Yep. And everyone I meet asks me the same question."

"It's gorgeous."

"And rare, apparently." Harper tucked into the waffle in her lap, licking the Nutella from her lips. "Auburn hair and blue eyes aren't really a thing, or so I've been led to believe."

"It...suits you." Cait mentally face-palmed herself. What did that even mean? "I mean, it's different. And it's nice."

"Hard for me to understand when people say things like that.

I've been this way since birth." Harper grinned, laughing. "Your colour suits you, too."

"Okay, fair enough. I realise how stupid it sounded." Cait fell silent, internally screaming at herself for being so pathetic. Harper wasn't here to be flirted with, Cait had to stop. "Sorry."

Harper shifted closer, holding up some Belgian waffle on a disposable fork. "Stop saying sorry and just try this instead."

She fed Cait the bite of waffle, the richness of the dessert sending her taste buds into overdrive. "Mm. That's good."

"We should make this a thing. Once a week."

"Which?"

"Coming here and getting cosy on a bench. Some people would say we were out of our minds for sitting at a lake in the middle of winter, it has to be at least minus 3 this evening, but those people can mind their business."

"Those people certainly can. And, yes, I'd like to make this a regular thing."

"Cool."

Harper stared back out at the lake, giving Cait the perfect opportunity to just watch her. Even the way she chewed her food was mesmerising. *Get a grip on yourself.* But Cait couldn't pull her eyes away. She turned on her side ever so slightly—and inconspicuously—propping her head up in the palm of her hand.

"I bet you're looking forward to sleeping in your warm house tonight…"

"I am. With my things around me. Familiarity, you know?"

"I do. Do you have food and stuff in?"

"Yeah. I drove out to one of the supermarkets this morning when I left your place. Got the essentials in. I don't really want to venture out during the day if I can help it. Not unless I have plans, anyway. And I really need to get my business side of things up and running. I'm going to tackle my office tomorrow. Then I'll know where I am with things."

"If you need a hand, let me know."

"It's nothing strenuous. Callie put the desk together with me the other week. I brought my computer and other equipment up in the car when I officially moved in. It's just a case of putting things where they belong and what not."

Callie.

Cait didn't like hearing her name during conversations with Harper. It always seemed to bring the mood down.

"But thanks for the offer." Harper offered Cait more Belgian waffle, smiling as Cait moaned at the taste. She didn't make it a habit to eat this kind of stuff, she didn't particularly want a middle-aged spread as she moved further into her forties, but she could indulge once or twice with Harper. She spent enough time on the go to burn it off in seconds. "So, you said you're out with friends next week?"

"Yeah. Looking forward to it."

"Good. You should. Friends are exactly the kind of people to help you break the routine."

"What is it with this routine thing?" Cait's forehead creased. "And why are you so determined to get me out of the B&B as much as you possibly can?"

Harper stopped chewing, her eyes drifting towards Cait. "Sorry, I'll mind my own business."

"I didn't mean that to sound so harsh. But I do still wonder why?"

Harper shrugged. "You're a gorgeous woman who spends her life working. Forgive me if I think you deserve more."

Cait's heartbeat thundered in her ears.

"But if you don't want to change that, I'm not going to force you to. I just thought it may have been nice for you to get out more."

Harper was right. She always was.

"You're right."

"No. I'm involving myself in the business of someone I don't even know. I'm sorry if you feel like I'm pushing you to do something you don't want to do. That wasn't my intention."

Harper got to her feet, discarding the empty paper tray that once held their delicious waffle. As she returned to the bench, she flopped down and sighed.

Cait rested her hand over Harper's. "Your intentions are good. I know that."

"I think maybe it's time to head back," Harper said. "I was planning an early night so I'm fresh in the morning."

"Sure. Okay." *There you go ruining things again,* Cait internally chastised herself. "Let's get back up the hill."

Harper nodded, getting to her feet. "But I have one more question before I butt out for good."

Cait was all ears. "Okay."

"What are you looking for in a relationship?"

Wow. Cait hadn't expected that question. But she knew exactly what she wanted. She always had. That was the sole reason it had never really worked out with anyone before.

"What do I want?" Cait paused. "I don't just want a lover or sex with no meaning. I want a best friend. Someone who makes me laugh. I want someone who is their own person but works *with* me to create a beautiful kind of happiness. I want a laugh I hear all day and a smile I can fall asleep to. That unexpected connection that knocks you off your feet, and in time, a love so raw that it physically hurts when you're apart."

Harper smiled, her head cocked slightly. "I love that you know exactly what you want."

"Basically, I want something I'm not sure exists."

It was true. Cait could think up all her hopes for a relationship in her head, but she was yet to find a single person who wanted the same or someone she imagined could provide that. She did see hints of the qualities she was looking for in Harper, but they'd clearly met at the wrong time, so it wasn't meant to be.

"What do you want in a relationship?" she chanced, throwing the question directly back at Harper.

"The same as you."

Cait quirked an eyebrow. "You can't just use my list because you don't have your own. That's not fair."

"No, it's the truth," Harper said. "I've always wanted that stupid kind of love. The love that takes you away from your friends because you're too busy just sitting at home staring at your partner and her beauty. I want to spend my weekends cooking together. Movies, blankets, so wrapped up in one another that you lose all sense of time and where you are. But I don't know. Callie knocked my confidence big time, and I'm not sure I could give that to someone else again."

"Did Callie give you all those things?"

"No, not really. Now and then we would spend the day at home together, but a lot of the time, she wanted to be around other people. If we went out to lunch, she invited friends. If we went out to dinner, she wanted to meet up with her girls afterwards at a club. And I think that maybe she just never really wanted me. Not how I wanted her."

"She didn't deserve you," Cait whispered, the air around them thick with emotion.

"Maybe not. I don't know. But after she cheated, after she told me that we'd gone stale...I feel like I'll never be good enough for anyone else. Like, did she feel as though she couldn't approach me and tell me she was unhappy? That I was doing something wrong? I must have just been a terrible girlfriend. Why else would she cheat on me?"

"Why do you believe that *you* did something wrong?" Cait hated hearing Harper talk so low about herself. In Cait's opinion, it couldn't be further from the truth. She could spend her entire day just sitting in Harper's company. If Callie didn't want that, she was a fool.

"Have you ever been cheated on?" Harper asked, tears in her eyes.

"N-no."

"Then you couldn't understand. When the woman you love cheats on you, it tears you apart. And even if down the line you believe that ending it was for the best, that sense of being worthless sticks with you. It doesn't even matter if deep down you knew it wasn't working, the fact that the person you shared your life with touched another woman, someone who wasn't you…it really fucking hurts." A sob escaped Harper's mouth as she wrapped her arms around herself. "She said yes when I asked her to marry me. She wanted to buy a home with me. So to find out that she'd given everything that was only for you to someone else…" Harper paused, her bottom lip trembling. "I hope you're never cheated on, Cait."

Cait was at a loss for words. This side of Harper, the raw and vulnerable side, only left Cait wanting to sweep her up in her arms and hold Harper until she took all her pain away. "Come here." Cait wrapped her arms around Harper, a soothing hand on her back. "I didn't mean to upset you," she whispered as she turned her face into Harper's neck, her warm, soft skin. She never wanted this hug to end. "Let's get you home and away from me. I'm only making everything worse."

Harper tightened her grip. "No. You make it all better."

CHAPTER EIGHT

CAIT LISTENED INTENTLY AS HER FRIENDS UPDATED HER ON THEIR lives. The odd text message had kept them all in contact but sitting around drinking wine together felt normal. Honestly, Cait loved it. It felt…like she was living her life. And as the week drew to a close, with Harper firmly in her sights, Cait wanted to experience this more often.

Really, Harper had encouraged her to do this. But as she sat here this evening, it dawned on her that she would rather be with Harper. Her energy was electric, her smile brightened Cait's entire day, and her laughter was contagious.

Harper had survived her first week here, her house was taking shape, and Cait was thrilled that she was beginning to feel more comfortable. She had truly intended to only be a friendly face for Harper, but as the days passed, she found herself wanting more. More than being a neighbour, more than being a friend.

That connection she felt with Harper had only intensified as they sat on the lake last Sunday, and then with less contact this week, Cait was left yearning for so much more. A part of her worried that she was completely off base in sensing that Harper was slowly creeping closer to her, but she didn't believe she was.

The slight touch of a hand, the lingering looks…Cait wasn't stupid. Harper, in all of her beautiful, playful glory, *was* flirting.

Was Cait concerned about that? Absolutely not.

"I still can't believe you showed up tonight," Mandy, one of Cait's oldest friends, said as she topped up her wine glass. "And I have to say, you're looking brilliant."

Cait sipped her wine. "Thanks."

"I always have it in my head that you're sitting at home with a bowl of crisps watching Bridget Jones."

"I don't have time to do that. But it sounds like my kinda night."

Mandy leaned in with a suspicious look in her eyes. "Do you remember Liz from the top of the hill? Daniel's sister?"

"Liz?" Cait cast her mind back, drawing a blank. "I don't believe I do."

"Oh, you do. Blonde, leggy, same year as us in school," Irene, another friend, cut in.

"Vaguely."

Mandy cleared her throat, placing her palms flat on the table between them. "Well, turns out…she's one of your lot. Daniel caught her with a woman a few weeks ago."

"Caught her? She's a woman in her 40s. There's nothing to catch."

"You know what I mean." Mandy rolled her eyes. "Anyway, Daniel was telling Barry about it. And Barry may have thrown your name into the conversation."

"Why would he do that?"

Mandy's forehead creased. "Because you're single and so is she…"

Cait blew out a long breath. Her friends never ceased to amaze her. "Wow. So now I'm the local desperate lesbian who gets pimped out?"

"Don't be dramatic. I just told her you were looking. Because you are, right? Now that Jude has put on his big boy pants and taken on a role at the B&B, you're definitely looking."

Cait paused for a moment. Was she looking? Yes, but not in Liz's direction. "I'm not looking, exactly. I…have my eye on someone else."

"There's no one else here, Cait. Come on, we live in a tiny town, you have to be realistic about these things."

"Mandy Routledge, are you telling me you want your best friend to settle for the first woman that looks her way?"

"If you'd have asked me that 10 years ago, I would have said no. But we're not getting any younger, pretty lady."

"I'm aware of that. My knees ache every night."

"And I'm sure you want to get some action in before you need replacements, don't you?"

"From Liz who I don't even know? No, thanks."

Mandy nodded, resting back against her chair. "Fine. But at least tell me you'll consider it. I even got her number for you."

Mandy wasn't giving this up, but Cait wasn't going to give in, either. "I'm sure she'll find someone. But it won't be me." No, Cait had Harper on her mind. Entertaining another woman would be both unfair and a waste of time. "And we're not here to discuss my non-existent love life. We're here to catch up."

"Fair enough. I'll order us some cocktails while you ladies have a look at the menu."

Now that was something Cait could get on board with. Food and drinks with friends. Real friends. They may like to interfere, Mandy especially, but they all had Cait's best interests at heart.

Cait took a menu from the holder, opening it on the tapas dishes. "Right, ladies. Let's eat."

❄

Harper braced herself against the sink in the kitchen. She just needed a moment to breathe. Callie was sitting on the couch, helping herself to the bottle of wine she'd brought with her, away with the fairies when it came to having a clue about the wrong she'd done.

Harper wasn't prepared for this. She didn't know what to say to Callie once she sat down with her to talk. And the worst of it? Callie wasn't even due here today. But now that she was here, Harper wanted this over and done with. After a four-year relationship, they at least deserved to talk, to understand what went wrong. Tonight was apparently the night.

Harper rolled her head on her shoulders, grabbing the beer she'd opened moments ago. Her home was nearly complete, the new couches delivered yesterday afternoon, and the carpet had been fitted by Darren yesterday morning. Knowing that it was taking shape meant that Harper felt better here. And because this was *entirely* her own space, she didn't feel uncomfortable with the fact that Callie was sitting on her brand-new couch. This was Harper's home. Callie should remember that and show some respect.

"Okay, come on. You've got this," Harper whispered to herself as she turned and headed for the living room. She eyed Callie, a large glass of red wine in one hand, her long legs crossed. "How was the drive?"

"Longer than I expected. I don't remember it being so boring the last time you and I drove up here."

"Or the time you rocked up with what's her face?"

Callie offered a sheepish smile. "Ruby."

"Right. Ruby." Harper took the opposite end of the couch, the space between her and Callie calming her nerves further. She didn't know why she was nervous; she wasn't the one who'd fucked this all up. "So…"

"First, I want to say I'm really sorry for bringing Ruby here. It wasn't my place to do that, and I can understand why you were so angry last weekend."

Everything within Harper recoiled at the mention of Ruby's name, the hairs on her arms standing to attention. She felt her emotions surging to the surface, but she wouldn't let them defeat her. She had to show Callie that she wasn't interested in her lame apologies. If she hadn't done it in the first place, no apology would be necessary. "Why did you do it?"

"Trying to show off maybe? I don't know."

"Show off to who? Ruby?"

Callie lowered her eyes, resting her wine glass on her thigh. "Ruby likes the excitement of things. Sitting home at night watching TV doesn't quite do it for her."

"So, you shag her in other people's beds instead?"

Callie sighed. "I know what I did was unforgivable, Harper. And I know that I'm pushing my luck by even being here, but I am sorry."

"Fine. Yeah."

"Harper, do you think maybe we could be friends?"

Not in a million years.

"To be perfectly honest, I don't know why you'd want to remain friends. I wasn't good enough for you when we were together, so why would I be good enough for you now?"

"I lost my way. I thought I needed something more than what we had. And, I don't know, everything just became routine with us. The same thing day in, day out."

"I don't follow."

"Oh, come on. It got to the point where we ate the same thing each week on a particular night. Our bedroom routine was the same, our showering routine was the same. Just...everything. There was no spark there anymore."

"No spark?" Harper's eyes widened. "I was so in love with you, Cal. I would have done anything for you. If you'd just told me how you were feeling, I could have changed all that. You know I would have done and tried anything to make us happy. And I thought we were."

"We were. But it just wasn't enough in the end. And I know I'm just as much to blame for that as you, but she gave me attention. She flirted and asked how my weekend was. She invited me to dinner, to clubs...I was always her main focus."

"And I sat at home alone thinking you were working late, when really, you were sleeping with her." Harper didn't want to cry, but Callie was making her feel really shit right now. "I'm sorry I didn't make you happy. But you're happy now, and that's what matters."

Callie shifted on the couch, placing her glass of wine down as she took Harper's face in her hands. "You did make me happy. And to this day, I know it's *you* I should spend my life with and grow old with. But I messed up and I can't take back what I did."

Callie's breath washed over Harper's lips, her eyes fluttering closed. It was a brief kiss, neither stirring nor haunting. What registered with Harper was the complete nothingness she felt as it happened.

"I'll always love you, you made me happier than anything in this world, but we're moving on, babe."

Harper pulled back, nodding. "Yeah, we are." She wiped a stray tear from her jaw, lowering her eyes to her lap. "But thanks for coming by. For being honest. I just wish things could have been different."

"Could they be?" Callie asked, her eyebrow lifted. "Do you think maybe—"

"That I'd take you back?"

Callie nodded slowly.

"No, Callie. We're done. I could never trust you again." That was half the truth, but the part Harper had left out was the most important part. Cait Taylor. Of course, Cait had no idea how much Harper was thinking about her, wanting something more, but in time, she would. "Ruby is who you chose. Be happy with her."

❄

CAIT'S HAND rested on the sash window, her heart slowly sliding into her stomach. The walk up the hill had been refreshing, and it gave her time to think while she was alone, but everything she'd planned in her head and everything she wanted to say to Harper had disappeared.

This shouldn't hurt as much as it did.

Harper...was nothing to her. Not really. And yet, Harper meant a lot to her. She'd sat tonight with friends telling them all about Harper Grey. But now, here she was, standing outside Harper's home, watching her kiss her ex-girlfriend. Cait knew it was her; she remembered her from their stay at the B&B.

While Cait wanted Harper to be happy, she wasn't sure that would happen with Callie. It wasn't her business, Cait understood that, but she didn't want to see Harper get hurt.

This isn't your problem. She was only ever your friend.

Cait backed away from Harper's window, realising that she had been standing around far longer than could be deemed acceptable. The last thing she needed was to be caught by Harper, peering through her window. She hadn't done it intentionally; she'd just seen a light on as she reached the top of the hill and hoped maybe she could catch Harper for half an hour. That hadn't happened, and if Callie was back on the scene, it wouldn't likely happen ever again.

Moving as quickly as her heels would allow, Cait reached the B&B and shoved her keys into the lock. The office light was on, so Jude was still working, but she just wanted to change into something more comfortable and have a cuppa before she called it a night. It was Friday, ten in the evening, and Cait was ready for bed. As rock and roll as always.

It's no wonder she's not interested in you. You have zero sex appeal and a dreadful personality to match.

"Cait?" Jude's voice filtered down the stairs. "Is that you?"

"It's me. I'm home early," she said, her voice low so as not to wake any already sleeping guests. "Everything okay here?"

"Everything is fine. We had a walk-in earlier, but it's otherwise quiet. It'll pick up soon once the weather clears up."

"To be honest, I'm enjoying it being less busy for now. It means I'm not shattered each night."

"Yeah, I know what you mean." Jude smiled, turning out the light in the office. "You headed up?"

Cait slipped out of her heels, relief flooding her body as her toes relaxed into the thick pile carpet. "Yeah. I need sleep."

"You're a bit early…"

Cait was aware of that. "I thought maybe I'd stop off somewhere on the way home, but I didn't bother."

"At Harper's?" Jude followed his sister up the stairs, his voice smooth and understanding. "I'm surprised she didn't take you up on the offer of joining you and Mandy."

"She's…busy."

"Oh. Well, I'm glad she's finding her place here and keeping busy."

Emotion welled in Cait's throat. Harper was busy with her ex, not busy with her life. "Yeah, me too."

Jude must have noted the tremble in his sister's voice, his hand on her wrist as they reached the top of the stairs. "What's going on? You're upset."

"I'm fine. It's been a long day, nothing else."

"You're my sister, Cait. I know when something's wrong. Talk to me."

"You know how you've been bringing up Harper since the moment she arrived, telling me how I should put myself out there?"

Jude nodded.

"I really like her, Jude," Cait said, a single tear falling. "And when I say that, I mean that I can picture us together next Christmas, decorating the tree and stuff. Mulled wine. Cookies. Snuggles. I see it all the time."

"That's great." Jude grinned, but it faltered when Cait didn't share his enthusiasm. "Isn't it?"

"I was going to call in and see her on my way home from dinner. I'd sat at that table all night thinking about her while Mandy was trying to set me up with Liz, so I really wanted to see her."

"Liz? Daniel's Liz?"

"That's the one."

Jude shook his head. "She's not your type. No way."

"Agreed, even though I have no idea who she is."

"So, what's the issue with Harper? I mean, I know you're reluctant because of the time you have to put into this place, but Harper seems like the kind to understand. And she's definitely into you. You're joined at the hip lately."

"I was about to knock on the door when I heard talking. I may have peeked through the window. I didn't want to disturb her if she had company, and she did. She had her ex over."

"So?"

"So, they looked cosy. And that's fine. But if she's kissing someone else, I have to get her out of my head, Jude. If they're making a go of it, I'd never stand in the way of that. She *was* engaged to the woman after all."

"Shit. I'm sorry."

Cait lifted a hand, rubbing Jude's upper arm. "It's fine. It's not the end of the world."

"You'll still be friends, though."

"Maybe. I don't know."

"Cait, you can't throw away your friendship because she's back with her girlfriend."

Her girlfriend. Cait shuddered at the thought. Harper wasn't available, and that was the end of that. "They probably won't need me around. Harper won't if she has Callie back. But like I said, Harper's happiness is what matters. She's so great; I don't want her to spend her days moping around. She should be happy, and Callie must make her happy."

"Sleep on it, okay? Everything may feel different in the morning." Jude gave Cait a knowing look, but there really wasn't anything to sleep on.

"Maybe, but it doesn't change the fact that she's back with her ex."

"Sorry, kid." Jude enveloped Cait in one of his warm hugs,

rubbing her back. "But you're willing to get back out there, so don't let this stop you. Maybe Harper just wasn't meant to be."

But she was. She was so meant to be.

"Yeah. You're right."

CHAPTER NINE

Cait rubbed at her temples, resting against the counter in the kitchen of the B&B. She wasn't prepared for guests this morning, but she had no choice other than to suck it up and get on with her day. This was her life; it always would be.

Jude's voice could be heard outside, welcoming guests for breakfast, but Cait didn't have the capacity just yet to make herself known. Jude knew she was here and working but behind the scenes was best for the time being. She could pretend to be happy in a couple of hours once people milled about and enquired about their potential day ahead. That was when Cait would plaster on that fake smile she'd mastered over the years.

"Sorry about last week, Cait." Tom offered her a slight smile, flipping the bacon on the grill before perfecting his fried eggs. "That bloody Renault has to go. I'm throwing money at it for nothing now."

Cait snapped out of her daze, giving her full attention to Tom. "Don't worry about it. These things happen."

"I know, but I left you in the dark."

"Jude stepped in. His bacon isn't half as good as yours, you get it just right, but the guests didn't complain. It was lucky we didn't have any regulars in."

"Is that a hint for some bacon on toast, Cait?"

The thought of it sent a wave of nausea through her. When she was worried or upset, Cait struggled to eat. "No, thank you. I'm okay."

"I could rustle up some black pudding to go with it." Tom eyed Cait, his signature smile settling her worries, his highlighted hair styled with a quiff. "You know you want to."

"I'll grab some when breakfast is finished, okay?"

Tom curtsied. "It shall be waiting…"

Cait shook her head, her ponytail tickling the back of her neck as she laughed. Tom had joined the B&B just over a year ago, and his breakfast rating was exceptional on the review sites. He was a nice guy with a love for cats; what more could she want in an employee? "I'd better get out there and give Jude a hand."

"Nonsense. Sit in here and give me all the gossip."

Cait's lips curled into another smile. "I'd love to, but I have work to do and zero gossip."

Tom sighed dramatically. "God, this town needs a bit of fire in its belly. It's painfully boring at times."

"Oh, actually." Cait spun around. "Do you know Liz?"

"Daniel's sister?" Tom enquired.

"Why am I the only person that doesn't know who she is?" Cait really needed to take her head out of her arse and pay more attention to the town and its people.

"She's one of us, you know."

Cait threw up her hands. How did Tom know but she didn't? "You could have told me."

Tom stood with a hand on his hip, waving his spatula around the air between them. "Quite frankly, I can't believe you didn't know, Cait. She's one of the only women around here who people think is straight that isn't married."

"Is she on social media?"

"Of course. She's been on mine for years." Tom lowered the grill, grabbing his phone from a high shelf away from the kitchen appliances. "One sec."

Cait didn't know why she was asking about Liz and her social profiles; it wasn't as though she was interested in her. But Tom looked excited, so she would at least humour him for a few more minutes.

"That's her on the left. You know her best friend, too. Jill. Works the river cruises down the bottom."

Cait's eyes widened. "Oh. Her."

"It sounds to me like you've met before." Tom eyed Cait suspiciously.

"Two Christmases ago," Cait explained. "She showed up here absolutely sloshed. I don't know how she made it up the hill, but she basically fell through the door when I opened it. Asked for a room because she couldn't find her keys."

"And did you give her one?"

"I did. I couldn't let her go home alone only to sit on the porch. It was the year we had that bad snowstorm. And she was in heels. I'll always remember that."

"Well, she seems nice. I've bumped into her a few times. She asked me if she could tag along at Cumbria Pride last year, but I wasn't going. I'd just split up with 'he who shall not be named.'"

"Ah. Him."

"He's back with his ex, you know. God, he makes me sick."

Cait cleared her throat. She didn't want to hear about exes and relationships this morning. Seeing Harper with Callie last night still hurt deep in the pit of her stomach.

"Sorry, I think Jude is calling me. Can we talk about this later?"

"Go and be the town's best owner. While I be the town's best breakfast maker."

Cait smiled. "That has a lovely ring to it. Maybe I'll stick it on the next lot of promotion I have done."

"It'll pull them in. And if we stick your face on the flyers, you'll have all the lesbians at your door!" Tom winked, spinning around as he flipped his sausages. "Ooh, I love a gay wedding."

Cait loved Tom's enthusiasm, but he had more chance of

seeing Jesus Christ appear before him than Cait finding someone. After last night, she couldn't bring herself to think about the possibility of dating. What was the point? It only left Cait disappointed.

Jude bumped into her as she left the kitchen, looking flustered. "Hey, sorry I was wondering if you could give me a hand? I've got a call waiting for a booking, last night's walk-in forgot to order breakfast, and one of the cleaners has lost her keys to the rooms."

Cait took a calming breath. "Okay, which cleaner?"

"Margaret."

Cait smiled, shaking her head. "That'll be the third time since Christmas that she's misplaced them. And they always end up being in the same place."

"Any ideas?"

"Yep. In the fridge in the lounge. Check there and if not, let me know, and I'll go searching."

"The fridge?"

"She brings her own milk each morning. Oat."

Jude frowned. "We provide oat milk here."

"I know. I've told her. She said she likes to bring her own in case I let her down." Cait shrugged. At least that was one thing sorted. Now they had less to deal with. "I'll take the walk-in. You take the call for the booking. Which room?"

"Walk-in is staying in room 7. And she's sitting at table 3."

"Okay. Good. Now you can stop panicking." Cait placed a gentle hand on Jude's shoulder. "Go and take the call, and then I'll have a coffee if you're making one."

Jude smiled, rushing out of the breakfast room and towards the stairs. They both knew better than to let a booking slip through their fingers. If they didn't call back as soon as possible, their potential guests would simply go elsewhere.

Cait approached table 3, a sense of anxiety swirling in her belly. She recognised the head of blonde hair.

Callie.

"Oh, hi." Callie offered a pearly white smile. "I'm so sorry I forgot to book breakfast last night."

"That's okay," Cait managed to keep her tone in check, removing her small notepad from the back pocket of her jeans. "What can I get you?"

"I'll have a full English if it's not too much trouble."

"Not at all. Can I get you more coffee or fresh juice?"

"No, I'm okay. Thanks."

Cait nodded, keeping her eyes focused on the notepad. She pretended to write something down, but she was merely avoiding eye contact with Harper's girlfriend. "Won't be long. If you need anything, give me a shout."

"Actually," Callie started, "I wanted to say thanks."

"For?"

"You're Cait, right?"

Oh God. "I am, yes." Cait did find Callie's eyes this time. They were sincere, gentle, but Cait knew what this woman had done to Harper in the past so the kind eyes wouldn't wash with her.

"Harper was telling me that you've been helping her out."

"We're a community around here. We don't like to see people struggle."

"Thanks for looking after her. I made a right mess by putting the heating on when I popped up one weekend."

Cait cleared her throat. "Yes. Harper said."

"But I've made it right now. That's all I could do."

Please don't hurt Harper again.

Cait's emotions caught in her throat. She couldn't be around this woman. Harper deserved better. "Well, I'm happy you two worked stuff out. I should get this order in for you."

Cait rushed into the kitchen, handing over Callie's order to Tom. He looked at her with narrowed eyes, her distress clearly written all over her face.

"What's wrong?"

"Nothing. Order for table 3. That's the last one. If you need me, I'll be in the office."

"Cait?"

"Too busy to stop and chat, Tom." Cait rushed back out of the kitchen, heading straight for the office. She should stick around and serve Callie, but she wasn't sure what would come out of her mouth if she did.

CHAPTER TEN

Harper braced herself as she stepped out of the house, the windchill epic this morning. She had a video call with a client at nine, but she was out of milk for her morning coffee. That wasn't ideal; Harper lived for her coffee, but she couldn't drink it black. She needed a touch of milk and two sugars for her first in the morning, its ratio changing as the day went on.

She wrapped her scarf tighter around her neck, the mist visible over the mountains and the lake as she looked to her left. To her right, the place that had the milk. The milk she really needed this morning. *God, I hate today!* But it would improve. It had to. She had a potential new client about to go on her books, web design his requirement, and the past week had really seen an uptick in her services. She must have been doing something right.

As she crossed the small road separating her house from the B&B, Harper glanced up at the old Victorian house. The buildings around here were impressive, all built with a stacked slate that was more than worth its value on the market. It was like something from a quaint Christmas film. If anything, after this week, it was the one thing keeping Harper here.

Liar. Cait is the reason you're happy here.

But she hadn't seen Cait in a week. Not a peep out of her.

Harper assumed Jude had gone back on his word of helping out at the B&B, so she'd decided to wait until Cait came to her. She was a successful woman with a lot of people wanting somewhere to stay, so Harper and her life troubles were the least of Cait's concern.

She blew out a deep breath, taking the steep incline towards the nearest shop. A pint of milk, and she would be out of the cold for the rest of the day. She'd thought about heading down to the lake to clear her head, but it really was fresh today. Too fresh. Tonight wouldn't likely be any better, the frost on the ground this morning strengthening that fact. This place was idyllic, but… Christ, it was also cold.

Harper eyed the shop she wanted, crossing the main road quickly even though there wasn't a soul in sight. Maybe she would grab a paper while she was there and see what was going on in the local area.

Today marked the third Friday since she'd arrived, the leak that led to the flood now the least of her worries. But not seeing Cait had Harper bored out of her mind. Cait made her think. She made her want to sit and talk about anything that sprang to mind. But Cait was preoccupied with her livelihood, so Harper really couldn't do anything about it.

Thrilled when she reached the shop, Harper removed her gloves and headed straight for the milk. Maybe she could jog back down the hill to warm herself up. She'd lit the fire before she left, and she had no plans to move from in front of it today.

Maybe I could get Cait's number from the door and see if she's free this evening. Harper didn't know what she would say. She couldn't exactly begin the message with "I miss you," but she had time to think about it. Cait would be busy with the morning breakfast rush right about now anyway.

"Hi, good morning." Harper beamed a smile at the shopkeeper. "Cold, isn't it…"

"What else did you expect?" the older, greying man asked.

"Well, I didn't really know. I used to live in the city, so the rural life is literally biting me."

"You'll get used to it. Just keep wrapped up warm and summer will be here before you know it."

Harper took her glass milk bottle from the counter and grabbed a newspaper, handing over some coins. "Good advice. See you!"

As she stepped out onto the street, Cait landed in front of her.

Cait stared, her bobble hat adorable as it sat perfectly in place, dark curls poking out from the bottom. "H-hi."

"Hello, you." Harper's heart fluttered. Cait looked beautiful but cold. "I thought you'd been kidnapped."

Cait frowned. "Why?"

"Because I haven't seen you in over a week. I mean, it's closer to two but I haven't been counting."

"Right." Cait rubbed her forearm, looking down at her feet. "Busy, I guess."

"But that's good," Harper said, hiding her disappointment. "It means you're a success."

"Maybe, yeah. I don't know."

Harper studied Cait for a moment. This conversation seemed strained. "Well, it seems like you're in a rush or you don't have time, so I'll let you get on."

"Yeah. Bye, Harper." Cait side stepped her, disappearing into the shop.

It was at that moment that Harper decided to hang around outside. They could walk back down the hill together. Keep one another company.

When Cait came back out of the shop, she looked puzzled.

"Thought we could head back down together..."

"Oh. Right, okay." Cait took a quick pace, rushing in front of Harper as they left the shop front.

Harper wanted to enquire, to know if she'd done something wrong, but Cait was hard to read this morning. Harper had never felt so uncomfortable around her.

"Hey, I was wondering if you're free this evening?"

"I'm not. Sorry."

"Tomorrow?" Harper chanced.

Cait slowed her pace, sighing as she turned around. "I'm really busy at the minute. And I will be until God knows when."

"I thought things slowed down at this time of year?"

"Seems I got it wrong. But that's what I'm good at doing, so it's no surprise really."

What did that mean? "Well, it's good that business is doing well, I guess."

"Yeah. Great." Cait backed away down the hill. "Look, I really have to rush. But it was nice seeing you."

Cait turned to leave, but Harper wasn't quite finished yet. "Cait?"

"Yeah?" Cait's voice shook, her inability to face Harper confusing.

"Is everything okay?"

"Sure." Cait's eyes remained focused ahead of her. "But I really do need to get back. Guests are waiting on their papers."

That was a lie. Harper hadn't seen a single person pick up a paper when she stayed at the B&B. She pushed off her foot, jogging down the hill to meet Cait. "Wait. Just for a moment."

"Harper…"

Harper turned Cait around, shocked and saddened to see tears falling down her rosy cheeks. "Hey, what's wrong? I don't like seeing you upset."

"I'm fine. It's nothing."

"It's not nothing if you're crying in my company. Did I do something to upset you?"

"No. You're perfect."

Harper was taken aback. Nobody had ever called her perfect, nor had she ever professed to be.

"I just…my work with you is done, Harper. You're thriving at home now, and Darren says all work is complete."

"Well, yeah. But unless I was some kind of project for you, I don't understand why you're dropping me. I thought we were friends."

"We are. But you have your life, and I have mine."

"You've still not broken the routine then?"

"I was considering it. I thought I knew what I wanted," Cait said, brushing stray hair from her eyes as an ice-cold wind whipped around them. "But I was wrong. So, I'll stick to what I know and work myself into the ground."

"That's no life to live. You could be having so much fun."

"I had my fun with you when you arrived here. And now it's back to work. It's my livelihood, and I can't slack, Harper."

Harper understood. She'd taken up far too much of Cait's time. But she did appreciate it. If only Cait would allow her to show that, Harper may not feel as guilty as she did this morning. "Okay." She nodded. "Well, my door is always open if you ever want to hang out."

"That's a delightful offer, but you know..." Cait threw her thumb over her shoulder. "Back to the grindstone."

Harper watched Cait disappear down the hill, her mind drawing a blank when it came to understanding what had just transpired. Cait Taylor was never unwelcoming, but that was the impression Harper was getting this morning. She'd say maybe Cait wasn't a morning person, but she'd seen her over several mornings now, and she'd always had that sweet, wonderful smile. Today, it was nowhere to be found.

❄

"I'LL PUT our review up on TripAdvisor the moment we get home, Cait. It's been another fabulous stay with you and Jude."

Cait forced a full smile. Mr and Mrs Penny had stayed at the B&B many times over the years. "That's great. Have a safe trip home, okay? And we'll see you soon."

"You will. We'll be back for the summer. You know that."

"Send me an email with some dates. I'll make sure the suite you want is available."

"Look at that, Ron. Isn't she just wonderful?"

"As always."

Cait kept the fake smile plastered on her face until her guests had climbed into their car, her body weary from the lack of sleep last night. It wasn't any one thing in particular causing it, but knowing Harper was just down the street with her girlfriend didn't help in any way.

"I'm off to the supplier." Jude grabbed his coat from the stand by the door. "Need anything while I'm gone?"

"A new existence?"

"You're still thinking about Harper…"

Cait wrapped her arms around herself, needing something to keep her grounded. "Bumped into her this morning when I went to collect the papers."

"How was she?"

"Fine." Cait lifted a shoulder. "She asked if I was free tonight or tomorrow, but I declined her invitations."

"You can't avoid her forever, Cait. You should at least stop by and tell her why you're not willing to give her the time of day anymore."

"That's not what I'm doing. She just caught me off guard this morning. Next time, I'll be friendlier."

"If there is a next time." Jude looked at her knowingly. "Considering she's back with her girlfriend, I haven't seen sight nor sound of her around here."

Cait frowned. That was true; Callie hadn't been around. "No. Me neither."

"Maybe it didn't work out. That's something to consider."

"Perhaps I could stop by this evening. Apologise for this morning. It'll give me an idea as to whether her girlfriend is there or not. Surely if she is, she'll be around this evening."

"Sherlock would hire you any day."

"Oh, piss off!" Cait shook her head, managing a laugh. "I'll get the invoices finished and then I'll get my housework done. Do you mind if I take a few hours this evening?"

"Take all the time you need. I don't have any plans."

"But this is the second Friday in a row that you've had no plans..."

"Because I'm needed here. If it all goes pear-shaped and you're home early, I might call in at the pub to see the lads, but, if not, it's no big deal."

"Thank you."

Cait watched Jude leave, the harsh air pushing its way through the door as he went. She'd never been one to investigate anything, but something told her that Harper could be worth it.

CHAPTER ELEVEN

HARPER YAWNED, HER EYES BURNING AS SHE FOCUSED ON THE template she was working with. Graphic design was her life, but web design seemed to be all the rage at the minute. As she contemplated taking a short break, maybe stretch her legs, her Mac started to ring, followed by her phone, her iPad, and her watch. "Jesus. Is there any need for everything to alert me?"

She grabbed her phone, answering the call direct, and relaxing back in her chair. "Hello, best friend. I thought you'd forgotten I existed."

"I could say the same right back at you."

"But you wouldn't do that because you know how busy I've been with moving." Harper grinned. She knew Autumn would be rolling her eyes and cursing under her breath. "Right?"

"Yes. Fine. Whatever you say."

"So, what's up?"

"Wanted to check in with you. How's it all going up there in the land of icicles and frozen nipples?"

"Well, my nipples haven't fallen off, so that's something." Harper laughed, bringing her knees up to her chest in her office chair. She missed Autumn and the banter they shared, but it wasn't like they lived a million miles away, so it wasn't the end of the world. Autumn would beg to differ though, judging by her reaction and how she'd sobbed as she waved Harper off. "How is back home?"

"Boring without you."

"I'm sure you're fine. You can be with all your girly friends now that the lesbian isn't around."

"That's nonsense."

Harper shrugged. "Tell that to them and the way they used to snarl at me when I was around. I'm sure they thought I was trying to recruit you to the dark side. But I wouldn't do that to you; it's honestly not worth it. Women are the fucking worst!"

"Yeah, I didn't think you'd be taking it so well."

"Oh, I'm fine. I just have no desire to entertain another woman for the rest of my life."

"Look, I know it must be hard, but now that she's out of your life…and moving on by the looks of it, you can get on with your own life. And it must be gorgeous up there."

"She was here last weekend. Showed up."

Autumn fell silent.

Harper frowned. "You there?"

"I…yes, I'm here. So, she told you then?"

"She tells me all kinds of shit she thinks I want to hear. You'll have to be more specific."

"About the engagement?"

What engagement? Harper had called that off the moment she found out about Callie's infidelity.

"I'm so sorry."

"Autumn, I've no idea what you're talking about."

"Ruby proposed."

Harper's heart thundered in her chest. How could this be happening? "What?"

"They went away for the weekend a few weeks ago. Ruby has it all over social media. I know you don't follow her, but I thought one of the girls may have told you. Seems it's left to the best friend when it comes to that sort of stuff."

"What's Ruby's surname?" Harper couldn't check Callie's, she'd already blocked Harper from all of her accounts, but maybe Ruby hadn't been so clever.

"Fuller."

Harper pulled up her page, searching for Ruby's profile. She wasn't sure she wanted to come across the post she was looking for, but it might put an end to everything Harper ever felt for Callie. When her eyes landed on Ruby's profile picture, Harper's anger bubbled. "The fuck?"

"Harper, close the page. You don't need to see that stuff."

She studied the image, horror tearing through her at the speed of light. "I…it's…that's my fucking bedroom! Here!"

Autumn gasped. "No. It can't be. Why would it be?"

"The reason I didn't call you is because I've been dealing with some issues at the house. I had a leak downstairs, but it's all sorted now. It wasn't as bad as I thought it would be once I took the carpet up."

"Shit, I'm sorry."

"It was Callie who caused the leak in the first place. She admitted to bringing Ruby here the week before I moved in. She only admitted it though when I found a fucking bra in my room." Harper swallowed down her anger and emotion. If she cried for this woman one more time, she would scream. "But this? A proposal in my fucking bedroom?"

"Crap. I've made this worse, haven't I?"

"I'm sure I would have come across it at some point." Harper's entire body slumped in her chair; this was too much to take. This tipped everything completely over the edge. "But you know, thanks and that."

"Can I come and visit you?" Autumn asked. "We can sit around in our pjs and talk shit about them both."

"I'd love you to come and visit me, but I don't want to sit around talking about her. I'm done with everything she is!"

"Okay, well, when is best for you?"

Harper relaxed slightly. Knowing her best friend was visiting made this seem less daunting. Nobody would be any wiser as to where Callie was proposed to, but Harper knew. She always would. Callie was sitting at home laughing at her, no doubt about it.

"Come up whenever you like. I'll be home. I'm just getting used to things at the minute."

"I'll drive up first thing in the morning. Spend Saturday and Sunday with you. I'll drive back Sunday night once the traffic has died down."

"That works for me. I'll put your favourite pillows on my bed. It's been a while since we've hung out like that."

"See you early tomorrow afternoon, okay? Send me the address, and I'll bring alcohol. We could both use a blowout."

"Bye, bestie. Love ya!"

"Love you too."

As Harper ended the call and placed her phone down, tears slid freely down her face. Autumn wouldn't know that, she didn't often show emotion in front of other people, but, God, she needed to let it all out. Just last week, Callie had been in this house, asking if Harper would take her back. And now? Well, it seemed a leopard really didn't change its spots.

❄

CAIT STOPPED, glancing across the road at Harper's house. It really was a home to be admired; Cait still kicked herself for not putting an offer in when it was up for sale. But she stood by her word—Harper would treat it well. And she deserved the incredible space inside.

As Cait placed one foot on the road, uncertainty rolled through her. Was it wise to call and see Harper? What if Callie was home? Cait didn't know what Harper and Callie had discussed, but Cait knew that Harper had an inkling Cait was attracted to her. It was too obvious when they were down at the lake together. An evening that seemed like a distant memory now.

She steeled herself, rushed across the street, and approached Harper's front door. The garden gate was already open, just another obstacle removed from Cait's pathway to Harper. She lifted her hand and knocked lightly, clearing her throat in preparation for what she would say.

What would she say? She had no idea.

The door opened slowly. Harper peered around the slight gap, frowning. "Is everything okay?"

Cait smiled. "Yes. I just wanted to call by and see you."

"Why? You didn't want to speak to me this morning, so I don't know why you've changed your mind."

"Could I come in and explain?" Cait asked, aware that Harper wasn't in a great mood. The reason was most likely Cait's cold shoulder this morning, but she really didn't want it to be that way. So she would explain her predicament to Harper, and then let her be. "Please?"

Harper nodded, opening the door. "Fine."

Cait breathed a sigh of relief, stepping past Harper and closing the door. She knew better than to hang around outside when the fire was keeping it warm inside. And with the bitter wind chill this evening, Cait really didn't want to bring it in with her.

She moved into the living room, fully complete with new carpets and brand-spanking new couches. Cait's breath caught when she eyed the roaring fire, the thick fleece throws, and a rom com playing on the huge TV.

"You look settled."

"Finished working for the day. Got nothing better to do, so I may as well sit and scoff at the pathetic film I'm watching."

"O…kay." Cait straightened herself; Harper didn't want her here.

"Sorry, I've had a bad day. You didn't deserve that." Harper lifted a hand, an apologetic look in her eyes. "So, you wanted to speak to me?"

"Is Callie home?" Cait asked, not wanting to cause a rift between them. "I can come back if it's not a great time."

"Callie? Home?"

Should Cait tell Harper she'd seen her here? Or maybe just start with the fact that Callie was at the B&B? "Never mind. She's obviously not here."

"Cait," Harper said, pinching the bridge of her nose. "Why the hell would Callie be here?"

"I...I thought you were back together."

Harper barked a laugh, dropping down onto the edge of the couch. Cait chanced her luck, taking a seat beside her. "That woman is only around when she wants to hurt me that little bit more. I really don't know what I did for her to hate me so much."

Cait focused on Harper. She had to be truthful. "She was here last weekend. Kissing you."

"What?" Harper's brow knitted. "How could you possibly know that?"

"I saw."

"And how exactly did that happen?"

Cait swallowed, lowering her eyes. "I was coming home from dinner with friends. I wanted to stop by and see you because... well, it doesn't matter why. I realised you had company. I know I shouldn't have looked through the window, I really wish I hadn't, but I did."

"Right."

"So..."

Harper dropped her head into her hands. "She came here. Turned up with a bottle of wine and told me she'd gotten a room for the night. She said we needed to talk and that she wanted to apologise for everything."

"That's something...I guess." Cait didn't like where this was going. Even though she'd seen what she did, it still made her stomach roll. "And now?"

"She's engaged," Harper said barely above a whisper. "She kissed me, asked if there was any chance, while she was engaged."

"Wow."

"Not only that, her girlfriend proposed the weekend they were here."

"Oh."

"In my bedroom." Harper brushed a tear from her jawline, shaking her head. "She's made a complete idiot of me."

"Hey," Cait said, shifting closer and settling a hand on Harper's forearm. "I'm so sorry she did that to you."

"It's never-ending. But that was the last straw. I no longer give a shit about anything she does, so long as she stays out of my life."

"You were going to take her back?" Cait asked, hiding her surprise miserably.

"No. I told her there was no chance. The kiss just happened, and it wasn't even really a kiss."

"That'll teach me to jump to conclusions."

Harper wiped her cheeks, blowing out a breath. "I just thought you'd had a busy week. But even though she did kiss me…what does it matter?"

Cait took a calming breath. Harper was watching her expectantly, but she needed a moment before she laid her cards on the table. The last couple of weeks had been miserable without Harper around, but Cait truly didn't know where they stood with one another. Harper had said in no uncertain terms that she didn't want a relationship, but was that forever? Or just for now?

"Cait?"

"Sorry. I didn't think this would be so difficult. It would appear I'm really out of practice."

Harper twisted in her seat, giving Cait her full attention. But that only made her nerves skyrocket. "Is something wrong, Cait?"

"No, nothing's wrong. Not with you, and not with this." Cait paused. "Harper, we've only just met, but I feel like I've known you my entire life. And I respect your choice to want to be single, but do you think that maybe down the line, when you're happy, that maybe you would consider going on a date with me?"

Harper stared straight through Cait. Silence.

"I'm sure it's all in my head, but at the lake, those things you said…"

"It's not all in your head."

Okay, that made things easier. Now Cait just had to pray that Harper would one day entertain the idea.

"But there is nothing I could bring to your life that you don't already have. I just…I have to really look at myself, see how I can improve."

"Improve what?"

"Well, whatever Callie didn't like. Because I know it'll only happen again with the next woman I meet, and I don't think I could go through what she's put me through ever again."

"Callie is gone. And I know she hurt you, but you have to understand that some people are just like that. It doesn't mean you did anything wrong. I see how much you've enriched *my* life already, so I'm really struggling to find any areas for improvement with you."

Harper turned her hand over, lacing their fingers together. "You're really sweet."

"No, I tell the truth."

"Maybe one day. I don't know."

As much as Cait loved that it could potentially happen, Harper didn't seem overly enthusiastic about the suggestion. Perhaps Harper was just trying not to hurt Cait's feelings, but she preferred honesty in any situation. "You know, I don't want you to just tell me you'll consider it if it's not what you want."

Harper sighed. "If only you knew just how much I do want it."

Cait smiled, but Harper looked emotionally drained. She wouldn't put any more pressure on her about this. Cait had opened up about her intentions, now the ball was in Harper's court. "Well, I've said what I needed to say. I'll leave you to enjoy the rest of your night."

"Do you like Kendal Mint Cake?" Harper asked, her eyes brightening ever so slightly.

"What kind of question is that? I grew up on the stuff."

Harper got to her feet, blowing out a long breath. She rolled her head on her shoulders and stared down at Cait. "Fancy some? With this film?"

"You...want me to stay a while?" Cait suppressed the grin she felt curling on her lips when Harper nodded. "You're sure?"

"Only if you promise to finish the entire bar with me?"

"That's not difficult. I always have a bar at home and one hidden for back up."

"Uh-huh. Just the kind of thing I'm looking for."

CHAPTER TWELVE

Harper was running late. Autumn was due any moment now, and she was only just leaving the local shop. Autumn had told her she would bring the alcohol, but Harper figured she should at least stock up on some herself; it wouldn't do any harm. But if she got back home and Autumn was waiting for her, Harper would never hear the end of it.

In all honesty, Harper was in a world of her own today. She'd gone to sleep last night thinking of Cait, and she'd woken this morning in the same situation. But for a change, she felt positive. She knew all about the spark she and Cait shared, but to actually be asked if there was a chance she may one day consider dating Cait? That hadn't been on Harper's mind. It had crept in once or twice as a fanciful daydream, but it didn't hang around long enough to stick. Except today…it did.

Harper moved quickly as she descended the hill, her eyes catching the upstairs window at the B&B. She could see Cait's silhouette, her breath quickening as she stopped to admire the view for a second. It looked as though Cait was twirling in a mirror, and Harper was certain she probably looked stunning.

And then her phone pinged, ruining the moment she was sharing with herself. Bastard.

A: I'm here. You're not. What gives?

H: 2 secs. I was at the shop.

A: Hurry up. I'm freezing my bollocks off!

Harper rolled her eyes, locking her phone as she jogged the rest of the way home. Autumn was always dramatic when it came to arrivals; it looked like today wouldn't be any different.

When she spotted her best friend leaning against the garden wall, Harper could hardly contain the laugh that worked its way to the surface. Autumn stood in a thin denim jacket and a skirt. "Are you taking the piss?"

"Excuse me?"

"Autumn. It's like minus 50 here. I hope you've brought warmer clothes with you."

"I'll be in my pjs. It'll hardly matter." Autumn popped the boot of her car, taking a hold-all from it. "Be a love and carry that thing in for me."

Harper bent to lift the bag, almost pulling her back out. "Shit. What's in that?"

"My life."

"You're only here until tomorrow. You're off your head!" Harper dragged the hold-all up the path, searching for her keys in her pocket as she balanced the alcohol under her arm. "But God, I'm so happy you're here. We have stuff to talk about."

"Please let me sit and slate that whore and her home-wrecker all night. Please!"

"Nope. Callie is the least of my concerns," Harper said, holding up a hand as she ushered Autumn inside. "Welcome. Make yourself at home."

"That's the plan." Autumn kicked off her shoes, dragging herself into the living room. "I love this house. It's gorgeous. And very…not you."

"Hey! I'm a new person now." Harper scowled, her hand on her hip. She left Autumn's hold-all in the hallway, closing the front door and locking up. "And I'm not as miserable as I was when I spoke to you yesterday."

"Why?"

"Autumn, I've met someone. She's amazing, she's gorgeous, she has the sweetest smile, and I'm fully prepared to fall over myself for this woman."

"And this all happened since yesterday?"

"Well, not exactly. But she came over last night and asked me if I wanted to go on a date…"

"Wow. Okay. Sit down, I want to know all about it."

"Can I get you something to drink first? Cup of tea?" Harper got to her knees, adding more wood to the fire. Autumn was shivering, but Harper knew she wouldn't mention the fact after how she'd been greeted. "Cold drink?"

"I'll have a coffee, love. Warm my hands up."

"And what about the rest of you? Your knees are blue."

Autumn glanced down. "No, they're not!"

"Could have been."

"Anyway, I'm not interested in me or what I'm wearing, I'll warm up in no time. What I want to know is all about this woman you're head over heels for."

"I'm not head over heels."

"But you could be?"

Harper remained silent for a moment. She knew with one hundred percent certainty that Cait could be the best thing to ever happen to her, but she also knew herself well enough to know that she had the potential to fuck it all up. Harper didn't want to even tempt fate by saying too much to Autumn. The results could be devastating.

"If we get on, yes. No reason why I couldn't."

"Something changed just then," Autumn said, sitting forward with her elbows on her knees. "You were thinking…"

"I just have a lot to consider, Autumn. As much as I'd love to knock on her door now and take her out to dinner, I'm not in the right place. We both know that, and I think Cait does too."

"Fair enough."

"But I do really like her. She's just great. She has this spark in her eyes, Autumn. You know, like she wants more in life but doesn't know where to turn?"

"And it's taken you moving here for her to realise it?" Autumn quirked an eyebrow. "You must be special."

"Not necessarily, no. I just feel like she wants more."

"With you?"

"No. In life." Harper busied herself in the kitchen, making coffee for them both. She grabbed her phone from the counter as she brought their drinks through, placing the mugs down on the coffee table. "She owns the B&B up the road. It's literally her life."

"Ooh, I'd love to own a B&B."

Harper frowned. "You would?"

"Oh, yeah. It must be nice and cushy."

Harper didn't get that impression at all. Cait was always run off her feet. "Then you're sadly mistaken. She works her arse off."

"And you want to get into a relationship with someone who dedicates her life to work?"

"Beats being with someone who dedicates her life to shagging around."

Autumn nodded as she settled back onto the couch, pulling the handle at the side to release the footrest. Harper's best friend looked like she belonged there. "Good choice, pal."

"The couch or the woman?"

"Huh. I'm undecided. I have to meet this mysterious Cait before I can give you my blessing on that front."

Harper gulped, taking her coffee from the table. Cait probably wasn't into that. And Harper could hardly blame her. Autumn wouldn't be dating Cait, so what did it matter the opinion she had? "She's probably jam-packed this weekend, but maybe in the future."

"Probably?"

Harper tugged her earlobe. "I don't know what her plans are. She was here last night, but I kinda turned down her offer of a date."

"Okay, you've lost me." Autumn held up her hand. "Do you want to date her or not?"

"I do. Absolutely, I do. But like I said, I'm not sure I'm ready yet. I feel like I only left Callie a minute ago."

"So?"

"So, Cait deserves more than that. I need Callie completely out of my head before I give my all to Cait."

Autumn narrowed her eyes. "You're still thinking about that bitch? Why?"

"I'm not thinking about her. But I'm still reeling from what she did to me, Autumn. I mean, she was here just last weekend. She was asking me if there was a chance we could ever be together again. And it doesn't matter that I told her no. She still asked that question and kissed me while she was engaged."

"Fuck her. She's dead to me."

"Me too. Mostly."

"Mostly?" Autumn scoffed.

"Look. We were together for four years. I was planning the wedding of all weddings. I'd even finished the invitations, and she'd picked out the chair cover colour. It's not as simple as just erasing her from my mind. Surely you understand that?"

"I do. Kinda. But this Cait woman may not hang around while you decide what you're doing with your life. And if she met someone else, could you blame her?"

"No, I couldn't."

"So, it's time to do what's right for you. Fuck the rest of them. You were always too good for Callie. I wish you could see that."

"But not good enough for her when it came to being happy and content. It's all a bit fucked up."

"She'll never change. And I think her being here last week only shows you that. If you're thinking for one second about taking her back, I can't be your friend. I love you to death, but if you entertain her for a second longer, we're going to have issues."

"I'm not stupid." And Harper really wasn't…not usually. But Callie had been her one moment of weakness. Everyone had at least one, didn't they? "She's more than out of my life. But do you think I'm ready? Honestly?"

"Depends."

Harper sighed. "On what?"

"Whether you're willing to give this woman the benefit of the doubt and realise that not everyone is the same as Callie."

"I don't need to give Cait the benefit of the doubt. She's perfect. I'm not sure she's stepped out of line once in her life. And I trust her. I don't know her, and I trust her."

"Then you asking me if you're ready is a waste of breath, my friend."

"Okay, so…maybe I could see if she's available tomorrow, and I'll do Sunday dinner. What do you think?"

"I think that's a nice idea. It's nothing too drastic and it will give you a feel for what could potentially happen. Did you want me to leave earlier?"

"No, I'd really like you to meet her…but just don't throw 20 questions at her."

"I wouldn't do anything to jeopardise this for you. You know that."

"I know."

❄

Cait checked her makeup in the mirror beside the front door to the B&B. Tonight hadn't originally been in her plans, but here she was, heading out to dinner. Jude had encouraged her and Mandy had demanded Cait show up at the restaurant in question, but she couldn't be sure she was doing the right thing. She knew it wouldn't come to anything, this was merely a date she'd been guilted into, but Mandy was right. Cait would never leave another woman sitting alone in a restaurant. Even if it had been Mandy who promised Liz that Cait would show.

Cait could deal with her best friend at a later date, she deserved one hell of a reprimand for doing this to her, but Liz was waiting at the restaurant three blocks away, so Cait really had to rush.

"You look great, Cait." Jude appeared behind her as she checked she didn't have any lipstick on her teeth. "And I'm really happy you're going on a date."

"It's not really a date when I'm not keen on the idea, is it?"

Jude shoved his hands in his pockets. "You never know. Liz could be great and you two could get on really well."

Jude was right, but Cait was still holding onto the idea that Harper may one day be ready. "Maybe."

"I know what you want deep down, but how long are you willing to wait?" Jude asked. "A few weeks? Until next year? You deserve more than that, Cait. You deserve to find someone now, not when it suits Harper."

But that wasn't how Cait felt about it all. She could completely understand the predicament Harper was in, and, in some ways, she appreciated Harper's honesty. Cait didn't want to spend her time in the arms of a woman who wasn't entirely sure yet. She also didn't want to put herself in a position where she could fall for Harper only for that sentiment to not be returned. "I should go. Liz will be waiting."

"That's the spirit."

Cait sighed as she reached for her long black overcoat. As the draught seeped through the door, she was beginning to regret her choice of little black dress and heels. It was winter, not the height of summer. "I shouldn't be late."

"Are you sure you don't want a lift to the restaurant?"

"It's three blocks away, Jude. I'll be there in five minutes."

"It's a cold one tonight..."

"I need the fresh air. Maybe I'll realise the mistake I'm making before I get there." Cait could realise the mistake ten times over, and she still wouldn't let Liz down. It wasn't her fault that Mandy had meddled in something that didn't concern her. So Cait would enjoy dinner and pray to God Liz didn't expect anything more. "See you in a few hours."

She didn't wait for another remark from Jude. The sooner Cait forced herself out of the B&B, the sooner her nerves would subside. Maybe she could take a few positives from this evening. If nothing else, it would give her an idea of what dating looked like these days. Harper, if she ever changed her mind, wouldn't see her as being so out of practice when the time came.

Cait crossed the street, the darkness comforting in some way as she approached Harper's house. This time, she would keep her eyes ahead of her. The consequences of peeking last time hadn't done her any favours. If anything, doing so had only given her less time with Harper for jumping to conclusions.

But then Harper's front door opened, a flash of that beautiful auburn hair catching Cait's attention. Her stomach rolled; she hadn't really wanted to see Harper this evening. Not when she was about to go on a supposed date with another woman. Shit!

"Wow." Harper dropped the sack of rubbish in her hand to the floor, her mouth agape. "You look…wow!"

"Thanks." Cait gripped her clutch bag, removing her black leather gloves from her coat pocket. She may only be a short distance from the restaurant, but Jude was right. It was icy this evening.

"Off somewhere special?" Harper asked, her eyes travelling Cait's entire body. "I mean, whoever is in your company tonight had better be grateful."

"Just…dinner." It wasn't a lie, but it wasn't the complete truth either. "Do you have plans?"

"Autumn arrived this afternoon. We're just about to put a film on and catch up with one another."

"Well, have a lovely evening." Cait tucked a curl behind her ear, looking down at the floor.

"You know, I could walk you into town if you wanted me to…"

Cait lifted her head, frowning. "Why would you want to walk me into town?"

"So you're not walking alone at night. I don't like the idea of that." Harper quickly disposed of her rubbish in the correct wheelie bin, rushing to the door. "Wait there. I'll grab my coat and some shoes. Autumn won't mind."

"Harper, it's fine."

"Cait." Harper sighed. "Just let me walk you into town."

"It's a date." Cait's words tumbled from her mouth, something she instantly regretted when Harper's shoulders visibly slumped.

"Oh," Harper said. She quickly picked herself back up again, but Cait had seen the disappointment. She knew how Harper felt; she didn't particularly want tonight to happen either. "Well, I… uh." Harper's flustered words filtered quietly through the air between them. "H-have a lovely night. I hope the lucky lady appreciates the effort you've put in. You look gorgeous."

"It probably won't come to anything." Cait tried to justify her reasons, perhaps even her expectations, but Harper looked as though she was ready to end this conversation. "Just…getting a feel for it all again."

"I still don't mind walking you." Harper lifted a shoulder slightly, her eyes not finding Cait's.

"Really, it's fine."

"Okay." Harper stepped back, almost losing her footing as she stumbled over the threshold. She caught herself on the door, gripping it as she balanced herself. "Bye, Cait."

Cait remained still for a moment, considering her next move. She could call off the date and head back home, but she really didn't like that idea. Not only would Liz feel as though she'd been stood up, but Cait had gone to a lot of effort to plan her evening and her outfit. "It's just dinner," she muttered to herself. "And Harper isn't ready."

Cait took one final glance at Harper's house and shook her head as she finally found the strength to move her legs. The longer she stood here, the more she wanted to turn around and lock herself away, pyjamas her only comfort tonight. But Cait would push on and show her face. It wasn't the end of the world that she had to spend time with another woman.

❄

CAIT SET her cutlery down and pushed her plate away, full to bursting from the Italian meal she'd just shared with Liz. The restaurant was quiet considering it was Saturday, but the cold snap they were going through often meant less people milling about. The problem was, with less people around them, it felt more intimate. And that really was the last thing Cait needed.

Liz was delightful, hilarious too, but she really wasn't what Cait was looking for. Since they'd received their food, Liz had talked about nothing other than moving onto a cocktail bar with potential shots on the cards later on. While Cait loved Liz's enthusiasm for a good night out, Cait really wasn't a big drinker. She never had been. The B&B played a big role in that reason since she didn't have the luxury of waking up with a hangover every weekend, but, she preferred to be the sober one within her group of friends anyway.

"So, how was your food?" Liz asked, her soft eyes staring back at Cait. "I've only been here once before but that was impressive."

"It was lovely. I feel as though I need to lie down now, though." Cait took her wine glass in her hand, drinking the last remaining drop.

"No time for lying down, Cait. Those cocktails are calling our names."

Cait offered a slight smile, relaxing back in her seat. "As much as I'd love to, I really shouldn't. Tomorrow is check out day for the current guests. I have to be available from breakfast onwards."

"I'm sure Jude can look after the guests." Liz's hand suddenly shifted, snaking towards Cait's that sat on the tabletop. "I feel like I still don't know a lot about you."

That can only be a good thing. Cait didn't often offer up a lot of information about herself. There really wasn't much to tell. "I really can't. I'm sorry."

"Okay, so how about we get ourselves another bottle of wine for the table? Here is good enough if you're okay with that?"

"By all means, you enjoy another bottle. But I think I'll settle for a cappuccino."

Liz lifted her hand and called for the waiter. Once she'd ordered their drinks, Liz focused back on Cait. "I can't believe we've both lived in this town all our lives and we're only just getting together now."

Getting together? Oh, no. That wasn't what was happening here. Not at all. "I spend seven days a week working. I don't really usually have time to do this."

"But you made an exception for me. I'm so happy about that." Liz reached further forward, her fingertips touching Cait's. But Cait felt nothing. No spark. No connection. No…nothing. "And we should definitely do this again."

"Could you excuse me for a moment?" Cait threw her thumb over her shoulder towards the wooden bathroom door. "I'll just be a few minutes."

"Of course. Yes." Liz grinned, watching Cait as she left the table with her clutch bag in hand.

When Cait reached the safety of the bathroom stall, she took her phone from her bag and brought up her messages. Before she left Harper last night, they'd exchanged numbers. Right now, she was more than happy they'd done so.

C: Hi, it's Cait. Can you call me to get me out of this date?

Cait sent off the message, waiting until she received the little read receipt at the bottom of the bubble, but it didn't come. She tapped her foot against the floor, blowing out a deep breath. She didn't expect an immediate response from Harper, so she unlocked the door, put her phone away, and washed her hands. Harper would surely call soon. She had to.

Cait focused on herself in the mirror. She didn't have that brightness in her eyes that she did when she was with Harper. She didn't feel that fire in her belly as they embraced. She really didn't feel a single thing about this date.

It's not a date, Cait told herself. *It's simply dinner with another resident of the town.*

Cait steeled herself and left the bathroom. Liz was watching her just as she had moments ago. And while she felt good about herself when another woman was drooling over her, this was not the woman she wished to be sitting with.

"Sorry about that." Cait spied her cappuccino waiting for her. She added half a sachet of brown sugar and stirred, avoiding eye contact with Liz. "So, what do you do when you're not working?"

"Usually down the pub with the girls. I play darts on weekends."

"Nice." Cait had no idea what else to say to Liz. They really didn't have very much in common with one another. "Have you played for long?"

Liz blew out a deep breath. "Must be coming up to 20 years now."

"I can't say I've ever picked up a dart."

"You should try it sometime. Maybe that could be our next date. Darts and beer."

Okay, Cait couldn't do this any longer. It was painfully clear how incompatible they were. And yes, she wasn't looking for someone that was entirely like her, but, still, some kind of similar interest would help. "Liz…"

"Yeah?"

"I'm sorry, but this really isn't working for me." Cait felt terrible, but she couldn't prolong this for another second. "Mandy set this date up without my knowledge."

Liz's eyes widened. "You mean you've been sitting here for the sake of it?"

"I didn't want to let you down," Cait explained. "But I've still had a lovely evening."

"Well, if I wasn't already into you, I certainly am now. That's a really nice thing you did by showing up."

Cait blushed, lowering her eyes. "I'm really not in a position to date. Mandy shouldn't have taken it upon herself to lead you to believe otherwise." That wasn't quite the truth, and Cait hated lying, but Liz wouldn't know any better if Harper suddenly appeared in the picture. She hadn't seen this woman in two years and even that was by sheer chance; she doubted she would start to bump into her at every turn now. "Let me get the bill. It's the least I can do."

"No, we'll split it."

"Please, I insist." Cait had never felt so guilty before. She may have meant well by showing up tonight, but she'd still led Liz on. "It's the least I can do after wasting your time."

Liz's features softened. "Believe me, you haven't wasted a second of my time."

Please stop saying things like that. Cait focused on her bag as she took her credit card from her purse. She'd been honest with Liz, but that didn't seem to matter to the other woman. Liz clearly still wanted to continue this.

"I'll pay at the bar, okay? Did you want to walk back up the hill together, or?"

"You haven't even finished your cappuccino."

"I couldn't eat or drink another thing. Really." Cait eyed the waiter, getting to her feet and crossing the restaurant.

She felt Liz's eyes on her, burning through her back. When Cait glanced over her shoulder, Liz sat with her hands clasped under her chin, taking in Cait's entire form. Maybe dating wouldn't be so hard after all. If she suddenly had two women interested in her, she was surely doing something right.

She looked down at her phone. Harper hadn't responded to her message. That could only mean one of two things. Harper really was busy with Autumn…or Harper didn't care to assist Cait in getting out of her date. Cait really hoped it wasn't the latter, but something in the pit of her stomach told her that Harper closed her door this evening quite upset.

Cait could only apologise. What for, she didn't quite know, but she would still call to see Harper tomorrow if she had the time. But for the time being, Cait would make her way back up the hill to her home where she could chastise herself for playing unintentional games with Liz.

CHAPTER THIRTEEN

Harper stood staring at her empty fridge, blowing out a frustrated breath when she realised she had absolutely nothing in for a Sunday dinner. She knew she'd need a few bits and bobs from the shop, but not an entire fridge of food. Right now, she didn't have the patience for a supermarket on a Sunday. With reduced hours, it was every person for themselves.

She took the notepad attached to the side of her fridge and flopped down onto a kitchen stool. The sooner she got a shopping list together, the sooner Harper could feed her and Autumn.

Her best friend had been a godsend last night after Harper had bumped into Cait. She hadn't expected it, but the idea that Cait was going to dinner with another woman was overwhelming. Just a few hours before, Harper had been fully prepared to invite Cait over today, but how could she do that now when she had an ulterior motive? How could she possibly ask Cait to join her for dinner when she was trying to get a feel for the woman she was more than interested in? She would be no better than Callie or Ruby if Harper knowingly got closer to Cait when she was potentially involved with another woman.

Autumn had warned her that it could happen, but Harper hadn't expected it to happen quite so soon. No less than 24 hours after Cait had shown up here. Honestly, it didn't feel great. And though Harper thought sleeping on it would alleviate the turmoil she was experiencing, it hadn't made a difference. She was still angry with herself for not taking Cait up on her offer immediately. If she asked again, Harper wouldn't hesitate for one second.

"Good morning, my little country bumpkin." Autumn yawned, stretching her long body. "Whatcha doin?"

"Making a list."

"And checking it twice?"

Harper wasn't in the mood this morning. "Christmas has been and gone, kiddo."

"Ah. Still feeling the effects of last night?" Autumn approached Harper, settling a comforting hand on her shoulder. "I did warn you."

"I know you did. But just one day later? Really? She can't have been that interested in me. Maybe we just got caught up in one another and it never would have worked anyway…"

"Is that what you really believe?" Autumn wrapped her arms around Harper's neck from behind, almost squeezing the life out of her. "You seem really miserable."

"Can you get your huge tits out of my back please, friend?"

"Call yourself a lesbian!" Autumn unravelled herself from Harper, scoffing. "Aren't you supposed to be into tits and stuff?"

"I am. Just not my best friends when they're crushing my lungs from behind." Harper spun around. "But they're great. I've lost count of the amount of times you've shoved them in my face on nights out."

"They're a good pair."

"I prefer a decent arse, anyway." Harper shrugged. "Cait has a great arse. I know I shouldn't look, but it's just there, being all round and wholesome and inviting."

"Have you invited her over yet?"

Harper shook her head, that feeling of self-anger rolling through her again. "No. What's the point?"

"Well, because you wanted to test the water."

"She went on a date last night in case you forgot?"

"I didn't forget. But if I'm not mistaken, Cait doesn't belong to this other woman. So, go in there and claim her for yourself."

Harper quirked an eyebrow. "*Claim* her?"

"Absolutely. Maybe she went on that date knowing you would be jealous. Maybe that was the plan. To help you shift your arse and make up your mind."

"Cait wouldn't date someone to do that to me."

"You're sure about that? Because a little jealousy never hurt anybody. And if anything, it makes the sex hotter."

"There is no way that was her intention. She's not that kind of woman."

Autumn sighed, pulling herself up onto the counter. She studied Harper's eyes, offering a slight smile. "You really think you've missed your chance?"

Harper's heart sunk a little. The way Autumn was looking at her only brought her emotions to the forefront. Deep down, Harper believed she *had* missed her chance. "I mean, we've only known each other for a few weeks, so maybe it was for the best that Cait found someone else."

"That's not what I asked you."

"But it's what I feel. I knew this would just end up seeming like a rebound. Perhaps Cait noticed that on Friday night when she went home. Maybe she's doing what's best for her."

"Did she give you that impression on Friday night?" Autumn asked, sending Harper's thoughts wild.

"Actually, no. She was so great and so cosy as I kinda snuggled a little closer to her. God, I almost kissed her, Autumn. I was so close to just kissing her and saying fuck it to all of my own worries."

Autumn lifted Harper's phone from the counter, handing it over. "Text her. Invite her over. The worst she can say is no."

Harper looked at the dark screen, chewing her lip. Cait would be busy, surely. And even if she wasn't, she wouldn't want to hear from Harper. "No. I'll leave it."

"If you don't text her, I'll call her."

Harper gripped her phone against her chest. She didn't want Autumn to meddle. That wasn't the type of relationship she wanted with Cait, if a relationship was at all possible. "Please. Just leave it."

"Harper," Autumn warned, her usual motherly tone grating on Harper. "Just do it. Jump in headfirst. What's the worst that can happen?"

"Oh, I don't know. I'll be heartbroken twice within the month?"

"You really like her, don't you?"

"Too much, I worry." Harper tapped her screen, surprised to find a message waiting from Cait. But as she checked the time to the side of the message, she discovered it had been sent last night. "Shit. She texted me last night."

"Well, that's something."

"Maybe. Maybe not." Harper, with a shaky hand, opened her phone. As she pressed the message app, Cait's name and message sat waiting at the top of her previous messages. "Bollocks!"

"What?"

"She was asking me to save her from the date she was on."

"And you didn't respond." Autumn ruffled her bed head. "Well, that's probably gone down like a lead balloon."

"Don't say that." Harper considered responding, but really, she wanted to see Cait. To apologise to her beautiful face. "Fuck! I really should have kept my phone on me last night. That's your fault, wanting a girly sleepover."

"Excuse me. I'm the guest here."

"So?" Harper frowned. "We've been best friends since nursery. There's nothing *guest* about you anymore. Damn it!"

"What are you going to do?"

"I have to go see her. Can you give this place a bit of a clean?"

"You want me to clean?" Autumn cackled, shaking her head. "It's Sunday. I'm not cleaning."

"I just mean put the recycling out and maybe fill the dishwasher."

"Fair enough. I can do that."

Harper shot from her stool, pulling on her Vans and grabbing her keys, followed by her wallet. As she shrugged her thick winter coat on, Harper turned back to face her best friend. "Wish me luck."

"Good luck, sugar puff."

Harper narrowed her eyes. "Was that a slur?"

"Piss off! As if! You're just stalling now. Get out!"

Autumn was right; Harper was one hundred percent stalling. When she came face to face with Cait, Harper would be an absolute nervous wreck. She felt it building as she stepped out of the house, the wind chill once again assaulting her skin. She really had to get used to the weather; she wouldn't make it here otherwise.

Harper took the short walk to Cait. The incline went on forever as she put one foot in front of the other, but then Harper found herself standing on the street outside the B&B, staring up at the sign before she was prepared. *Cait's Rest*.

Just the thought of Cait in her little dress and heels last night had Harper's heart rate soaring. Her body burning, her cheeks reddening. She hadn't expected to see such an incredible woman standing before her while Harper walked into the garden in her socks and sliders, but Cait was...*wow*.

She cleared her throat and walked through the open door to the B&B. She dinged the small bell next to the rack of flyers, blowing out a breath while she waited for someone to greet her.

Unfortunately, it was Jude who approached her from down the hallway. "Morning, Harper."

"Hey. How are you?"

Jude shrugged. "Fair to middling."

"That's good...I think." Harper tugged at her cuff, lowering her eyes. Jude always made her feel uncomfortable, but she wasn't about to turn around and walk out without seeing Cait first. "Is Cait around?"

"She's up in the office finishing off for the morning."

Disappointment settled in Harper. "Oh. Well, I won't bother her. Could you tell her I came by, please?"

"Go up to her. Second floor, first door on the left," Jude said, stepping aside. "I'm sure she'd be happy to see you. She's been working all morning while I took care of the checkouts."

"Are you sure?"

"Completely. Go on up."

Harper nodded, taking the stairs two at a time. She really just wanted to apologise and then she would let Cait get on with her work. She'd never disturb her if she was busy. As she took the second flight of stairs, fingers on the keyboard could be heard.

The office door was open, so Harper quietly approached and tapped her knuckles against the doorframe. "Hi."

When Cait turned, thick rimmed glasses framing her eyes, Harper lost her breath. She was a total sucker for a woman in glasses, and Cait was no exception. "Hi, Harper."

"I didn't want to disturb you, but Jude said you wouldn't mind."

Cait swivelled her chair away from the screen. "No, it's fine. I'm pretty much done for the day. Is everything okay?"

"I've only just got your message from last night. Autumn wanted to have a girl's night, whatever that means, so I left my phone in the kitchen."

Cait's smile was gentle. "You don't have to explain. You had plans, and I shouldn't have contacted you. I'm sorry."

"No. You should have. I mean, I want you to contact me."

"O…kay." Cait frowned, her soft brown eyes behind her glasses confused. "So?"

"I'm headed to the supermarket for some things. I'm planning to make a Sunday dinner, and I'd really love it if you could join us."

Cait chewed on the end of her pen. "Oh, I don't know. You

have your friend over, and I'm sure after last night I'm the furthest thing from your mind."

"Last night?"

Cait cleared her throat. "The date."

Harper leaned against the doorframe, smiling fully. "Hey, if you've found the woman you want, that's great. It doesn't mean we can't hang out anymore. At least, not unless she's the clingy insecure type who doesn't like you being around other women."

"It wasn't like that," Cait explained. "It was a date I didn't want to go on but felt bad for not showing up at."

Cait was far too sweet. "You went to a lot of effort considering you didn't want to be there."

"I never get to dress up anymore. Forgive me for wanting to let my hair down a little."

"Oh, I'm not complaining. You looked remarkable."

Harper noted the blush as it crept across Cait's neck. "Thanks."

"So…dinner?"

"Okay." Cait smiled. "What time do you want me there?"

"Whenever you like but dinner will be ready around 3."

"I love to." Cait got to her feet, her office chair wheeling itself backwards as the weight lifted from it. Cait held out her arms. "Hug?"

Harper would never turn down a hug from Cait Taylor. To do so would be ludicrous. She nodded, taking Cait in her arms and holding her close. She felt Cait breathing in deeply, and Harper quickly followed suit. There was no denying that something was coming soon for the pair of them, Harper just had to let her own walls down long enough to let this woman in. But Cait shouldn't have to break through them. She deserved more. They both did.

"I wanted to be with you last night…"

Harper turned her face into Cait's neck, trying desperately not to kiss the skin so close to her lips. "I wanted to be with you, too."

And then Cait slowly pulled back, holding Harper's gaze, the electricity between them charged. "What's going on here?"

Harper lowered her eyes but Cait immediately lifted her head, her hands holding Harper's face. "I don't know. I just know it feels good when I'm with you."

"In case I haven't made myself clear," Cait said, tilting her head ever so slightly. "I want you."

Harper's pulse quickened. It boomed in her ears. "Y-yeah?"

Cait exhaled a steady breath, a gorgeous smile playing on her lips. "Oh, yeah."

"Then I should make dinner extra special this afternoon. I wouldn't want to disappoint with my cooking."

"Honestly?" Cait quirked an eyebrow. "I'm not sure anything else matters. You grabbed my attention the moment you stepped into this town."

CHAPTER FOURTEEN

Cait wrung her hands as she stood to the side of Harper's house, out of view for the time being. She wanted to go inside, wanted to spend the afternoon with Harper, but an unease settled in her stomach. She couldn't fathom why. Perhaps it was the exchange they'd had in Cait's office earlier. She wanted to hold onto that feeling. Harper's breath against her neck, her arms wrapped around Cait and holding her like nobody had held her before.

God, she wanted so much more of that.

The sheer difference between her date and how she felt around Harper was stark. So stark that Cait had repeatedly kicked herself from the moment she woke up. How stupid she had been to go to that restaurant last night. And how awful it must have been for Harper to see her walking a path to another woman.

Okay, Harper didn't wear her heart on her sleeve a lot of the time, but Cait had the opportunity last night to stay a while with Harper. To talk to her and discuss what they were doing. Instead, she allowed herself to placate another woman. One who she didn't really care for in terms of the dating scene.

Cait didn't want to be wined and dined followed by cocktails and any other alcoholic beverage that came to mind. No, she wanted to cuddle on the couch with a trashy film. She wanted to lie with Harper in her arms while she read a soppy romance novel, Harper sleeping soundly against her. Mandy could suggest that Cait needed to get out more until she was blue in the face, but Cait knew exactly what she wanted, and right now, she was done waiting.

But then she remembered that Autumn was at Harper's. So the plan to go in there and kiss Harper was out of the question. But she could make her intentions known once more. Get an idea for how Harper was feeling today. It wouldn't surprise her if Harper had an opinion on the fact that she went on a date just 24 hours after Cait had asked Harper on a date. *She probably thinks I've been around the block.* No. Cait knew Harper would never think that.

Instead of allowing her thoughts to take over her entire day, Cait stepped through the garden gate and knocked on the door.

It swung open, an unfamiliar face greeting her. "Hi. You must be Cait."

"And you must be Autumn."

"Correct. Come on in. We've been waiting for you."

Cait frowned. "Am I late? I'm so sorry."

"No, no. You're not late," Autumn said, lowering her voice. "But Harper has been waiting for you. Trust me."

Cait smiled weakly. What the hell did Autumn already know? Had Harper divulged everything they'd discussed so far? "Well, if she needs a hand in the kitchen, I'm happy to help out."

"She needs a hand." Autumn grinned. "Definitely. I'm hopeless when it comes to cooking."

Cait removed her coat, hanging it on a peg in the hallway. As she kicked her boots off, Harper cursed and yelled.

"Is everything okay?" Cait poked her head around the door, concern overtaking her initial worries momentarily. "Harper?"

Harper turned, sucking her fingertip as she grimaced. "Think I lost a finger."

Autumn snorted. "Well, that's no good for you lesbians, is it?"

Cait held back the urge to laugh. Harper looked as though she was in some pain. "Can I give you a hand?"

"You might need to give her a finger," Autumn interjected, every pair of eyes in the house widening as Autumn laughed, a slight blush creeping onto her cheeks. "Or two."

Cait was certain she was blushing harder than she ever had before, but Autumn was beginning to look just as mortified. At least they were on an even footing for the time being. It certainly helped with Cait's nerves when it came to meeting the best friend of Harper.

Cait focused on Harper, crossing the living room, the plush neutral carpet cosy beneath her feet. "Let's get you cleaned up."

"I'm sorry about her," Harper spoke quietly, turning her head to find Cait's eyes. "She can't help herself."

"It's fine. She broke the ice." Cait smiled fully, shaking her head as Harper's eyes sparkled. "What did you do?"

"Cutting the carrots. It flew off the board and took my skin with it in the process."

"Okay, maybe we need a fresh knife. And tossing that particular carrot in the bin is probably a good idea, too."

"You think?" Harper's lips twitched into a smile. "I mean, my skin tastes pretty good."

"I'll bear that in mind..."

"You will?"

"Mmhmm." Cait looked away. She had to focus on Harper's bloodied fingertip. Not only was it dripping on the counter, but Cait didn't like seeing Harper in this state. In all honesty, she hated blood. "Come on. Clean up." Cait focused on Harper's hands. Long slender fingers, the softest skin, her nails trimmed to perfection. "You don't do much with your hands, do you?"

"Excuse me?" Harper quirked an eyebrow. "I'll have you know that I'm *very* good with my hands."

"I don't doubt that. But it doesn't change the fact that they don't look as though they've seen a hard day's work in their life."

"And there was me admiring your beauty while you insult me in my own home."

"It wasn't an insult. It was an observation. The softer the better."

"Oh yeah?" Harper smirked. "Why is that?"

"Much more pleasant for me when I'm holding your hand." Cait lifted her head, finding Harper's eyes. The intensity was enough to send her to her knees, crystal blue and far too inviting for the moment. Cait held Harper's hand under the tap, watching the water cascade over her fingertip. She wanted to kiss it. Her fingers, her knuckles, her skin. She wanted to kiss Harper all over. "That should do it. Do you have a plaster I could put on?"

"Depends if you're willing to be my nurse or not while you do it."

Cait contained the fire she felt roaring inside her. Autumn could be heard singing to herself in the living room, but the lower level was far too open plan for Cait to do what she really wanted to do. For every second that Harper looked directly into her eyes, Cait struggled to breathe.

"For the love of god!" Startled by Autumn's voice, Cait jumped a little, dropping Harper's hand. "Can I use your office for ten minutes?"

"F-for what?" Harper asked, her eyes finally straying from Cait.

"My arse-wipe boss isn't capable of working without me there. He needs a file. Says it's not on the system, but it is. I have a backup on my drive."

"Sure, yeah. But use my laptop, not my computer." Autumn disappeared up the stairs with her rucksack, heavy footsteps followed by a door slamming shut. "She's always that quiet." Harper grinned. "Hardly know she's here."

"About that plaster for your finger?" Cait lifted a brow. She really needed Harper to busy herself elsewhere. She couldn't concentrate on anything if she didn't. "Are they in a cupboard somewhere?"

"I'll get it." Harper took the kitchen stool, standing on it as she reached into the back of a cupboard. Cait watched Harper's arse, round and full, her jeans straining against the muscles when she moved a particular way. "Here. Got some." Harper jumped down from the stool, almost crashing into Cait as she did. "Sorry. I didn't realise you were behind me."

Cait took the plaster from Harper, peeling back the paper from the sticky residue. Harper held up her finger, smiling as Cait focused on her beautiful face. With the plaster securely in place, Cait cleared her throat. "So, now that we've stopped the drastic bleeding, should we finish preparing dinner?"

"Y-yeah." Harper spoke, her voice hoarse. "Maybe you should take over cutting the vegetables."

"That seems wise."

Harper crouched, removing the meat from the oven. Cait inhaled, her stomach growling when she caught sight of the leg of lamb sitting on the worktop. Complete with rosemary sprigs, garlic, and other roasted vegetables, she could hardly wait to tuck into it.

"That looks divine."

"I haven't cooked dinner for a long time. But it's kinda therapeutic. Takes your mind off stuff."

Guilt rolled through Cait. "Harper, I'm really sorry about last night."

Harper finished moving the roasted vegetables around, putting the lamb back into the oven. She wiped her hands on a tea towel and shook her head. "I've told you, you don't need to apologise. And you don't need to explain either. I'm just sorry it didn't work out for you last night."

"And if I told you I'm glad it didn't work out?" Cait stopped cutting, the knife resting against a carrot on the board. "If I said that I'm not interested in dating any other woman?"

"I'd say I'm happy about that." Harper cocked her head, her eyes narrowed. "Why did you go?"

"Mandy set it up. She texted me yesterday morning to say

she'd booked a table, and I couldn't not show up. It wasn't my date's fault that my best friend had done that."

"What was so wrong with her?" Harper asked, resting her hands against the worktop.

Cait lowered the knife in her hand, wiping her own hands as she rounded the island in the middle of the kitchen. "She wasn't you, Harper. I'm not sure she made me laugh once."

"You didn't do it to make me jealous?"

Cait smiled weakly. "Do I really strike you as the type of person who would do something like that?" The insinuation saddened Cait. She would never dream of doing anything to hurt Harper. It wasn't Cait's style at all.

"No." Harper lowered her eyes, chewing her bottom lip. "No, I don't think you would."

"Look at me." Cait placed a hand over Harper's, lifting it and linking their fingers. "I know you're not ready yet, but when the time comes…if you still want that date, I'll be here waiting."

Harper's eyes flickered a darker shade of blue, her body turning towards Cait. As Harper's free hand settled on Cait's hip, she lost her mind. She lost all sense of time, fisting her hand in Harper's t-shirt.

"Cait…" Harper inched closer, leaning her head forward. "I'm sorry I said no on Friday night. I'm just worried that I'll make a mess of it with you, and of all the people in the world, you deserve that least."

"I'm a big girl, Harper. I know what I want, and it's definitely you."

Harper's lips brushed Cait's, soft and gentle as they touched. But Cait needed more. She needed a whole load more than that.

She tightened her grip on Harper's t-shirt, pushing her back against the counter. Without a second thought, she crushed her lips against Harper's, revelling in the taste of this woman. Cait couldn't say she'd ever thought about how it would feel to be with a woman again, her previous memories had faded a long time ago, but Harper and her soft lips were breathing life into her.

Assuring her. Silently telling Cait that this was everything she never knew she needed.

Harper pulled back, pressing her forehead against Cait's. "God, I've been wanting to do that."

Cait smiled, leaning into another kiss. As she lingered, smiling against Harper's lips, Autumn cleared her throat.

"I leave you alone for five minutes and this is what happens?"

Cait turned her head away from Harper, pressing her fingertips to her lips as her eyelids fluttered closed. Autumn was the least of her concerns. Now, she had to figure out a way to keep her hands to herself until Harper gave all this the go ahead.

"I didn't hear you coming down the stairs," Harper said, her voice honey-like as she dropped her hand from Cait's waist. "You're like creeping Jesus."

"Sorry." Autumn shrugged. "But at least this is one less thing to worry about. We don't have to sit around the table of tension now for dinner."

"Come again?" Harper relaxed her shoulders, her backside still resting against the counter. Cait mirrored Harper's movements, folding her arms across her chest.

"You and your puppy dog eyes. Worrying about whether you'd cocked it all up with Cait." Autumn rolled her eyes. "I'm going to go out on a limb here and say that you didn't cock anything up."

"No, she didn't." Cait smiled, side glancing at Harper. "One day at a time, okay?"

Harper wrapped her arms around herself, offering a fragile smile. "Okay."

❄

HARPER STOOD AT THE SINK, rinsing plates before she stacked them in the dishwasher. Cait was enjoying a moment to herself in the living room, and Autumn was beside Harper, clearing away the kitchen. She knew Autumn had things to say on the tip of her tongue. She only hoped that her best friend would at least be discreet when the time came to offer those thoughts.

Autumn handed another plate to Harper, watching her intently.

"What?" Harper asked.

"Nothing."

"No. You have something on your mind, so please, just come right out with it." Harper didn't have the energy to mind read this afternoon. She needed to nap after the food she'd just eaten.

"I think I might head off a bit earlier than planned."

"Because?"

Autumn smiled, sighing lightly. "I'm not sure I'm needed here anymore, Harper. I came to visit because you needed someone. I think you have that someone now."

"Don't be ridiculous. Cait is just hanging out with us."

"Really?" Autumn lifted an eyebrow. "Because I don't ever recall kissing one another when we used to hang out. Is that what people are into these days?"

"That was just…an *in the moment* kinda thing."

"Mmhmm." Autumn pursed her lips, dropping cutlery into the washing up bowl. "She's really nice, by the way."

"I'm glad you like her."

"I think she's absolutely the right person for you. I mean, she's nothing like Callie. So that's something, right?"

"I think that's what attracted me to her. Callie was too much for me at times. Cait is…laid back. I don't want a relationship with someone who is constantly questioning why I'm doing what I'm doing. Someone who expects me to drop everything for them. I mean, I would for Cait, but she'd never expect it."

Autumn glanced over her shoulder. "No, she wouldn't. She's great."

"You're sure it's not too soon for me?"

Autumn rested a hip against the counter, blowing out a deep breath. Harper knew she would be honest with her, but she wasn't entirely sure she was prepared for the answer. "I think that you have an opportunity to be happy here. That may come straight away; it may take several months. But I think if you're going to show an interest in anyone, it's Cait you should be looking at."

"She's the *only* one I'm looking at." Harper chanced a look in Cait's direction, smiling as she wrapped a lock of hair around her index finger.

"I know. I've just had dinner with you both and I could have easily not been here. You wouldn't have noticed."

"I'm sorry," Harper said, lowering her eyes. "I didn't think kissing her was on the cards today. My head is a bit of a mess."

"Understandable. You thought you'd ruined it this morning, so I can see why you're not sure."

"It's not that I'm not sure, I am, but is Cait? Is she sure I'm the right person?"

Autumn cocked her head, smiling. "I can't answer that, love. That's something you'll have to talk to Cait about."

Harper's stomach rolled. She *hated* talking about her feelings. Before Callie, it wouldn't have been so difficult, but laying it all out in front of Cait had terror tearing through her. Could she really give her heart away again so soon when it was so recently broken?

"Or maybe you need to take some time to think about all of this. I think you both look good together, but only you know if you're ready, Harper. Only you know how you feel inside."

Harper looked up to the ceiling, holding back the tears she felt welling in her eyes. "God, I hate feeling like this."

"I hate seeing you like this…"

"I just feel worthless, Autumn. I feel like everything that happened with Callie was my fault. And I know it wasn't, I know I couldn't have loved her any more than I already did, but it still fucks with your head."

Autumn wrapped her arms around Harper, placing a soothing hand on her back. "I really hate her for what she did to you."

"Me too." Harper sniffled. "I had my life planned out with her."

"You still love her, don't you?" Autumn pulled back slowly, searching Harper's eyes. "I know she hurt you, but you still love her."

Harper lowered her eyes. Autumn always saw through the mask she wore lately. "I don't know."

Cait cleared her throat, standing between the stone floor of the kitchen and the plush carpet of the living room. "I'm sorry, I have to go."

Harper's heart sank. Cait had just heard everything. "Sorry, we were just talking about—"

Cait cut in, holding up a hand. "You don't have to explain. But I do have to go. The booking system is down, and I need to get it fixed before tomorrow morning."

Harper simply nodded. "Okay."

"Bye, Autumn. It was lovely to meet you." Cait smiled, but it didn't reach her eyes. "Safe drive home, okay?"

"Y-yeah," Autumn said, taking Harper's hand inconspicuously. "I'll see you next time I'm up."

"Maybe, yeah." Cait turned, the sound of her taking her coat from the hook in the hallway finalising the fact that she really was leaving. "Bye," she called out as she left, the door clicking shut behind her.

Harper slumped back against the sink unit, placing her head in her hands. "Fuck!"

"She didn't seem too upset."

"You know what? It doesn't even matter anymore. This is a fucking waste of time."

"What is?" Autumn frowned, pulling Harper into the living room. "Cait?"

"No. She's worth every second of my time. But I'm wasting my time in thinking I could make her happy. She hasn't been in a relationship for a long time. I'm sure she wants all of the romance and new beginnings that comes with it, and I don't think I'm in the position to give her it all. I'm not sure I ever will be."

"Remind me to fucking kill Callie when I get home. You're so much better than all of this. How she's made you feel." Autumn gritted her teeth, her nostrils flared. "God, I could wring her neck!"

"She's not worth it."

"Oh, she is. It'd certainly help me to sleep better at night."

"Look…" Harper paused, her eyes taking in her beautiful living room. "I'm going to be fine. I know I will. I have a gorgeous home, a good job, and a best friend most people would give a kidney for."

"Is that enough for you?"

"That's more than what most people have, Autumn. I'm not greedy."

"But you deserve love."

"And in time, I may find that. If I don't, it's not the end of the world." Harper would give anything to be in love with a woman who adored the ground she walked on, but while Callie lingered in her mind, it wasn't possible. And in reality, she wasn't sure anyone would ever adore her. "For now, I should love myself."

"I don't know where my best friend has gone, but I don't like this." Autumn slumped her shoulders, shaking her head. "But if this is what you want…"

"It's not what I want. But it's how it should be. For now. Just…trust me."

CHAPTER FIFTEEN

Cait sat on a bench close to the edge of the lake, a few people milling about, wrapped up from head to toe in winter clothes. It was slightly milder today, the temperature a degree or two higher than usual, but she still felt the icy air seep through the wool of her gloves. It still crept up the sleeve of her coat, sending a shiver through her every now and then. But it was pleasant; she really couldn't complain. The sun was shining, the brightness was a welcome relief from the cloud that had plagued the town earlier in the week.

She lifted her scarf higher, covering her mouth and nose as she watched a couple at the edge of the water with a small child. The lake was a huge part of her life for so many years, and Cait loved to watch small children fall in love with it too. The boats bobbed up and down in their spaces, a slight ripple on the water from the barely recognisable breeze. Nobody seemed to be interested in a lake cruise this morning. But that was to be expected.

Cait picked up her hot chocolate from beside her on the bench, her eyes closing as she removed the lid and the heat warmed her lips. She'd had a quiet week overall, the guests who were currently staying not really requiring much help. In some ways, it left Cait twiddling her thumbs; in others, it meant she could relax in her own section of the house.

She'd managed to get through three romance novels this week alone, and in Cait's world, that was unheard of. Her housework had been finished before the middle of the week arrived, and Cait had even had the time to change her bedroom around. She'd been meaning to get it done for a while now, but with little to no time on her hands, it simply hadn't been possible. Now, it looked great. More spacious. Cosy.

Looking up at the bright sun, Cait leaned her head back and smiled. If she focused hard enough, she could feel a slight warmth, her skin tingling as she imagined the summer the town would have. They didn't always have the best weather, rain often scuppering tourists' plans, but so long as you had a waterproof jacket in your possession, you really couldn't go wrong here.

Her phone started to ring in her pocket, breaking Cait from the world of her own she was in. "Hello?"

"Hey, what time are you due back?" Jude asked, his voice soft. "Some of the lads are off to the pub, and I was wondering whether I could grab a few hours to myself?"

"Of course. What time do you need me back?" Jude had really been great over the last few weeks, Cait was certain his liver would thank him for it, but he deserved a night out with friends. "I can head back now if you want me to?"

"No, I don't need to leave for a few hours."

"Okay, well, I'll be back in an hour or so."

"Thanks, Cait. I owe you one." Jude ended the call before Cait had the chance to respond.

He really didn't owe her anything. They were working as a team, and it was successful. Now that Cait had zero plans on any particular day of the week, it really didn't matter if he was around or not.

Harper hadn't been in touch since last Sunday. And now, five days on, Cait didn't expect it would happen any time soon. But

Harper had a lot on her mind, her ex-fiancée to be precise, so Cait wouldn't get in the way.

Cait had heard Harper and Autumn's conversation in the kitchen, and she'd also lied about needing to get back to the B&B. As they'd all shared dinner, Cait *had* had every intention of hanging around until Harper kicked her out, but she couldn't share a space with someone who didn't know if they still loved the woman who'd cheated on them.

Cait had never really been in a position to understand, she hadn't been in a long-term relationship like Harper had, so as the weekend approached, she was still struggling to grasp how Harper could still possibly love that woman. Callie had turned Harper's life upside down; she deserved nothing from her. Least of all headspace.

But it wasn't any of Cait's business, and that became increasingly clear as the week wore on. As much as she would love to be with Harper on those nights when it were possible, cosied by the fireplace, she couldn't bring herself to call. If Cait was in a relationship, she needed to be the only one on Harper's mind.

Cait got to her feet, gripping her hot chocolate as she stepped closer to the water. She'd thought about booking a self-driving motorboat for her and Harper last week, and the thought had flashed up once again this week, but Cait couldn't bear the thought of being rejected.

She turned her watch towards her. She had time if she wanted to go out on the water for an hour. It had been a while since she took herself out onto the lake with just herself for company. Cait quickly sent a message to Jude, disposing of her hot chocolate as she approached the pier where the self-driving boats waited. The lake was definitely calm enough today, and a safety boat was on hand should she need help getting back. But Cait knew this lake like the back of her hand. She knew exactly the path to take.

As she neared the team who would recite the safety brief, she recognised one of the women. And then it dawned on her. Tom had mentioned that Liz's best friend Jill worked on the cruises.

"Cait Taylor, as I live and breathe."

Cait may not have remembered Liz, but she remembered Jill. They'd gone through a phase of hating one another during high school, Jill being the bitchy bully for a good two years before another girl knocked her front tooth out. From that day on, Jill had retreated, and school had been more positive for it.

"What are you doing here?" Jill placed a hand on her hip, a scowl on her face.

"Well, hiring a boat. Since it's the boat hire spot."

"Alright, no need to be snarky. What boat are you after?"

"Self-drive." Cait took her credit card from the pouch in the back of her phone, eyeing Jill as she took the card reader from its charging holder. "Just an hour, please."

"You're okay going alone? I could call Liz. She'd be down here faster than you could blink."

"No, thanks. I'm perfectly fine going out alone."

Jill stepped closer. "What happened with you two? I was confident you'd hit it off."

"I didn't arrange the date. I'm sure Liz has told you all about it."

"She was upset. And I don't like seeing my best friend upset."

Cait smiled fully. "And I'm not sure what you think you're doing, but you're not the school bully anymore."

"I was never a bully," Jill said, quickly stepping back and brushing herself down as though Cait had just taken a naked flame to her clothing. "Cheeky cow."

"If you could just let me know the boat name, I'll be out of your way."

Jill shook her head, taking the reservation book from the hut at the edge of the pier. As she made notes, stapling Cait's receipt to the edge of the paper, a clearing of the throat shocked Cait. She turned to find Harper staring back at her, her blue eyes bright but the tip of her nose red from the cold. "Oh, hi."

"Hi, Cait." Harper adjusted her hat, her cheeks now reddening. "I was wondering if you were headed back home. We could walk together?"

"I'm not going back yet. I've just hired a boat."

"Oh. Well, have a nice morning." Harper turned to leave, shoving her hands in her coat pockets.

And then Cait felt terrible. "Harper?"

"Yeah?" Harper stopped and turned around. Cait couldn't be sure, but Harper looked as though she had tears in her eyes.

"Did you want to join me? Plenty of room for another..."

Harper's face fell slightly as she swallowed hard. "I, uh..."

Jill sighed. "Are you getting on the boat or not, love?"

"We are, yes." Cait reached out for Harper's hand, offering a smile. "Come on. These little boats are great for seeing the lake."

❄

HARPER SWALLOWED REPEATEDLY, her mouth ridiculously dry as she sat on her hands. She looked down at the life vest strapped to her upper body, it didn't feel like much. Would it really save her if this boat capsized? The thought of that alone sent a wave of horror through Harper, and as she looked out of the tiny window, she was much closer to the water than she would have liked to be.

Cait steered, quietly taking in the lake. A slight smile played on her lips, but Harper felt tension between them. The problem was, in this moment, Harper couldn't care less about the tension. She was too busy remembering if she'd told everyone she loved them. If she died today, would they know?

As Harper blew out a slow steady breath, Cait side glanced at her. "Had you come down to hire a boat of your own?"

"Nope."

"Just taking a walk?" Cait asked.

"Yeah. Walked eleven miles according to my watch."

"It's easy to get taken in by this place. And the lake is gorgeous when you come out on a boat."

"To be honest, it's nice enough from land." Harper really

wished she could enjoy it how Cait was, but it simply wasn't possible. If she looked down at the water once more, she was going to vomit.

Cait shrugged, focused on the path she was taking. In all honesty, Harper was happy with that. They didn't have to talk at all if it meant Cait was busy concentrating. "But you have to admit, being on the water is therapeutic."

No, it was a nightmare.

"Wouldn't you agree?"

"Just…please stop talking." Harper couldn't concentrate on anything other than her breathing while she sat on this tiny, barely stable, white boat.

"Did you want to take over?"

"No." Harper bounced her knee up and down, adjusting her hat. "You just do your thing. Pretend I'm not here."

Cait cut the engine in the middle of the lake, smiling as some kayakers passed them by. She turned to face Harper, wearing a frown. "You should have said if you didn't want to be here with me. I thought I was doing the friendly thing by inviting you, but, that's not the way I'm seeing it."

"No, this has nothing to do with you." Harper smiled weakly. "And if you could start the engine again, that would be great. I don't really want to sink out here. Closer to shore, I'd have a fighting chance."

Cait sat with a confused look in her eyes.

"I have a fear of water," Harper explained, aware how ridiculous she sounded. "And I didn't realise just how low in the water this boat was."

"Why didn't you say? I never would have insisted you join me if I'd known."

Harper lowered her eyes. "I'll face my fears if it means I can spend some time with you."

She knew there was a deeper meaning to her words, but it didn't matter what fear she was facing—the fear of commitment, the fear of loving Cait for it to not be returned, or the fear of water. Right now, all of the above was rolled into one, the intensity enough to have Harper's heart bursting out of her chest.

"If I have to sit here shaking, I'll do that."

"W-why?" Cait's voice trembled.

"Because Sunday when I kissed you was supposed to be the start of something for us. But I let everything else get the better of me, and I fear I've hurt you in the process."

Cait reached out for Harper's hand, gripping it tightly. "You haven't hurt me. But I can't go into this with you if you're still thinking about her, Harper. I'm sorry."

"I'm not thinking about her."

"Your conversation with Autumn would suggest otherwise." Cait smiled weakly, chewing her lip. "But if you can be honest with me, I can give you whatever space you need."

"The one thing I don't want is space, Cait. Certainly not from you. I've spent this week thinking about what I want, and it's definitely to spend more time with you, not less. But I know how it must have seemed on Sunday, especially if you walked in midway through a conversation."

"Yes, that's a downfall I have. As you know, I'm good at jumping to conclusions. But that wasn't what I was doing on Sunday. It seemed easier for me to go home and let you figure things out with Autumn instead."

"If I gave you the impression that I was uncertain about Callie, I'm sorry. It's just that everything is a bit of a mess for me at the moment. And I don't want it to be, but I don't know how to sort through it all in my head."

"Maybe you have to get on with your life. Forget about her. I don't know."

Harper had to agree with Cait. She'd sat at home alone all week and it hadn't done her a single favour, nor had it given her the answers she was looking for. But perhaps there were no answers to find. Perhaps Harper was supposed to move forward with her life. "I think you're right."

Cait's eyebrows shot up with surprise. "Really? I'm not usually the person people turn to for relationship advice."

"She's happy…don't I deserve to be?"

Cait grinned. "You do. One hundred percent."

"Right," Harper said, her body stiffening as another boat sailed past them, creating a slight wave in the water. In turn, it sent their own boat swaying side to side. "Oh, fuck." Harper's eyes slammed shut as she gripped the handle to the side of her, her heart racing. "No, no, no."

"Hey, you're safe. I promise."

Harper shook her head, her eyes still squeezed shut. "No, don't make promises you can't keep, Cait."

"Open your eyes, beautiful."

Harper's breath caught. Cait was something else.

She slowly opened her eyes, focusing on Cait's. "I really love being alone with you, but can we go back now?"

Cait offered the slightest nod, leaning forward and placing the slowest of kisses to Harper's lips. If Harper wasn't fearing for her life, she would have melted to the boat floor. "Come on. I don't want you to feel this way when you're with me. I want you to be happy."

Harper's eyes flickered closed briefly, a smile teasing her lips as the sweet taste of Cait lingered. "Something tells me I'm going to be."

❄

Cait and Harper took a slow pace as they left the lake, the beginning of their ascent up the hill now imminent. While Cait loved this walk, more so with Harper, she felt as though her legs would give out at any moment. She hadn't for one second expected she would have the opportunity to spend some time with Harper today. She also hadn't anticipated the kiss they would share out on the lake. But Cait loved how eager Harper was to spend time with her, willingly getting onto that boat even though the thought of it terrified her. It meant a lot.

But it wouldn't be necessary a second time around. She'd witnessed that sheer terror in Harper's eyes when she cut the engine. She could have offered some positive statistics about the likelihood of drowning in the lake, but she thought it best not to. Harper didn't need to know that drownings were unlikely even though the place where they sat out there had been 70 feet deep. So Cait had refrained from frightening Harper any more than she already unintentionally had.

As they passed by the local fudge shop, Cait took the chance and linked her fingers with Harper's. Relieved when Harper didn't shy away, Cait pulled her closer, squeezing her hand in appreciation. This meant so much to her. And right now, she was wishing Jude hadn't made plans with his friends at the pub.

But it didn't matter. Harper had discovered that Cait wasn't out to hurt her, so they had all the time in the world to spend the evenings together. She was just happy to be in her company for a little while. Cait was taking whatever she could get.

"Did Autumn get home okay last weekend?" Cait turned her head ever so slightly, gripping Harper's arm as they weaved through a group of walkers.

"She did. And all week she's called me, asking if I've seen you yet."

"Why?"

"I knew the moment you left that I'd said the wrong thing. And I'm sure you don't believe that for one second, but Autumn has a habit of putting me on the spot when I least expect it. You'd just kissed me, and I didn't know what the hell was going on. Last Sunday as I watched you sitting in my living room…it felt too good to be true."

"I felt that way, too."

Harper visibly relaxed, her shoulders no longer tense. "Yeah?"

"Of course," Cait said. "Harper, I think you forget that I

haven't been in a relationship in a long time. The last thing I expected was for you to walk into my life."

"It was just a lot to take in. But I never meant to make you feel as though I was unsure. I'm so sure."

Cait stopped on the pavement, turning to face Harper. "But are you? Really?"

Harper smiled as she leaned into a kiss. Her hands gripped Cait's arms, her breath warm. "I promise you I'm sure."

Cait exhaled a deep breath, her bottom lip trembling as her emotions tried to get the better of her. But she wouldn't allow it. This was a happy time, not a time for tears. "Then I'm really looking forward to this with you."

Harper lifted a hand, brushing Cait's cheek with her thumb. "Can I see you tonight?"

"I'm on call. Jude is going out with friends."

Harper nodded, not hiding her disappointment very well. "Okay. Maybe another night?"

"Definitely. Let's arrange something." They made their way up the hill, passing by a bakery, the aroma of fresh bread warming Cait inside. "Whenever you're not working."

"I'll always make time for you. If I have to work through the night so I get the day with you, I'll do that."

Cait's insides swirled. Harper really was about to make her entire year. Cait felt it. "You know, I'll just be sitting at home tonight."

"O…kay." Harper's eyes narrowed.

"So, maybe you could just sit at home with me, too?"

Harper wrapped her arm around Cait's lower back as the B&B came into view. She was wearing one hell of a smile, her eyes sparkling. "Tell me the time, and I'll be there."

CHAPTER SIXTEEN

"Hey, it's me." Harper spoke low into her phone, checking her outfit in the mirror. "You won't believe this..."

"First of all," Autumn paused. "Why are you whispering?"

"Oh. I don't know." Harper did a twirl in the mirror. She couldn't say she'd ever twirled in her life. "I didn't realise I was."

"Well, go on. What's the big news?"

"I saw Cait today." Harper could barely contain the grin that spread across her mouth. She really was on cloud nine this evening. All Cait's fault, but Harper would allow it. "We went on a boat trip together."

"Okay, this is a development. Did she call by and invite you?"

"Well, no. She was down at the lake...and so was I."

"Interesting."

Harper frowned. "What is?"

"That you both just happened to be there at the same time. Have you been following her, Harper? Sneaking a look whenever you can?"

"Don't be ridiculous. I'd been out walking. I needed to clear my head. This guy I'm working with is an absolute ball ache."

"Right."

"And Cait happened to be there when I was heading back. Totally innocent, I swear."

"I'm not convinced, but whatever."

"Anyway…I think everything is fine between us. She didn't even seem upset with me. But that's why she's so great. She's not an angry person."

"No, she didn't strike me that way when I met her."

"I'm going over to her place in the next thirty minutes." Harper wasn't sure what this night would involve, but she knew Cait would be there, and that was all that mattered. "I need some words of encouragement."

"Why?"

Harper sighed. "Because I'm the one who told her I wanted to see her again. I'm the one who took that step, like I should have last weekend, and now I'm panicking."

"Please don't say you're thinking of backing out."

"No. There's no way I'm backing out. If I back out once more, I may as well come home."

"Correct answer."

With a final once over, Harper used a light spray of her favourite perfume and headed for her bedroom door. She had a little time to spare—time she could use for a pep talk from her best friend.

"I think you should know that Callie and Ruby split up."

Harper frowned, stopping midway down the stairs. Her hand gripped the wooden rail, her knuckles white. "What?"

"They split up."

"How? I mean…why?" Harper wasn't particularly interested in Callie or her life, but she really had to work on her relationship keeping skills. They were piss poor.

"Someone may or may not have dropped a line or two to Ruby."

"About what?"

Autumn fell silent, telling Harper everything she needed to know.

"Please tell me you didn't."

"Sorry, but I'm sick to death of seeing that woman come up smelling of roses."

Harper dropped to the stairs, pinching the bridge of her nose. Autumn couldn't help herself at the best of times, but she really hadn't expected her best friend to send a message to Ruby. In some ways, she was grateful; in other ways, she wished she didn't have to deal with them again. "Why couldn't you just leave them alone?"

"Because Callie walked all over you in her fake Louboutin's, and I'm more than over seeing her get the girl. She's full of shit and lost the best thing to ever happen to her when she broke your heart."

"But I'm fine. I don't care what they're doing. It really doesn't interest me."

"Still, I couldn't sit back and watch the soppy selfies and the 'me and my world' posts on social media. It makes me gag."

"What did you actually tell Ruby?" Harper asked, getting back to her feet. She didn't have time to sit around discussing her ex.

"That Callie showed up at your place. Asked if you'd take her back. I may have slipped the date in, too. You know, so Ruby was aware of the fact that it happened *after* she'd proposed."

"This better not come back to bite me. I swear to God!"

Autumn cleared her throat. "Why would it?"

"Because…I don't know. But if either of them shows up here, I'm leaving them in the garden until *you* arrive to explain yourself."

"They won't show up."

"Maybe not. But I really don't need them in my life in any way at all. So, you'd better pray that they leave me alone."

"Don't worry. They will. I told Ruby that you're involved when she said that Callie was welcome to you. And I must be a mind reader because you are involved now."

"Well…" Harper paused. "I'm not sure that's true just yet, but

I'm not going to do anything to mess this up with Cait, so in time…I will be."

"Right, well, you should be getting ready to leave. Wouldn't want to keep Cait waiting."

"I have time."

"Did you shave your legs? And your lady garden?"

Harper wrinkled her nose. "My…lady garden?"

"You never know. It could be your lucky night."

"Um, I'm just going to Cait's for a few hours. Get to know her a little better. There will be no sex, I can promise you." *Plenty of time for that,* Harper thought. And what a wonderful thought it was.

"But she might want a little fondle," Autumn explained. "You don't want her to get down there to find she needs a hedge trimmer, love. It's better to be safe than sorry."

"Okay, I'm hanging up now. We may be best friends, but I'm not discussing my trim with you."

Autumn gasped. "So you *did* check that it wasn't something that resembled Japanese knotweed?"

"Goodbye, Autumn." Harper ended the call, leaning back against the living room wall.

She couldn't recall getting from the bedroom to the living room, but she had somehow made it without falling down the stairs. Now, she just had to keep her legs steady and get this show on the road. Cait was waiting.

And, yes, Harper *had* been through her beauty regime.

It's always better to be safe than sorry.

❄

CAIT WRUNG HER HANDS, inconspicuously watching the road outside her living room window. Harper was due here at any moment, but something inside Cait told her that she may not show. Cait was sure Harper would contact her if she couldn't make it, but if that message or call came through, Cait would be hugely disappointed. After spending an hour or so with Harper this afternoon, she really wanted this evening to go ahead.

When Cait had left Harper at her front door and walked back to the B&B, the smile she wore hurt her face. Once again, Harper was having a positive effect on Cait. She always did, even when Cait felt hopeless in terms of discovering something more, but today, it was heightened. Today, it was different. Harper appeared more determined. More certain of what she wanted.

Cait turned her watch towards herself; Harper was technically late. *She's not coming.* Cait's shoulders dropped ever so slightly, her evening with Harper probably too good to be true. But then a body trudged up the road, a familiar bobble hat covering beautiful auburn hair. Cait's belly swirled, those butterflies flitting around so effortlessly. *Oh God.* Cait couldn't believe Harper had actually shown.

She pulled her front door open, rushing down the stairs to meet Harper at the entrance to the B&B. It wasn't ideal living here, she could be interrupted by a guest at any moment, but Cait had no other choice. She was sure Harper didn't mind either way since being here meant they couldn't live any closer to one another.

Harper lifted her head, her eyes bright as she smiled at Cait through the closed door. Cait's heart thumped a little bit harder, a shaky hand reaching for the lock of the door. When she opened it, Harper's light perfume wafted towards her. "Hi. Come in."

Harper tugged her hat from her head, slight auburn curls falling loosely around her shoulders. "Sorry I'm a few minutes late. I had a call."

"Don't worry. Just happy you're here."

Harper scuffed her boots against the doormat, squeezing past Cait and into the hallway. "It's a bit milder out there tonight."

"It's the cloud. Keeps the freezing temperatures away." Cait locked up before turning back to face Harper. The shy smile she wore had Cait itching to reach out and touch her, but tonight was just some time to get to know one another. "Should we get upstairs before one of the guests seeks me out and finds a reason to talk to me?"

"If you want, yeah." Harper stood back against the wall, evidently waiting for Cait to take the lead. "I didn't bring anything. I wasn't sure if I should or not."

"No need. Just yourself is perfect." Cait leaned in, placing the slightest of kisses to Harper's lips. When she pulled back, Harper had her eyes closed and her lips parted. "Come on. No need to give the guests a free show." She took Harper's hand, dragging her towards the stairs.

As they reached Cait's area of the house, Harper kicked off her boots at the door, shedding her coat before Cait had got the key in the lock.

That sense of apprehension had left Cait. It had been replaced by appreciation for how comfortable Harper felt being here. Cait knew how hard this must be for Harper, it couldn't have been easy learning that not every woman was Callie, but Cait hadn't ever been in that position so she could only be honest and open with Harper and pray the rest followed naturally.

Tonight was important for them both. Tonight could be the beginning of something incredibly beautiful. God knew Cait was ready.

"Have you eaten?" Cait asked, inviting Harper inside. "I had some fresh bread delivered a couple of hours ago and got some cheese from the local shop. I thought maybe we could have some grilled cheese."

"Where I come from, that's just cheese on toast, right?"

"The way I make it…not quite."

"Okay, well I'm up for trying it however you make it." Harper shoved her hands in the pockets of her jeans, smiling. "If it's anything like your eggy bread, I think I'm in for a treat."

"You should come by one morning for breakfast. I'll rustle us some up."

"I think I might take you up on that offer." Harper followed Cait into her kitchen.

"Have a seat," Cait said, the ingredients already sitting on her small kitchen counter. "Sorry about the space. I had to work with what I had when I was turning this level into my own."

"It's cosy. I love it."

"It's not quite at the standard your place is, but it does me well. It's a typical single woman half-sized flat."

"Well..." Harper cleared her throat. "Are you planning on keeping it that way, or?"

"Keeping it what way?" Cait turned, wearing a frown.

"A typical single woman half-sized flat..."

"Unfortunately, I cannot change the size of it. But a single woman space? I'm hoping not." Cait's hands grew clammy as Harper stalked towards her. She couldn't say she'd ever felt so giddy around another woman, but that could be down to the fact that she often suppressed the feeling. Cait had never wanted to get too deep into a relationship because of the dedication the B&B required. But with Harper, the total opposite had happened. "Harper..."

"Mm?" Harper took Cait's hand, backing her up towards the worktop.

"You're okay with all of this, right?"

"You mean, being here with you?" Harper quirked an eyebrow. "Without a doubt."

"I mean..." Cait paused, revelling in the sensation of Harper's hands now on her hips. "I'm not always going to be available. I have to work a lot. I don't know what's going to happen from one day to the next. You know?"

"I'm well aware of the work you put into this place, but that doesn't mean I'm about to say thanks but no thanks to you, Cait."

Cait chewed her lip. "You're sure?"

"I'm very sure. I work a lot, too. The only difference is, I can work crazy hours. I can work around *you*."

"I wouldn't ever ask you to do that."

Harper nodded. "I understand that. But if I'm going to sweep you off your feet, I have to be prepared to change things up a bit. Break my own routine, just like you."

"Kinda funny if you think about it," Cait explained. "How we're about to break our own routines but together."

Harper smiled, lowering her eyes as a blush crept up her neck. "I'm sorry for messing you around, Cait. And I know I've only been here a month, but I was pretty certain even in the beginning."

"I don't want you to be pretty certain; I want you to be absolutely certain. Meeting you…it means so much to me, Harper. So much that if you're not sure about this, we shouldn't continue."

"I am."

Cait curled two fingers under Harper's chin, lifting her head. "I know you are. I wouldn't have you in my home otherwise."

"You're very private, aren't you?"

"You're not?"

"I am, but it's different for me. I spend a lot of my life online, and maybe I've been foolish to give so much of myself away, but I admire how you can be so discreet with your life. Not many people have that ability anymore. Posting their life online for the world to see."

"I don't have social media. Only an account for the B&B. My life is exactly that. Mine."

"I know; I tried to find you. Maybe I'll take a leaf out of your book."

"It certainly makes life easier," Cait said, turning back to the ingredients and cutting slices from the fresh bread. "But if it's part of your business, I can understand why you have to be online."

Harper shrugged, blowing out a deep breath. "It's toxic most of the time."

"Then you shouldn't think about it and just spend time with me instead."

"Sounds like a much more appealing way to spend my time," Harper said, clearing her throat. "So, uh, Autumn called me when I was getting ready to leave."

"How is she? She's really nice. I'm glad you have her." Autumn reminded Cait of Mandy in some ways. Except Autumn seemed to be a less meddling best friend than Cait's own. She was yet to chastise Mandy for planning a date on her behalf but right now, she had more pressing things to see to.

"She's fine. She kinda did something, and I don't know how it's going to go for me."

Cait lowered the knife, wiping her hands on a towel beside her. "What did she do?"

"Sent Ruby a message."

"Ruby?"

Harper hopped up onto a kitchen stool, resting an arm against the small breakfast bar across the back wall of the kitchen. "Sorry. Ruby is Callie's girlfriend. Fiancée. Whatever."

"Why did she send her a message?"

Harper sighed. Cait immediately noted the unease in her eyes.

"Harper?"

"To tell her Callie showed up at mine. And everything else that followed."

Cait winced. She could see why Harper didn't appear to be happy about it. What good would it do any of them in knowing that?

"And I don't know." Harper lifted a shoulder. "I feel like it wasn't necessary. They're both as bad as the other, so I'm surprised Ruby ended things with Callie."

"They split up?" Cait arched an eyebrow, surprised by that little piece of information Harper had slipped in. "Wow."

"Kinda hypocritical if you ask me. Ruby was happy to ruin my life by cheating with Callie. She knew we were together. I don't see what the issue is in Callie trying it on with me. They're both guilty of hurting other people at one time or another."

"I have to agree."

"I just don't have the energy for whatever may result from it, you know?"

"I'm sure they'll let you be. You didn't do anything wrong.

Callie asked you if you would take her back, and thankfully, you said no."

"Thankfully?" Harper echoed.

Cait nodded as she smiled, approaching Harper. She stopped between Harper's legs; her arms draped over her shoulders. "Thankfully, because now *I* get you."

"You do." Harper grinned, turning it into a smirk as she leant forward and kissed Cait. "You definitely do."

"I wouldn't worry. So long as you're happy here, you don't have to let it concern you."

"Oh, it's not. Not really. I just wish Autumn wouldn't have got involved. But she has, so she can deal with it herself."

"And you? What will you do?"

Harper narrowed her eyes, taking her bottom lip between her teeth. "Keep kissing you?"

"That is one hundred percent the right answer." Cait gripped the back of Harper's neck, pressing their foreheads together. She wouldn't get too carried away this evening, but Harper's lips were quickly becoming her favourite taste of all. "Something you can always do is kiss me."

CHAPTER SEVENTEEN

HARPER TAPPED HER FOOT AGAINST THE SLATE FLOOR IN THE KITCHEN, blowing out a deep breath. She'd woken this morning feeling a million and one things for Cait, not a single one of them budging from her mind. It seemed as though every time they were together, everything intensified between them. Even just a simple smile from Cait had Harper melting in front of her. So, rather than continuously question it all, Harper was going to embrace it.

Next week was Valentine's Day, and Harper had an idea up her sleeve. She would need to speak to Jude before she got overexcited about the prospect of spending it with Cait, but she was sure he wouldn't mind working. Unless he had plans of his own, and then Harper was in trouble.

Cait had made it no secret that she wanted to take Harper out on a date, but Harper preferred something a little more…intimate. They could head into town, spend triple what they would any other night of the week, or they could enjoy dinner alone at Harper's, all the bells and whistles provided.

Harper gripped her phone, anxiety swirling around in her belly as she brought Cait's message thread up.

H: Hey, are you around at all?

C: Sorry, I'm about to leave for the supplier. I'll be back in an hour.

H: That's fine. Let me know when you're back, and I'll call in for a coffee with you.

C: Well, my day just got significantly better.

H: Charmer!

Harper grinned, zipping her coat up as she took her keys from the table to the side of the door. Cait was gone; the coast was clear. She may have only bumped into Jude once or twice since he almost tore her head off at the B&B, but he seemed friendlier. And right now, that was exactly what Harper needed.

With the front door slamming shut behind her, Harper jogged up to the next block, relieved when she found no sign of Cait's car. The main door was open, but Harper wasn't sure where to look first. So, she stepped inside the warmth and cleared her throat. "Hello?"

Footsteps came from down the hallway, Jude offering a friendly smile. "Hi, Harper. Cait's not here."

"I know. It's you I called to see."

Jude frowned. "Oh. Well, what can I help you with?"

"I kinda wanted to do something with Cait next week. I was wondering if you could give her a bit of a kick up the arse when it happens?"

"I'm fairly certain she'd kick me back ten times harder." Jude folded his strong arms across his chest, leaning against the doorframe that led to the lounge. "But sure. What day?"

"It's the evening, if that's okay. And it's totally fine if you have plans…but I was wondering if you could give her the night off next Thursday?"

Jude nodded. "Sure. I don't see why not."

"Thanks."

"Wait. That's Valentine's Day…"

Harper reddened, lowering her eyes. "I know. And it'll probably end up going completely wrong, but it's a date. The thing is, Cait doesn't know about it. I want to surprise her."

"You want to surprise my sister." Jude's features softened as a smile played on his mouth. "You really like her, don't you?"

"I do. And I wish I'd done this sooner, like, the day I arrived here, but I feel like I'm in the right place now. I didn't want to let her down when we first met. And since that day at the lake, we've just been getting to know one another. You know?"

"How can you be so sure it's the right thing? You've only been here for a month or so."

Harper shrugged. "Sometimes we just know, I guess."

Jude nodded, pushing off the frame. "Cait means the world to me. And I know we got off on the wrong foot, but I've never seen her so happy every morning. More so when she knows she's spending time with you."

Harper's heart fluttered. "She means the world to me, too."

"And I'd give you the speech about how I don't want you to hurt her, but I know you wouldn't. If this wasn't serious for you, you wouldn't have gone to the trouble of coming here and asking me to give her the night off. You would have just planned something unexpected."

"I just want it to be perfect," Harper said, shoving her hands in her pockets. "I want to get it right; she deserves that. She deserves the world. She's just…never mind."

"No. Go on…"

"She's amazing," Harper breathed out, her voice trembling. "And I'd really appreciate it if you kept this between us."

"Count me in. It's about time she found someone who cared about her."

"I won't hurt her, Jude. I give you my word."

Footsteps startled Harper, a familiar perfume enveloping her. "What's going on here? You both look like you're planning my death."

Harper spun. She really hoped Cait hadn't heard any of what she'd said. "I've misplaced a USB, and I wondered if I'd left it here when I was staying. Thought I'd pop in and check."

"Oh. I don't believe the cleaners have come across anything. Did it have important stuff on it?"

"It's fine. I've got it backed up. Just wanted the USB to be honest." Harper shrugged. "Anyway, I thought you were at the supplier."

"It helps if I have the credit card with me. Realised I'd forgotten it when I got into town."

"Oh, well, I'll let you get on." Harper placed a gentle hand on Cait's shoulder, offering a smile. "Maybe I'll catch you later if you're free for that coffee?"

"If things aren't too hectic here, absolutely."

Harper stepped out onto the drive of the B&B, turning back and holding seven fingers up at Jude. He nodded, throwing in a wink for good measure. "See you both soon. Bye."

As Harper made her way back down the block, her insides swirled with delight. This time next week, she would be preparing to have Cait over for a surprise date. So long as Cait wasn't horrified when she walked through the door, the night surely couldn't go wrong.

❄

Cait relaxed back against the couch, her feet throbbing from the never-ending up and down she'd done all day. Jude had been great, holding the fort at the B&B, but Cait really couldn't bear the thought of ever walking into town again. She'd driven out of town for the supplier, but once she got home, Cait had to make several trips up the road. Yes, she loved the area and the views, but now, she was ready to call it a night. And it was only seven in the evening.

With breakfast prepped for tomorrow morning, Tom unable to make it into work, Cait knew it would be another early one. Honestly, she didn't have the strength to think about it tonight. Her back ached from spending the last two hours in the office, every invoice now filed away appropriately, and her calves burned. God, she could really do with a massage.

She took her phone from the arm of the couch, chewing her lip as she brought Harper's name up on the screen. She wanted to see her, wanted to relax and allow the day's events to evaporate from her mind, but Cait really wouldn't be any fun this evening. As she focused on her phone, her eyes fluttered closed. That was never a good sign. But she should at least let Harper know that she was ready to turn in for the night. She'd already had to cancel coffee this afternoon.

C: Hey, sorry about today. One thing after another here.

Cait smiled as Harper immediately started to respond. Not many women were so eager for Cait's attention.

H: Don't worry about it. I love your success. It means us women are doing something right, right?

Cait grinned. Harper was so enthusiastic that it rubbed off on her from an entirely different building.

C: Definitely. But unfortunately, I'm just about ready to close my eyes.

H: That's a shame.

C: I know. I was looking forward to seeing you. But this is the life of a B&B owner.

Cait instantly regretted sending that message. She may have been disappointed to have to cancel with Harper, but it didn't mean Cait had to put Harper off her completely.

H: I'm sure there will be plenty of other times…

C: You know, I appreciate your understanding. Not many others do.

H: What are you doing right now?

C: Sitting on the couch, trying to keep my eyes open.

H: What time are you planning on sleeping?

C: I need to make dinner. Then shower. Then bed. So, 9 maybe.

H: Text me when you're in bed.

C: Why?

H: Just text me.

Cait frowned as she stared down at the screen. Was Harper planning on coming over here and keeping Cait warm? She certainly wouldn't turn down that offer.

C: Okay. Give me a couple of hours.

H: I'll be waiting…

A shiver ran down Cait's spine at those parting words. Nobody had ever been waiting for Cait, but Harper? She definitely was. And it was a thrilling experience.

❄

CAIT SUNK down into the mattress, the cover pulled tight against her as the cold air snuck in through the gaps at the bottom of the bed. She couldn't sleep with the heat on; it made her feel stuffy the following day. That only left Cait dreaming about the possibility of having someone to keep her warm someday. But not just anybody. Only Harper.

She took her phone from beneath the blanket, bringing up her previous conversation with Harper. She tapped the reply tab, smiling as she got comfortable.

C: In bed. So?

H: Are you ready to sleep?

C: Without a doubt.

Cait expected a reply, instead receiving a call from Harper. She accepted the call, her body warming instantly as Harper's light breathing filtered down the line. "Hi."

"Hi," Harper responded. "It's cold tonight."

"What are you doing?" Cait asked, turning on her side and flicking off the bedside lamp.

"Same as you. Lying in bed."

Cait eyed her alarm clock. "It's only nine."

"Your point being?" Harper teased, her tone light. "You're the one who brought me to bed early."

"Huh?"

"You were going to bed, so I figured I'd be bored without you and decided to go to bed, too."

Cait really wished Harper were here with her. But it was far too soon to even contemplate that. "Hey, do you snuggle?"

"What kind of question is that? I'm a lesbian; of course I snuggle."

"Big spoon or little spoon?" Cait enquired.

"Big. I like to feel as though I'm being protective. Not in a creepy kinda way, but in a loving girlfriend kinda way."

Cait was more than on board with that. The sooner it happened, the better. She could picture it all in her mind. Harper with her arms wrapped around her, Cait nestled into her chest and sleeping soundly. She didn't imagine Harper snored, but, even if she did, Cait wouldn't mind. It would be nice to know that someone was beside her through the night. And then Cait imagined the opposite. Her holding Harper, stroking the skin of her hip, breathing in her shampoo. God, it was all she wanted right now. Not lying here alone.

"Cait? You there?"

"I'm here," Cait breathed out. "I was just thinking."

"About what?"

"How happy you've made me feel in the short amount of time that I've known you."

She felt Harper smiling down the line. "It's what I'm here for. Don't ever forget that."

"And I wish I'd seen you tonight."

"I wish I'd seen you, too."

Cait fell silent again, the sound of Harper's soft voice soothing her into a world she really wished to be in. If Cait closed her eyes and just listened, it almost felt as though Harper was beside her. Holding her exactly the way she said she would. Protecting her and warming her body. And if she concentrated, she could feel Harper's arms around her. She could smell that gentle perfume Harper wore. Everything about this evening was perfect.

"Tell me something about you," Harper said, interrupting the perfect visions Cait was conjuring up in her own mind. "Anything."

"I've never left this town…"

"Never?"

Cait smiled faintly, her eyes no longer wishing to remain open. "No. Never. I don't even own a passport."

"Wow. So, you've never been abroad? To Europe for a holiday?"

"No. I hate the sun. We get so little of it here that I'm used to the ideal temperature. And I love the rain. I could stand in it for hours when it's summer."

"Is that something I'll have to do with you?"

Cait snuggled down, bringing the blanket up to her chin. "It depends if you're planning on sticking around in my life for that long."

"Planning to be around much longer than that."

Cait's body thrummed with an electricity she'd never felt before. Harper brought out everything she could possibly ever want in herself. The priority being the happiness she felt. "You're sure?"

"If you asked me to come over and hold you right now, I would. I'm not just in this for the fun. I'm in it for the long haul."

"How can you be so sure about me?" Cait asked, avoiding what Harper had previously said. If Cait thought about the offer too long, Harper would be climbing into bed with her right now.

"I think I've always been sure in some way. You just have this pull I can't seem to drag myself away from. And you're sweet, kind. You have every quality I could hope for in the woman I'm dating…but I don't think you see it in yourself."

Cait's eyes filled with tears. "You're right. I don't."

"Then I want you to listen to me, okay?"

"Okay."

"You, Cait Taylor, are the most beautiful woman I've ever met. Your dedication to everything around you is astounding, and I'll never forget the help you offered me when I moved here.

But it's not only that kindness I saw. I saw the deeper you. The part of you that wanted more from life. And I'm going to be with you to experience that. I'm going to laugh with you and snuggle with you and just be myself. Because that's all you've ever seen from me. Myself. No mask, no lies. Just me. And you liked it..."

"I did like it. I still do."

"I've learned to be myself around you. Something I never felt I could be around Callie. She always demanded something more, something false. But you got me at my worst, and I'll never forget that."

If Cait could wrap her arms around her phone, she would. "I wasn't looking until you knocked on the door."

"Good. Because the thought of you being taken really sucks."

"I've never been taken, Harper. I've spent my life pushing everyone away."

"But you won't push me away, will you?"

Cait sighed lightly. She couldn't even if she tried. "No. Never."

"This could be something really beautiful," Harper whispered. "And it's kind of ideal that we met in the winter."

"It is?" Cait's eyes remained closed as she inhaled the fresh scent from her bedding.

"Mm. It gives me a reason to cuddle you whenever I want to."

"Oh it does, does it?"

Harper fell silent for a brief moment. "I mean, when that's something you want, yeah."

"I'm just playing with you, Harper. I know exactly what you mean. Something about the winter just makes everything around me feel more romantic."

"I love me some romance. Just so you know."

Cait yawned. "I will bear that in mind."

"Hey, you should get some sleep. I don't like knowing you're tired."

"I'm fine." Cait yawned again, her eyes beginning to water. "Just keep talking."

"No. Because if I do that, I'm going to scale your drainpipe and climb into your bedroom."

Oh, that would be wonderful. "It wouldn't be the worst idea anyone has ever put to me."

"Goodnight, Cait." Harper's voice remained soft and gentle. "Put me two pieces of eggy bread on at eight. I'll be there. I have a busy day tomorrow with work."

"I'll put that extra bacon on that you like."

"Night, beautiful." Harper sighed, clearly refusing to end the call.

Cait wanted to speak, she wanted to respond, but Harper calling her beautiful had knocked the wind well and truly out of her sails.

"Go to sleep, Cait. If your body is telling you to, you should listen…"

Cait didn't respond. Instead, she wandered off into a world filled with Harper and her beautiful smile. Her infectious laugh. Her calming presence.

As Cait's body started to feel lighter, succumbing to her sleep inevitable, Harper sighed lightly and whispered, "You're so pretty."

CHAPTER EIGHTEEN

With a slightly elevated heart rate, Cait grabbed the bouquet of roses from her kitchen counter, blowing out a deep breath as she stopped behind her front door. She would leave soon, no doubt about it, she just needed a moment to herself.

She wasn't second guessing all of this with Harper, no way, but they hadn't even discussed the fact that it was Valentine's Day. In all honesty, Cait had almost forgotten. She was hardly used to remembering the date for a particular reason; it usually came and went without a second thought.

If the B&B were full around this time of year, she would put in some effort. Scattering fresh rose petals across guests' beds before they arrived, perhaps a complimentary box of chocolates for the happy couple. But in reality, Cait had always hated this day. It only reminded her of everything she didn't have.

Of course, she loved seeing married couples and those newly dating giving one another the 'come to bed' eyes, but it still stung deep down. As wonderful as everyone always described Cait, she'd never had that someone special in her life on the most romantic day of the year.

But in Cait's mind, she didn't need a day dedicated to romance and costly gifts. If she was involved, that romance and gift giving was a year-round kinda thing. If she was in love, it was more and more each day, not just on a particular day that had been commercialised to the hilt.

As Cait placed her hand on the door handle, a light knock startled her. She wasn't expecting any visitors. She didn't even know if Harper would be home when she eventually convinced herself to stop by. Harper had been crazy busy with work over the last week or so, but Cait was thankful for any time they managed to spend together. It didn't always work out, though. And as she stood here this evening, Cait was wondering if it would be something Harper would eventually regret about them.

Three times this week, Cait had turned down a dinner invitation on the lake with Harper. She simply didn't have the time to stop what she was doing and leave the B&B. And with Jude gone for three days earlier this week, Cait didn't have the option to ask him to step in. So now, she had to hope that Harper wasn't having second thoughts because of the lack of time Cait had dedicated to her. It really would break her heart.

Another knock came, reminding Cait that she had a visitor. She opened the door to find Jude standing on the other side. "Hi. Everything okay?" Cait kept the bouquet hidden behind the door. If Jude was about to require her help, she didn't want him to know that she hoped to spend a few hours with Harper. It would only leave him guilty. "Did you need a hand?"

"No," he said. "I actually came here to see if you wanted to take what's left of the night off?"

"Oh. Well I was hoping to call and see Harper for an hour, if that's okay? I won't stay long. She's been mad busy all week."

"Sure. No rush to get back. I've just given room 3 directions to the Italian up in town, and room 2 and 7 are about to head out to their pre-booked dinners."

Cait breathed a sigh of relief. She really did want to see Harper just for a little while tonight. "Thanks. I'll leave soon."

"You know today is Valentine's Day, don't you?"

Cait opened the door fully, revealing the bouquet of rich red roses in her hand. "Yeah. I remembered."

"Wow. That's an extraordinary bunch."

Cait chewed her lip, ushering Jude inside her flat. "You don't think it's too much?"

"Too much?"

"Harper hasn't even brought up the fact that it's Valentine's Day, Jude. I don't want to knock on her door and be disappointed when she's not impressed that I'm there."

"Are you having issues?" Jude frowned.

"No, not at all. Quite the opposite, actually."

"Then I don't understand why you think Harper wouldn't be happy to see you."

Cait shrugged, looking down at the flowers. "Just me being daft, I suppose."

"Sit down for a moment," Jude insisted, closing Cait's front door. He perched himself on the arm of her couch, a right bug bear of Cait's. "I know you haven't done this in a long time, but I'm sure Harper is really going to be thrilled to see you standing on her doorstep with those roses."

"What if she hates Valentine's Day?"

"Who the hell hates Valentine's Day?"

Cait placed the roses on her coffee table, careful not to ruin the petals. "At one time…me."

"No, you just didn't appreciate it as much as some people because you had no one to spend it with. But now you do."

"Yeah." Cait released a slow breath, running her hands down her thighs. She'd gone for a simple pair of jeans this evening, her favourite thick oversized sweater keeping her warm. "Just panicking, is all."

"Cait, go and spend the evening with Harper. And if things do go well, stay the night. We're not at full capacity, and unless a woman walks through the door tonight looking for me, I have no plans whatsoever."

"Maybe now that *I've* found someone, it could be your turn to do the same," Cait pressed, choosing to avoid what Jude had said. Just to see Harper would be incredible this evening; the thought of spending the night had Cait's heart rate through the roof.

"I'm good, thanks."

"You can't think everyone is the same as Melanie." Cait gave Jude a knowing look. Her brother didn't often say how he was feeling, but Cait saw it in his eyes. She always did. "It's been almost two years."

"And in those two years, I've never felt so free."

"Please consider it." She wouldn't get on Jude's back about his private life, but Cait wanted him to have what she was beginning to enjoy. She wanted him to have someone by his side, someone who cared about him. "For me?"

"I don't have time for a relationship. I'm turning into you, and that's fine by me."

Cait got to her feet, taking Harper's bouquet from the table. "Don't even joke about that. I wouldn't wish the loneliness on my worst enemy."

"Cait Taylor…has enemies?"

Cait rolled her eyes. She didn't have time for this any longer. "We all have enemies."

As she made a beeline for the front door, Jude cleared his throat. "I'm really happy for you, sis."

Cait turned, smiling. "Let me make sure it's going to last before we celebrate."

"Harper's great."

The greatest, Cait thought. "I won't be late, okay? Don't wait up. I have my key for the main door."

Jude smirked, eventually lifting one eyebrow.

"What?"

"Nothing. I just think it's bold of you to assume you'll even be coming home tonight."

"Hey, I may *feel* lucky…but I'm not *that* lucky."

Without another word, Cait left her flat and rushed down the stairs. She needed fresh, cool evening air to lower the temperature of her skin. Between hoping about what could be and worrying about the reception she could potentially face from Harper, Cait felt flustered.

Forcing her feet to move forward rather than back, she blew out a frosty breath and pushed on. Just another moment and she would see those striking blue eyes, that genuine and heart-warming smile. She would see Harper, and everything else would fall into place.

As she reached Harper's home, Cait stopped and looked up at the house. It wasn't quite in darkness, but the slight light trickling through the windows in some way suggested that Harper didn't want to be disturbed. Maybe she could leave the flowers on the step and knock before leaving. Maybe she should just go back home. Or maybe, just maybe, Cait could bite the bullet of not wanting to inconvenience Harper and make herself known.

Just knock. You have nothing to lose.

But she did. Cait hadn't realised it before right now, but she had *everything* to lose this evening. If Harper didn't invite Cait in, she would crumble into a thousand pieces in front of her.

Well, you won't know unless you knock.

Cait stepped through the gate to the side of the garden and curled her hand into a fist, knocking loudly. The scent of Italian food wafted through the door, and as Cait peeked her head to the left, she noted the lit candles and the romantic ambience.

Her heart sank.

Harper had company.

She turned to walk away, almost losing her footing as she twisted off the pavement onto the stones. But then the door opened, and Harper was calling her name. When Cait turned around, she couldn't help but notice the makeup Harper was wearing. She wasn't sure she'd seen mascara and eyeliner on her before, but it only made Harper's eyes all the more enticing.

"Cait?" Harper pulled Cait from the million thoughts she had whirring around her mind. "You okay?"

"I-I…yes." Cait got herself together. She couldn't crumble. She refused to look a fool. "I just wanted to bring you these, but this isn't a good time for you, so I'll just go."

"Not a good time?"

Cait glanced down at the flowers then back up at Harper. "You have company, don't you?"

"Uh..." Harper wore a look of confusion, glancing over her shoulder.

"It's fine. I should have known. It all makes sense now." Cait's hands started to tremble, her bottom lip ready to follow suit at any moment. "I shouldn't have called, I'm sorry."

"Cait, what the hell are you talking about?"

"You didn't mention Valentine's Day. And I thought that maybe it just wasn't your thing, or maybe we weren't at that point yet, but I understand now. You look really beautiful tonight." Cait paused, swallowing down the emotion in her throat. That solid lump that wouldn't budge. "Is it Callie?" With her best fake smile plastered across her face, Cait searched Harper's eyes. "It is, isn't it?"

"It's you." Harper stepped out of the house, taking Cait's free hand. "And if I knew this would be your reaction, I'd have told you about it last week."

"Told me about what?"

"Our first official date. On Valentine's Day. Just me and you."

Cait's emotions no longer wished to be suppressed as a single tear slipped down her cheek. Harper's thumb immediately caught it, a soft smile on her lips.

"You really thought I had plans with someone else?"

Cait chewed the inside of her cheek. She'd never felt so ridiculous. "I...no. I don't know."

"I'm surprised he even managed to get you here," Harper said, guiding Cait into the house. The warmth enveloped her immediately; something about Harper's place really did put Cait at ultimate ease. "And I can't believe he didn't let it slip out either."

"He? Who's he?"

"Jude. He knew all about it. I asked him to get you here for seven."

Jude was in on this? Wow, Cait really did have people who cared around her. Jude had always been there for her in many ways, but since Harper's arrival, they seemed to be closer than ever before. And Cait loved it.

"He's not usually very good at keeping quiet, so I'd take that as a compliment."

Harper nodded. "Noted."

Cait wasn't sure what to do with herself, the bouquet of roses still in her hand. She really was lacking in experience, but Harper didn't seem at all concerned. That was just another reason for the note she'd written on the card attached to the flowers.

Thank you for being you…

"I know we hadn't arranged anything, and we don't technically have any concrete plans, but these are for you." Cait stepped closer to Harper, holding out the roses. "And I'm really bad at this so forgive me for my nerves."

Harper grinned, taking the roses from Cait. Her slender fingers stroked the delicate deep red petals, tufts of gypsy grass within the bouquet adding that little something extra. "They're really pretty." Harper read the note, her eyes gleaming as she lifted her head and smiled. "Thank you."

"I'm sorry about just before. I wasn't sure you wanted me to even come over, you know?"

"No, I don't know."

"I cancelled plans with you three times this week, Harper. And as much as I really love being here with you, or anywhere with you for that matter, I understand that you probably need more."

"I'm good." Harper leaned in, pressing a kiss below Cait's ear. A shiver ran down her spine, soft breath tickling her skin. "And if you'd like to take your coat off, dinner is almost ready."

Cait couldn't comprehend what was happening. Not only had

she gotten the wrong end of the stick this evening, Harper had laid on what Cait knew would be a beautiful dinner. If she ever could have landed on her feet in the exact place she wished to be, it was here. In this house. With Harper.

❄

Harper topped Cait's wine glass up, an expensive red she'd looked up online to complement dinner. She could sit here and pretend to know what she was talking about when it came to wine and food, but Harper would only end up looking a fool by the end of the night. She didn't know the first thing about what went with which. And she wouldn't pretend to. Cait wouldn't appreciate that.

"Is everything okay with your food?"

"Are you joking?" Cait closed her eyes as she took another mouthful of the fettuccine Harper had actually made from scratch. A slight moan spilled from Cait's full lips, her eyelids fluttering open once she'd swallowed. "It's amazing."

"To be honest, I didn't have a clue what I was doing. Thankfully, I found a pretty straightforward recipe to follow, so I couldn't really get it wrong."

"This is just as good, if not better, than Piccolo down the street."

"Oh, I'm sure it's really nothing like the real stuff."

Cait lowered her fork, sliding her hand across the table towards Harper's. "Really. It's exceptional."

"Well, I'm glad you're enjoying it," Harper said, satisfied by Cait's hand in her own. "And if the wine is no good, let me know, and I'll open something else."

"The wine goes perfectly with it all. Trust me, this is great."

"So, did you really think I had plans with someone else?" Harper had thought about it since Cait walked through the door, but they were adult enough to discuss it. If it were Callie sitting across from her, Harper knew she would be soon eating dinner alone. But Harper should have seen that as a sign as the months went on. If Harper ever questioned anything Callie did, the late nights at the office, her ex would fly off the handle. Maybe it was the guilt, who knew?

"I think I just panicked. I didn't expect you to come out looking the way you do, and I didn't expect all of this. But I'm really sorry, if that counts for anything."

Harper lifted a shoulder. "No apology needed."

"And nobody has ever done anything like this for me before, so when I realised what was happening...I thought it couldn't have possibly been for me."

"All of this is *only* for you, Cait."

Cait lowered her eyes, swirling her fettuccine around her fork. "I've had a great night so far."

"Good. That was my plan all along." Harper finished the last of her food, pushing her plate away. "And I think the lack of seeing you this week only made me more excited for this evening. I barely slept last night."

"Why? Is everything okay?"

"For the first time in a long time, everything is more than okay."

"Good. That's good." Cait finished her own food, placing her plate on top of Harper's. "I think I picked the right woman to take an interest in."

"How so?"

"Well, you can cook," Cait said, grinning. "And then to find someone who can cook, have a great smile, and a heart of gold. Jackpot."

Okay, Harper could certainly get used to hearing those things said about her. More so when they were coming from Cait's sweet lips. But she still felt a blush spreading across her chest, the tips of her ears heating. "Thanks."

"And I was wondering...well, it's something I've been thinking about all week actually..."

"Uh-oh. That's not a good sign."

"I want to take you kayaking."

Harper's heart slid so deep into her stomach that she was convinced it had just fallen out of her arse. "What?"

"Kayaking. On the lake. Not too far out, just along the edge." Cait's joyful voice might have been music to Harper's ears on any normal day, but this wasn't a normal day. As much as Harper wanted to overcome her fear, she wasn't sure she was ready yet. And the water would be so cold. If she fell in, she'd die from the shock. "Think of it as another date."

That only made Harper feel worse. How could she turn a date down with Cait? "I…okay."

Cait's eyes lit up. "Yeah?"

"If it's something I have to do to be with you, yeah."

"I don't want you to do it if it's going to cause you any distress, Harper."

Harper's mouth dried, her pulse hammering in her ears. "No, I'm sure it'll be fine. I'm not turning down another date with you. It'll give you a bad impression of me."

Cait relaxed back, sipping her wine. "It's really gorgeous on the lake."

"Yeah." Harper offered a weak smile. She wasn't sure she could bring herself to get in a kayak, but she could only try. "I'm sure it is."

Harper fell silent, blowing out a deep relaxing breath. But it didn't relax her. It only made her feel worse. The anxiety creeping through her veins was almost overpowering.

"Could you give me a minute?" Harper asked, pushing her chair back. "Need the loo."

"Of course."

Harper shot up the stairs, closing the bathroom door behind her. With her hands braced against the back of the door, she dropped her head between her shoulders, her knees trembling. She really wanted to do this, she knew she needed to get it out of the way, but what if she let Cait down? What if Cait realised just how boring Harper was when it came to expanding her skills with something new and what Cait would deem exciting? Harper couldn't bring herself to think about the possibility of letting such a beautiful woman down, but it might ultimately happen.

Maybe this was why Callie cheated. Maybe Harper was too miserable and scared to try something new. Perhaps Ruby was adventurous and spontaneous. Harper clearly wasn't.

A tear slid down her cheek, dropping to the floor. She looked down at her feet, the brand-new pair of Vans she'd ordered for tonight's special date staring back at her, and shook her head. This was pointless. She should tell Cait how she really felt. And then Cait could decide the best thing for herself. Harper would just hope that it wasn't too big of a deal to her potential girlfriend.

She scoffed, Cait would never choose this. The woman was from The Lakes. Water sport was probably in her veins. Harper, not so much.

As she wiped her cheeks and opened the bathroom door, the sound of plates being cleared away caught her attention. Cait was supposed to be relaxing this evening, not doing the dishes. Harper shot down the stairs, stopping when she reached the living room door. Cait had placed the plates on the worktop and was now crouched down in front of the fire as she added more wood.

"Thanks," Harper said, wrapping her arms around herself. "I keep forgetting to put wood on to keep the fire going."

"You'll get the hang of it."

Harper smiled. "Yeah, once I'm freezing my tits off."

"I thought maybe we could sit down together, watch some TV or a movie. Unless you had something in mind."

Harper would love that, but first she had to be honest about Cait's date. "About before."

Cait's forehead creased as she sat back on her knees. "Before?"

"The date. Kayaking. I just…I don't think I can do it, Cait. But that's not me turning you down for a second date, not at all."

"Is that why you left the table?" Cait asked, climbing to her feet. "Because you didn't want to say no?"

"Kinda. Yeah." Harper rubbed at her forearm, casting her gaze on the floor. "It was probably the wrong thing for me to do. You know, moving here. I'm not that kind of person, but I'm sure you are."

"I mean, I enjoy it when I go out on the water, but it's hardly the end of the world."

"I think this is where I went wrong last time," Harper explained. "In my last relationship." Cait took Harper by the hand, guiding her towards the couch. Once they were sitting comfortably next to one another, Harper blew out a deep breath. Cait, as always, was giving her the time she needed to explain herself. "You're probably looking for someone who is adventurous. And I wouldn't blame you—"

"What do *you* want, Harper?"

"You."

Cait's smile widened, her hands resting on Harper's thighs. "Then why are you so worried?"

"Because I don't want you to settle for someone like me if you need more. As much as I love being with you, which is so much by the way, I wouldn't expect you to be here if it wasn't what you really wanted."

"That night you knocked on the door to the B&B was the first night I'd felt something in so long. I'd noticed you before, of course I had, but that night? God, that night I *really* noticed you."

Harper smiled shyly, her eyes drifting to her hands in her lap.

"Whether we are together on land or on water doesn't concern me. It's that we're together at all. It's all I need, okay?"

"Sure."

"You're not listening to me, are you?" Cait gripped Harper's jaw gently, lifting her eyes. "I'm serious, Harper. This, what we've done tonight, it's been perfect."

"I just wanted you to myself. No interruptions." Harper didn't care if she sounded selfish, it was true. "I just wanted to be with you."

"So, tell me." Cait shifted closer. "What do you want for the rest of this night?"

"In an ideal world, you'd still be here in the morning, but I know that's not possible. So, for the time I can keep a hold of you, I'd love to just hang out. Watch a movie. I'm sure I have some dessert chilling in the fridge that I may or may not have whipped up myself."

"Oh?" Cait quirked an eyebrow.

"Raspberry and passion fruit tarts." Harper shot to her feet; she didn't want to ruin anymore of this night with her insecurities or her fears. Time with Cait was far too precious for that. "Let me get the kitchen cleared away while you put your feet up."

"Oh, no. We clear away together." Cait followed, her arms wrapping around Harper's waist from behind as she reached the sink. "And for the record…I'd love to still be here in the morning, too."

"Maybe one day, yeah?"

Cait's lips pressed against the dip of Harper's neck, her arms tightening. Harper knew this woman would have a soft touch. Not too gentle, just perfect. But the more Cait trailed her lips down Harper's skin, the more Harper lost her mind. "No. Tonight."

"What?" Was Cait saying what Harper thought she was?

"I'll stay the night. Tonight."

Harper's entire body lit up with desire. A desire she'd never felt with Callie. She turned in Cait's arms, studying her eyes. There wasn't a hint of dishonesty. "You're serious?"

"If I could borrow an old shirt or something, I don't see why not."

"What about work?"

Cait leaned in, her lips slow dancing against Harper's. "What about *you*?"

Nobody had ever put Harper first like that. Not really. And

though she didn't expect it all the time, she certainly wouldn't turn down Cait's offer to stay over. She may have worries, but she wasn't completely stupid.

"You mean...*us*?"

Cait nodded, her eyes fluttering closed as she leaned in again and whispered, "Yes. Us."

CHAPTER NINETEEN

CAIT CRACKED ONE EYE OPEN, AN EXPANDING FEELING IN HER CHEST as she felt Harper's arms wrapped around her. She never knew she needed another woman's embrace quite like this. The years she'd spent single were not overly concerning to her, but now that she'd woken beside Harper after a beautiful Valentine's dinner, Cait knew there was no going back.

She had always been fairly certain with the path her life was taking. Every morning she woke with breath in her lungs she knew she was incredibly lucky, but the certainty she felt in Harper's presence was different. It was like an anchor. A weight that kept her grounded but uplifted all at once.

Harper really had brought an inspiration out in Cait. What that inspiration was for, she didn't know, but the positivity Cait felt lately was something she was holding onto.

Harper shifted behind her, those arms loosening from around Cait's waist. But Cait wasn't ready for this moment to end just yet, so she took a hold of Harper's hand and gripped it against her. "Not yet. Stay here a while longer."

Harper relaxed again behind Cait, snuggling closer, her nose buried in the back of Cait's neck. "Sorry, I didn't mean to wake you."

"I was already awake."

Harper lifted her head, peering over Cait. "Why are you awake so early?"

"This is late for me."

"Right, yeah. You're probably already working by 7, aren't you?"

Cait stretched, rolling onto her back. "Pretty much but being here is so much more enjoyable than *any* morning I've had in a long time."

"Good to know." With her head propped up in her hand, Harper stared down at Cait. Those blue eyes would forever hold a special place in Cait's heart, no doubt about it. "Did you sleep okay?"

"There was a reason I loved this house when I viewed it." Cait sighed.

"And…"

"It's the calmness of it," Cait said, lifting her hand and brushing Harper's hair from her face. "Put you in the picture too, and it's all I've ever wanted."

"I'm really happy you stayed last night. After I'd spent the evening with you, I really didn't want to see you leave. I didn't want to come to bed alone. Just sleeping with you in my arms was amazing."

"I'm sure it wasn't much different before you moved here. You were in a long-term relationship."

"This isn't the same thing," Harper said with a determination in her eyes. She seemed so calm and focused this morning. Certain about what she wanted. "Nothing I've ever felt with you is anything remotely like what I had in my last relationship."

"I'm hardly exciting."

Harper feathered her thumb across Cait's cheek, leaning down and brushing her nose against Cait's. "You make me excited. For life. For a relationship again. For love…one day."

"I've never worried about being single, it suited me with the life I have, but I'd be willing to change whatever I could to keep you, Harper. Before I leave this house today, I need you to know that."

"You're perfect exactly how you are." Harper's lips ghosted over Cait's, that familiar smile she seemed to wear whenever their lips met presenting itself once again. "I wouldn't ever want you to change. This…it works."

"For how long, though?" Cait asked, fear of losing Harper settling deep in her belly. "I know this is new, more so for me than anything else, but how long will me cancelling plans be acceptable for?"

"I met you knowing full well what you do. And I still loved everything I saw. If you think for one moment that I'm going to get arsey because you have a business to run, then I'm not sure you know me at all."

Cait sighed, tears pricking her eyes. "I feel like I've known you forever."

"And isn't that how it's supposed to feel? Comfortable with minimal pressure. Relaxed and laidback."

"I-I don't know." And Cait really didn't. She was the last person to ask when it came to dating. "Is it?"

"To me, it is."

Cait loved this side of Harper. She loved the vulnerability in her eyes as she spoke openly and honestly about how she felt and what she expected from Cait. But most of all, Cait loved how Harper never pushed for anything. It made everything feel so much more natural between them. "You'll tell me if you need more from me, though?"

"I need this," Harper whispered, her hand settling on the bare skin of Cait's stomach. "Just us. Like this. Whenever I can have it."

But Cait wasn't thinking about the future any longer. She was thinking about the here and now. And right now, Harper had her hands on Cait's skin, the heat sending a roaring desire through Cait's entire body. Harper could have whatever she wanted this afternoon, tomorrow, next month, but Cait knew exactly what she needed this morning, and it wasn't Harper's words or her reassurance. It was her hands, her lips, skin-on-skin contact.

Cait placed a gentle hand against Harper's shoulder, pushing her down against the mattress. Now propping her own head up with her hand, Cait stared Harper down, studying her beautiful features. "I don't have anywhere to be until later today…"

"Y-you don't?" Harper swallowed, that vulnerability still there as Cait sat up and lifted Harper's old, baggy university T-shirt from her body. Cait had never been so bold. "O-oh," Harper said, her voice low as Cait crawled towards her, settling on top of her body. "Cait?"

"Yes?"

"Are you sure I'm who you want?"

Cait tilted her head, offering a small smile. "Are you really asking me that?"

"I just…if we do what I think we're about to do…" Harper paused, closing her eyes briefly. "I can't go through with it unless you're sure about me. I don't think I could handle that attachment to you only to lose it."

"Hey," Cait whispered against Harper's lips. "Look at me." When Harper did exactly that, the intensity of her stare made Cait gasp lightly. God, Harper was heartbreaking. "I'm sure about you. I'm sure about this. I know what I want." She sat up, curling her fingers under Harper's T-shirt. "I really know what I want."

Harper sat upright, gripping the back of Cait's neck and kissing her hard. Cait had no idea what was to come with Harper in her life, but the wetness that had suddenly gathered between her legs told her exactly what would happen before the morning was over.

Cait dragged her lips from Harper's, leaning back as she almost tore the T-shirt from the curvy body in front of her. Cait had always been a huge fan of curves, and as she focused on Harper's half naked body, her light pink nipples, Cait couldn't contain herself any longer. She needed Harper. She wanted this morning to last until the end of eternity because Cait knew the moment she gave herself to this woman, nothing would ever be the same again. It couldn't possibly be.

She should have felt embarrassed, she should be devastated that she'd made the first move, but Cait resisted the urge to care. She'd never been overly adventurous when it came to sex, and most of the time, which wasn't often, it happened under the covers with the lights off. But not this time. And never again. Harper really had brought out an entirely new world for Cait; one she hadn't necessarily dreamt of going to before.

If Cait just focused on the reason she was here in bed with Harper, if she just forgot about the fact that being single had always suited her, this morning could be earth shattering. In every way imaginable. If Cait could just reach out and touch Harper's pale skin, run her fingers through her thick auburn hair, it would keep her grounded.

Harper lifted one hand, bringing it up Cait's shoulder and towards her neck. "Tell me what you're thinking."

A shiver ran down Cait's spine at Harper's touch. Gentle, but with a passion twisted into it. Soft, but confident. "You."

"Good things, I hope." Harper grinned that adorable smile Cait was quickly getting lost in every day. "Because I know right now, I'm feeling only good things."

"I'm not sure you bring anything other than good thoughts..."

Harper wrapped both arms around Cait's waist, craning her neck and leaning into another kiss. This position, how Harper held Cait as she wrapped her legs around Harper's midsection... God, it was intense. The skin-on-skin contact kept Cait warm, the softest hands trailing up and down her naked back, nipples pressing together.

"I'm so happy you're here with me this morning," Harper said, her voice laced with desire. "You make me feel like I belong here. With you."

Cait touched Harper's cheek lightly, determined to enjoy every second of this. She had Harper within arm's reach, and there was no chance she was letting her go. "You make me feel that, too."

"Why are you single, Cait?" Harper's inquisitive eyes begged to know the answer. To tell her, honestly. "I don't understand."

"Maybe I've been waiting for the one." Cait was fully aware of how ridiculous that likely sounded, but nobody had caught her attention for most of her adult life. Cait didn't look, she didn't put herself out there, but surely that didn't mean nobody else was interested. Perhaps she just didn't have that intrigue most women did. Perhaps she was just…plain. "Maybe this day, this moment, is what I've been searching for all my life."

"You believe that?" Harper's voice shook, her eyes never straying from Cait's. "That I could be the one?"

Cait tilted Harper's chin, placing the softest of kisses to her lips. "I think you *are* the one."

Harper's hand settled on Cait's backside, gripping her with an undeniable urge to take this further. But Cait was too lost in Harper's eyes to even comprehend what was happening anymore. Before she could think, Cait found herself on her back, Harper staring down at her, her body pressing her into the mattress.

"I always wondered if I'd ever find someone like you," Harper said, her voice hoarse. "Someone who has the most beautiful personality. Someone who makes me feel as though I can be myself. Someone who wants the same things I do."

Cait held Harper against her, her voice soothing.

"I never thought I'd settle here. I wanted to, I really needed to, but I didn't think it was possible. I may not show it on the outside, not really, but I *was* broken when I got into my car and drove here. I hated the way she made me feel. But you, Cait…you put me back together without even knowing it."

And Cait really hadn't known it. Yes, she'd made her intentions known, but she didn't for one second imagine that Harper would see her this way. Honestly, Cait was overwhelmed.

"Sex is a powerful thing, Cait."

Cait's heart stopped momentarily. Was Harper going to turn her down now that she'd given her a speech?

"But you have already overpowered my entire world just by

being in it, and now…I really need to touch you." Harper shifted back, her mouth caressing its way up between Cait's breasts. Her breath caught as soft lips kissed along the swell of her left breast, Harper's fingertips gently touching the right. "You're like the breath I never knew I needed."

"I'd never hurt you, Harper."

❄

HARPER HADN'T EXPECTED this to happen this morning. Waking up beside Cait had been a dream come true, but to have her almost naked beneath her, milky skin soft to the touch, Harper felt as though she had struck gold.

This didn't happen to her. Not usually. Yes, she'd been lucky to meet Callie, but really, it had been nothing more than a curse. They may have had good times with one another, but Callie had stripped every ounce of confidence Harper possessed when she admitted her wrongdoing with Ruby. And she hadn't even apologised. Not really. At least, not when it mattered the most.

Harper still remembered that evening when she finally called Callie out. The lack of interest in Callie's once pretty eyes, the self-assured stance she held as she sucked every drop of confidence from Harper. It didn't feel as though it had happened long ago, and really it hadn't, but Harper knew she was exactly where she was supposed to be this morning.

She may have Callie in her head occasionally, but it was nothing to distress herself, or Cait, with. And after this morning, she wasn't sure she would give Callie another second of her head-space again. There was someone new in there now. Someone who didn't make her feel like she was in the wrong. Someone who didn't lay blame on her shoulders. No, this someone was exactly what Harper imagined as she was growing up. Cait. Her gentle smile. Her warm nature. Her honesty and dreams for the future.

And now Harper was ready to delve deeper into the woman beneath her. Literally *and* metaphorically. Because Cait really was the one who mattered most to her. Not Callie. Not the past. Just this moment. It was time to move forward.

Harper kissed her way down Cait's stomach, smiling when she reached a spot that clearly tickled. As Cait shuddered, her hands gripping the bedspread, Harper continued on her path to absolute bliss. Her fingers found the waistband of Cait's lacy, deep red underwear. Wasting no time, Harper slid them down Cait's thighs, dragging them from her legs and away from her body. Where they landed was anyone's guess; Harper's full focus was now on Cait. Where it would remain.

With her hands on Cait's thighs, gently palming her skin, Harper watched on in delight as Cait's legs fell open. Hot, wet heat caught her attention, Cait's glistening sex just begging to be touched. To be relieved of the pent-up tension they both felt. But Harper wanted another second to herself. To admire. To adore. To fall hopelessly in love with everything Cait was.

And then Harper's want came back tenfold as she crawled on top of Cait. Gorgeous, naked Cait. *Wow.* Harper had to stop and breathe for a second. She was fairly certain she would pass out if she didn't. And the last thing Cait needed was for Harper to not be fully present.

As she came face to face with Cait, their lips brushing, tongues dancing, Harper became enveloped by Cait in her entirety. She'd never felt a connection with someone that touched her soul; Harper had never truly believed something so strong was possible, but this moment had proven her wrong once and for all. This moment…was a dream. Vivid, but one that had the potential to end at any moment.

Cait brushed the back of her hand against Harper's cheek, and she immediately leaned into her touch. It was gentle, inviting, sending excitement coursing through Harper's entire body. Her sole focus was Cait. And as she looked into her pretty eyes, Harper knew Cait would become her sole focus for many years to come.

The heartbreak that consumed her lifted, that sense of not

being good enough diminishing with every blink of Cait's eyes, but it was the way in which Cait's chest rose and fell that captured Harper. Her breath was laboured. Her skin glistened. Cait wanted Harper in a way nobody had ever wanted her before. She hadn't realised that would mean so much, but it did. It meant that Harper had left an impression on Cait. It meant that, just maybe, Cait really did want to take this further. To see what future they could have.

Harper steeled herself, closing her eyes as tears worked their way towards the surface. She didn't want to cry. She didn't want to come to the conclusion that she *wasn't* worthless because she never should have felt that way about herself. Harper, deep down, knew that she could make someone happy. Callie, perhaps not, but Cait? God, she really wanted to make Cait happy.

Her hand slid between them, Harper's fingertips gathering Cait's wetness.

A gasp.

A writhe.

Cait really was worked up, and Harper took pride in that knowledge. She'd always strived to know what she was doing when it came to women and their bodies, but Harper wasn't sure it would have mattered this morning. Cait was desperate, that much was clear in the way she clenched her jaw, her eyes squeezed shut. "Hey, look at me," Harper dipped her head, whispering those words gently.

Cait's eyes fluttered open, a soft smile playing on her mouth.

"That's better."

Harper positioned herself against Cait, their bodies flush, clits pressing against one another's. Harper could barely contain herself as that intense sensation coursed through her, skin prickled with goosebumps. Cait gripped Harper's neck, pulling her down into a deep, heated kiss. As Harper ground her hips against Cait, the moan that spilled into Harper's mouth was almost as earth-shattering as she knew her orgasm would be. "Fuck."

Her hands braced either side of Cait's head, Harper ground harder, throwing her head back as Cait met every thrust with her own hips. "Y-you feel so good."

With soft hands gripping her backside, Harper knew Cait was close. It may be over no sooner than it was starting, but Harper could hardly blame Cait for not wanting to prolong this. They both knew what they wanted—apparently, they had for some time—so why wait? Why not enjoy this moment, and wait in anticipation for the next? It made perfect sense.

Harper shifted her leg, now straddling Cait's thigh as she focused on the woman beneath her. She needed to touch Cait, to sink inside her and give her exactly what she wanted…what her body demanded. As she rolled her fingertips over Cait's swollen clit, the woman beneath her cried out, taking her bottom lip between her teeth.

Harper leaned down, her forehead resting against Cait's. "You want more?"

Cait nodded shyly, a blush forcing its way across her cheeks.

Harper braced herself on her forearm, capturing Cait's lips as she pushed one finger inside, only to slip out and add a second. Fuck, it felt good. It felt better than good. It felt…exquisite.

"O-oh," Cait whispered, her hips rocking against Harper's hand. "Y-yes."

As one hand of Cait's gripped the bedsheet, the other wrapped around Harper's neck, Harper pressed her thumb to Cait's clit, her fingers sinking deeper. Cait's walls clenched and her thighs started to shake, all sense of time and space vanishing around Harper. She'd had many dreams over the years, but none compared to the dream she was living this morning. If anyone had told her she would be on top of this woman several months ago, Harper would have slapped them silly.

"I-I, oh…shit." Cait hissed, her back arching.

"Let go, beautiful." Harper's words filtered through the air, sending Cait's mouth agape as she came undone beneath her. "That's it. Let go." Harper took one of Cait's nipples into her mouth, sucking and nipping, heightening the pleasure that was surely surging through Cait.

Harper rocked against Cait's thigh, her own body faltering as she neared the peak. Cait's breathy moans had Harper losing her mind, but when Cait suddenly flipped them, Harper's fingers still buried inside, her eyes had darkened way beyond anything Harper had seen before.

Cait's face sat millimetres from Harper's. "Fuck me again."

Oh. That was bold. But Harper loved it. "Say please…"

Cait grinned, spreading Harper's legs and settling over one of them. "Please, fuck me again."

Harper's belly swirled with delight, Cait's fingers creeping closer to exactly where she needed them to be. She'd been so close just moments ago, and now Cait really needed to finish the job. "Gladly." Harper's fingers moved in and out slowly, the sound of Cait's wetness turning Harper on more so than before. But when Cait entered her with two fingers, her incredible breasts in full view, Harper forced back the urge to top Cait again. "Shit, Cait."

Cait rocked, her hand buried in the mattress as she put a little more strength behind her thrusts. From the outside it would appear carnal, but inside, Harper felt pure bliss raging through her. Every emotion was heightened, but before she could think about Cait and how she brought out the best in her, Harper was gripping the bedsheet while Cait whispered complete filth into her ear. *Mm, my kind of woman.*

"Fuck, I-I…" Harper relaxed her body, allowing her orgasm to take over her in its entirety. "Fuck, I'm coming."

A cry tore from Harper's throat, followed by Cait's guttural moans. Cait fell forward, panting as her face buried into the mattress. "Wow," She mumbled. "That was…"

"Intense."

CHAPTER TWENTY

The ticking of the clock on the kitchen wall had Cait driven to distraction, her every sense and emotion heightened this evening. It was strange—she would admit that—but Cait didn't know what to do to remedy the fact that she missed Harper tonight. A stark contrast to last night.

But Harper had work to do. She had so much going on in her life right now that Cait would willingly step back until the time was right. This morning had meant the world to Cait, she knew she wouldn't ever feel that way again with another woman, but Cait understood the pressure that came with having bills to pay. She also understood that Harper needed her own space to work in, one that didn't include Cait lounging around.

Cait laughed. She couldn't say she'd ever lounged around in her life. But with Harper, that was exactly what she wanted to do. She wanted to switch off once the clock reached 5 p.m. and put her feet up, Harper's arms wrapped around her.

But then her mind drifted back to this morning. To the moment Harper flipped them and kissed every inch of Cait's skin. She felt the fire rip through her, the desire to scream out in ecstasy. Harper Grey knew her way around Cait's body, no doubt about it.

Cait swallowed, crossing her legs as she pushed all thoughts of a naked Harper from her mind. Every part of her body throbbed with the reminder, something she had to curb right now. It wasn't as though Harper was here to take care of how Cait was feeling, so she would bookmark it for another time. A night when they had all the time in the world to continue where they left off this morning.

Cait removed the kettle from the stove, poured hot water over her teabag, and then set it down on a heatproof mat, leaving her tea to brew for a few minutes. She really needed to find something to do to pass the time this evening.

And then a knock at the door had Cait's hairs on the back of her neck standing to attention. It had to be Harper. Nobody else ever called by.

Cait rushed through the living room, catching her calf on the corner of the coffee table. She grimaced; the pain would subside as soon as she saw Harper's pretty blue eyes. But as she opened the door, Cait found herself bitterly disappointed. "Mandy, hi." Mandy threw an arm around Cait, guiding her best friend back into the living room. With the door kicked shut, a bottle of wine in Mandy's grip, Cait frowned. "Everything okay?"

"We need a night together." Mandy disappeared into the kitchen, wine glasses clanging together as she returned with them resting between her fingers. "I brought red. The one you like."

"Oh, uh…" Cait tucked her hair behind her ear. "I'm just brewing a cup of tea."

"Don't be so boring. It's Friday night."

"And I have to work tomorrow," Cait explained. "But you enjoy a glass, by all means. I'm fine with tea. I'm shattered anyway so was planning an early night."

"Look, I know you're a bit mad at me for setting you up with Liz, but I did it with good intentions."

Cait hadn't even remembered Liz. That sounded terrible, but Harper constantly infiltrated her every thought. Liz had been forgotten about the moment she left the restaurant. "Don't worry about it."

"No. I owe you an apology. I shouldn't have set you up; I knew you wouldn't like it."

Cait perched herself on the edge of the coffee table. "So why did you do it?"

"Because you spend your life in this place. And I know your flat is cosy, but aren't you bored to tears sitting here alone night after night?"

Cait had always been content with her own company. It meant less drama was likely to ensue. "No, not really."

Mandy cocked her head, smiling. "You always did like the simple life, didn't you?"

"I just don't need someone by my side to make me happy," Cait lied. "And I know you don't feel the same way, but we don't all have to be seen with someone on our arm to keep the locals from talking. I was always happy doing my job and then turning in for the night."

"Was?" Mandy quirked an eyebrow.

Shit. "What?"

"You said you *was* happy doing your job."

"I love this place." Cait smiled a half smile as her eyes took in her flat. It was small but it was quaint. It was typical Cait. "And the B&B is about to go into business with the health spa down at the lake…"

"You decided to take them up on their offer?"

"I did." Cait breathed a sigh of relief as she managed to knock Mandy off the scent of Harper. Cait didn't know what was going on yet, so the last thing she needed was Mandy jumping on board to give her opinion on it all. "Guests will be allowed to use the facilities for free. It'll mean a slight increase in the cost of a room, but it'll be so small that people won't notice. They will then be offered twenty percent off their bill if they decide to eat in the restaurant at the spa."

"Sounds like a good idea." Mandy nodded, sipping her wine. "But, back to you. We have to get you involved with someone."

"Mandy," Cait warned.

"No, I'm sorry, but I can't watch you continue on like this. It's depressing."

"Depressing? It's my life, Mandy. I don't know what you have to be depressed about. It really doesn't concern you."

"Cait, you could have been married with kids by now. Living in a house far away from here. Just…happy."

Cait bit her tongue. She loved Mandy dearly, they'd been friends since forever, but she knew where this was going. "Please, don't start this again."

"Have you even thought about maybe joining a dating site? One that has a little bit of everything…"

"I don't want a little bit of everything." Cait shot to her feet, aware that her tea would likely be ruined now. "So please, don't even go there."

Cait braced herself against the breakfast bar, blowing out a deep breath. Mandy had never really fully understood Cait's sexuality, claiming to be old school, but tonight of all nights, Cait wasn't in the mood.

As she turned, she found Mandy standing in the doorway. "Just try it. What's the worst that could happen?"

"Try it?"

Mandy sighed. "You never know. You might enjoy it. Men are…complicated, but maybe you'll change your mind when you meet someone."

Cait's forehead creased. She didn't often get angry, preferring to let things go 99% of the time, but had Mandy really just said what she thought she had? "A man?"

"Have you *ever* dated a man?" Mandy rolled her eyes, sloshing her wine in her glass.

"No, I haven't."

"Then how do you know you don't like them?"

Okay, Cait wasn't doing this. Not now, not ever. She'd had the most incredible time with Harper since last night, and Mandy would not bring that mood down for her. Whether she knew about Harper or not didn't matter, Mandy had no right to say what she had.

"Well?" Mandy pressed. "How do you know?"

"Mandy." Cait pinched the bridge of her nose, stepping closer to her best friend. "We've been friends for 36 years. Please, don't say something to ruin that."

"I'm sorry. I just don't understand what's wrong with you. I set you up with Liz. She's a woman. She's a lesbian. So, why didn't it go well?"

"Because she's just not my type. And just because she's not my type, it doesn't mean that I should look for a man. I've never been attracted to a man in my life, and I know I never will be. I don't need to explain myself to you, and I have no intentions of doing so, so please...don't make a fool of yourself." Cait turned, trying to salvage her cup of tea. "By all means, stay a while and catch up, but do not think for one second that I won't ask you to leave if you continue this ridiculous conversation. My own parents accepted me all those years ago, you can either do the same, or you can leave."

"Sorry, Cait." Mandy held up a hand. "I don't know where that came from. I just want you to be happy."

"I am happy. So happy you couldn't begin to understand."

"So that's it?" Mandy asked, returning to the living room and flopping down on the couch. "You're happy working yourself into the ground, and that's that?"

As Cait opened her mouth to speak, a gentle knock on the door interrupted her. Jude was probably calling by to say good-night, but maybe he could stay a while to keep Cait company. God knew she needed someone in her corner while Mandy was here. "Sorry, give me a minute."

Another light knock had Cait rushing to open the door. When she did, Harper and her intense blue eyes stared back at her.

"Hi. Sorry to just call over."

Cait stepped out into the hallway, aware that guests were just a floor below. "Is everything okay?"

"Of course, yeah." Harper fiddled with the set of keys in her hand, looking down at them, then back up at Cait. "Just wanted to see you for five minutes."

"Oh, well now isn't really a goo—"

Harper lunged forward, planting her lips on Cait's with a passion that tore through her. The door swung open as Cait lost her footing, but neither cared. "I'm sorry." Harper held Cait's face. "For showing up. But I just really needed to kiss you."

The clearing of a throat brought Cait and Harper from their own world. And as Harper glanced over Cait's shoulder, she winced.

"And you are?" Mandy stood, clearing her throat. "I mean, I'm assuming you know my best friend and you haven't just forced your way in here by accident."

Harper backed out of the door, shaking her head lightly. "Cait, I'll see you soon, okay?"

"Oh, no." Cait gripped Harper's hand, following her out into the hallway. "Why are you leaving?"

"I can't believe I just did that. I mean, I don't even know if you're out around here and I just show up, kissing you."

"You can kiss me anytime you like."

Harper blushed. "Yeah?"

"Mmhmm." Cait pulled Harper against her, gripping the lapels of her jacket. As she leaned in closer, she lowered her voice. "I think after this morning, you have every right to show up at my door and do what you feel necessary."

"Your friend doesn't look very happy to see me."

"That's Mandy. She decided to come over tonight to sort out my love life."

"R-right."

"And I was considering telling her about you, but well, you've just done that yourself." Cait's hands fisted in Harper's blue and grey flannel shirt. "You should come in. Because when she leaves, I get you all to myself."

❄

HARPER SAT in a single bucket seat in the bay window of Cait's living room, her eyes focused on the fireplace. She could feel Mandy watching her, the intensity of her stare sending a wave of anxiety through Harper, but this woman wouldn't intimidate her. After all, she wasn't who Harper was dating.

Cait had been called away ten minutes ago by Jude, completely understandable given the fact that she lived at her business, but Harper was now wondering if she should just leave and see Cait when she was available. She wanted to hang around, to potentially spend the evening with Cait, but Mandy was her friend, and Harper had no right to hijack their night together.

Harper cleared her throat, rising to her feet. "So, it was nice to meet you, but I should probably head home. I'll send Cait a message to let her know."

"Sit down." Mandy stared up at Harper, wearing a suspicious look.

Harper returned to her seat, confused by this woman's tone. She hadn't spoken two words to Harper since she'd arrived, but now she wanted company?

"Are you a lesbian, too?"

Harper almost choked on the air she'd just inhaled. "Excuse me?"

"Like Cait. Are you a lesbian?"

"Look, I don't know what the etiquette is around here, but that's really not the kind of thing you just come out and ask."

Mandy frowned.

"Are you straight?" Harper asked, relaxing back in the chair.

"What kind of question is that?" Mandy scoffed.

"So now you realise how stupid your own question was. I'm not sure why it matters, but since you met me when I had my tongue down your best friend's throat, you could probably hazard a guess."

Mandy huffed, filling her wine glass to the brim. "I want her to be happy. I want her to have what the rest of us have. A family and a husband—"

"Whoa." Harper sat forward as she cut Mandy off. Harper couldn't be sure, but after this morning, Cait didn't appear to want this husband Mandy seemed to think she had the right to speak of. "What makes you think Cait wants any of that?"

"Every woman does."

Harper clenched her jaw, breathing deeply through her nose. "I don't know Cait very well, not yet, but I'm not sure she would appreciate you saying this stuff."

"She doesn't know what she wants. She's always been like this."

Oh, she knows what she wants. Harper held her tongue. She would never disrespect Cait by discussing their relationship with another person. "I think maybe you should let Cait figure things out herself."

"Where did you come from? I've never met you. I've never even heard of you."

"I moved here recently."

"And how did you come to meet my friend?" Mandy sipped her wine as she crossed her legs.

"I had to stay at the B&B while I had some work done at my house. Cait was kind enough to take me in unexpectedly when I realised the place had flooded."

"So, you took advantage of her. That's what you're saying?"

"What? No."

"Mm." Mandy pursed her lips, giving Harper a look of complete disdain. "I think Cait and I need to have a little chat."

"And I think it's time that I left." Harper shot to her feet. "You know, for someone who is so wonderful and kind, Cait sure keeps shitty company."

Harper made a beeline for the front door, disappointed by Cait's best friend's interpretation of her. Sure, they didn't know one another, but offending someone on a first meeting really didn't do it for Harper. Chances were, this woman wouldn't ever support Cait. And that was sad. Harper couldn't imagine Autumn asking the questions Mandy just had.

As the door closed softly behind Harper, she leant against the hallway wall. Her palms rested flat against the smooth white paint, Harper's breathing returning to normal. She could have flown off the handle, but what would that solve? Not a lot, Harper had come to realise over the years. Shouting and screaming never solved a single thing.

With a final deep breath, Harper pushed off the wall and headed towards the stairs that would lead her out of Cait's cosy B&B. Surprised to find Cait heading up the same stairs she was descending, Harper froze.

"You're leaving?"

Harper nodded. "Yeah. I should get home."

"Sorry. We had an issue with the broadband."

Harper stepped down another stair. "Don't ever apologise. This place would fall apart without you."

"But now you're leaving…"

"Your friend is visiting. I really don't want to get in the way." Harper knew that wasn't quite the truth, but Cait would go into panic mode if she told her what she really thought of Mandy. "Go and enjoy a glass of wine with her."

"It's bad luck to cross on the stairs," Cait said, her voice hoarse as she eyed Harper with her deep brown eyes.

"Then I will take a step back and let the lady pass." Harper carefully backed up the stairs, holding out one arm as she bowed to Cait. "After you."

Cait stalked towards Harper, gripping her hand and dragging her into an alcove between two rooms. "Just…" Cait's lips found Harper's with an urgency, a want. Harper hadn't ever experienced something so intense as she had with Cait, and now that made her decision to leave even harder. Why couldn't Mandy come down the stairs and tell Cait she had to leave? Why was Harper the one appeasing people? "This morning was amazing,"

Cait said breathlessly. "And I really wish we could have spent tonight together."

With their foreheads pressed together, Harper's belly flipped. She felt exactly the same way Cait did, but how did she explain why she was leaving without causing unrest?

"Something is on your mind," Cait whispered against Harper's lips. "Is it me? Is this too much for you?"

Harper pressed her body against Cait, trapping her against the wall. What Cait was saying couldn't be further from the truth. "You'll never be too much for me."

"Can I see you through the week?"

Harper's smile grew. "Text me when you want to see me. I'll make myself available."

"And if I happened to text you when I've managed to kick Mandy out?"

Harper's tongue trailed Cait's bottom lip before slipping into her mouth. She put everything she had into the kiss; Cait had to know she wasn't leaving because she didn't want to be here. *God, this woman drives me crazy.* "I'll be here."

CHAPTER TWENTY-ONE

Cait wrapped a blanket around her, bringing her knees to her chest as she snuggled in front of the fire. The thick rug covering the wooden floor felt soft against her feet, but her head hurt. How had this morning been so incredible, and now this evening she was feeling lousy about everything else? Mandy was to blame; Cait never should have given her the satisfaction of hanging around. But that was Cait. Loyal to everyone except for herself.

Now that Mandy had left, Cait was overwhelmed by everything her best friend had said to her this evening. She shouldn't be surprised, Mandy never had known when to keep her thoughts to herself, but it seemed to hurt more this time around. Perhaps it was the unadulterated joy she'd woken to this morning, only for it all to turn on its head this evening. She didn't know. But as Cait pulled the blanket around her tighter, she really wished Harper were here.

Mandy was complicated. Though she had never intentionally hurt Cait in the past, her comments had stung. But Mandy was one of those people who didn't realise what they were saying half of the time. That didn't mean Cait condoned Mandy's opinion, but it did usually make it easier for her to let it go. Except this time, it continued to gnaw away at the back of her mind. Add to it the foolish decision to leave Harper alone with Mandy, and Cait could truly punch herself in the face tonight.

She wasn't sure why, but she got the impression that Harper had left earlier for a reason. Cait could only hope that Mandy hadn't scared her off and Harper was just too polite to explain that when she caught her on the stairs. If Cait had to make things right, she would.

A light knock on the door pulled Cait from the internal war she was having with herself. And then the sound of a key turning caught her attention. She glanced over her shoulder to find Jude staring down at her. "Hi. Everything okay?"

"Mmhmm. I have someone here to see you."

Cait frowned. "To see me?"

"Should I let her in?" Jude asked. "I don't think she would take no for an answer anyway."

It had to be Harper.

Cait smiled. "Let her in."

Jude stepped out of the room, only to be replaced by Harper. She stood with her hands in the back pockets of her jeans, her gorgeous rich hair flowing over one shoulder. "I was going to send a text, but thought I'd just show up instead."

"Close the door. Come and join me." Cait opened the blanket she was wrapped up in, offering Harper the space beside her.

"Are you okay? Or do you often sit on the floor like a weirdo?" Harper turned her head, meeting Cait's eyes with a smirk playing on her mouth. "I mean, it's fine if you *are* a weirdo. We'd go well together."

"It's warmer down here." Cait's eyes returned to the dancing flames, the skin of her face heated. "I was just having a minute to myself."

"Did you want to be alone? I can go if you'd prefer that…"

Cait took Harper's hand beneath the blanket. "No, I don't want you to go anywhere. Just…sit here with me a while."

And Harper did exactly that. Though they sat in silence, it was comfortable. Cait didn't feel the need to fill the air with pointless chatter, and she enjoyed having Harper's hand in hers. She had so many things she wanted to say to Harper, but she didn't know where to begin. Cait didn't do speeches. She hadn't ever found herself in a position where she needed to. But with Harper? With Harper, she wanted to be as honest as she possibly could. She wanted everything to mould into place naturally but with communication when needed.

She knew this evening required no communication, and she knew that Harper would sit in silence for as long as she believed it was needed, but Cait didn't want that. Not really. She wanted to know Harper, inside and out.

"When I came out to my parents, I never for one moment thought that they would understand. Mum goes to church every Sunday, Dad just…well, he's Dad. This town doesn't have the best track record with being welcoming to something different, but I got the shock of my life when everyone shrugged and went back to their lives. I mean, that was all I could have hoped for. But I expected my best friend to embrace it just like everybody else did."

"Mandy doesn't agree with it?"

Cait blew out a deep breath. "She's so hard to read, so I have no idea."

Harper cleared her throat, turning her body inwards and towards Cait. "I don't think she likes me very much."

Cait's stomach dropped. She knew something had happened while she was called away. "What makes you say that?"

"She was just…hostile towards me. And I guess I shouldn't really worry about that since it was the first time she'd met me, but it made me feel uncomfortable."

"What did she say?"

"Nothing in particular. She just mentioned that she would have a word with you about me. That I'm somehow taking advantage of you, I don't know." Harper ran a hand down her face. "But it really doesn't matter. So long as *you* don't believe those things, Mandy can think whatever she wants to think."

"I'm sorry she said that to you, Harper." Cait settled a hand against Harper's cheek, trying hard to keep her anger at bay. "I don't know what her problem is, but you know I don't think those things."

"And she couldn't convince you to feel that way?"

Cait brushed her lips against Harper's, smiling as their foreheads pressed together. "Never."

"Then we don't need to talk about it any longer. I'm sure you'll set her straight when the time is right for you. You're my main concern, not anybody else."

Had Cait ever been another person's concern? She couldn't recall a time.

"Thank you for coming to me when you needed a place to sleep."

"This was the one place I knew I'd be welcomed."

"And this is one place that you can *always* feel that way." Cait pulled Harper against her, stretching out her legs and resting her head on Harper's shoulder. "Just so you know…I used to check you out when you came here with Callie."

She felt Harper grin. "Damn, I wish I'd known."

"Oh, no. Nothing good could have ever come from you knowing, or me allowing myself to be attracted to you."

"Nothing?"

Cait shook her head. "No. Because then I could have been a homewrecker."

Harper snorted. "Turns out, you wouldn't have been the only one."

"Still," Cait said, wrapping an arm around Harper's shoulder. "This happened when it was supposed to. Neither of us have done anything wrong, so neither of us have to worry. You were single, and I've been single since forever."

"I still don't understand how."

"Does it really matter?" Cait asked.

Harper turned her head, pressing a kiss below Cait's ear. "No, it doesn't."

CHAPTER TWENTY-TWO

Three weeks later…

Harper whistled as she made her way up the hill, Kendal Mint Cake and other sugary treats gripped in her hand from her morning of perusing the local shops in town. She had a completely free weekend coming up, and if that meant she had to hang around waiting for Cait to have a moment's peace to herself, Harper would one hundred percent do that. She'd promised herself a morning stroll, step one accomplished, and now she was on her way to the woman who held her heart.

I'm out of my bloody mind! Harper laughed, but she struggled to care. How could she when Cait was the reason she was smiling constantly? How could she for one second panic about everything that was happening when Harper had never felt so content and thrilled by the path her life was taking? *Stop thinking and just enjoy this.*

And for once, Harper would take her own advice. After all, taking it from others never seemed to work out for her. So, she'd made the decision to do whatever felt right for her, and this did. It felt so right that the idea it could possibly be wrong seemed ludicrous.

As she arrived at the B&B, Harper glanced down at herself,

satisfied that she was wrapped up enough for Cait's approval. She'd been told off more than once for not wearing a scarf when it was chilly, but it only made Harper swoon harder. Cait cared. Not only about the sexual aspects of their relationship but about Harper's wellbeing. That meant so much to her. Cait had even sent a text this morning to check Harper had eaten breakfast—another thing she was trying to keep on top of. Callie had never done anything like that. She'd never cared the way Cait did. And as Harper pushed through the unlocked inside door, she realised Callie probably didn't have the capacity to care about anyone other than herself.

"Harper, hi." Jude stepped out of the communal lounge. "You here to see Cait?"

"I am. Is she busy?"

"She's up in the office. She's getting the last of her things ready for this afternoon."

Harper frowned. "This afternoon?"

"Go up. I'm sure she'll explain. Cait…panics."

Okay. What is she panicking about?

Harper decided she would find out herself. Jude had better things to do than stand around listening to Harper. "I'll go up."

"She could probably do with a bit of encouragement," Jude said, collecting some leaflets from the stand. "And I'm sure she'd love to see you."

Harper's heart fluttered. "Yeah?"

"Go up, Harper." Jude winked and vanished back into the communal lounge.

And Harper would do exactly that. If Cait was having a minor meltdown about something, Harper would love nothing more than to see her through it. Isn't that what she was here for? To calm nerves. To be a sounding board. To help in any way possible.

Harper bounded up the stairs, taking them two at a time. The office door was closed, but Harper could hear Cait talking to herself from behind the wood. She could stand here and admire that side of Cait, or she could put Cait out of her misery and hopefully help in some way.

Harper lifted her hand, knocking gently. "Cait?"

"Come in."

Harper pushed the door open, surprised to see a flustered looking Cait with her head in her hands. "Hi. Jude said it would be okay to come up."

"I could use a distraction for five minutes…"

Harper grinned when Cait's eyes finally met hers. "Then I'm glad I showed up when I did."

Cait spied the bag in Harper's hand. "What's in that?"

"Just some treats. And lunch, if you fancy some?"

Cait slumped back in her seat. "You've just reminded me that I need to eat. I couldn't tell if I was going to hurl or whether it was hunger pains."

"Have you had breakfast?" Harper quirked an eyebrow. "You were quick enough to text me this morning, but have *you* eaten today?"

Cait offered a crooked smile. "I had half a round of toast around seven-thirty."

Harper immediately emptied the bag out onto Cait's desk, shaking her head. "Right. Time to eat. And then you can explain why you're losing your mind in here."

"I have to meet with the health spa down at the lake in a few hours."

Harper glanced up, her palms flat against the desk. "O…kay."

"I just…I hate anything like this. Meetings, public speaking. Anything that doesn't involve me being here in my comfort zone."

Harper hadn't expected that. Cait always seemed to be so put together when it came to life. But Harper would admit that it was refreshing to see another woman who had fears. She'd always felt inadequate when it came to being full of self-confidence. "I think you'll smash it."

"I don't know why I'm so worried. I've known the owner of the health spa for several years."

"Is there anything I can do to help?" Harper asked, handing over a wrapped freshly made sandwich. She really hoped she'd picked the right one. "Other than ply you with food…"

"The food is perfect, thank you." Cait unwrapped her sandwich, grinning as she checked the filling. "I don't recall telling you my favourite sandwich."

"You didn't. I just guessed."

"You guessed turkey and cranberry?" Cait asked, her eyebrow arched. "That's impressive guess work."

"I got it right? Wow. That never happens."

Cait got to her feet, placing her sandwich down as she beckoned Harper closer. She leaned over the desk wearing a sweet smile, her lips brushing Harper's. "Maybe we're just in tune."

Harper's insides fizzed with delight. Cait was right on the money. "Mm. You're right."

"Sit," Cait said, grinning. "Because if you keep looking at me like that, I'm never going to have lunch."

"Depends what kind of lunch you were hoping for."

Cait cleared her throat as she shook her head. Harper loved it when she blushed. It meant she was causing the right kind of reaction. "Something substantial. And this sandwich will certainly hit the spot."

Harper took a seat, staring at Cait from across the table. She looked different in her blazer and blouse. She looked…professional. Snazzy. "You look great, by the way."

Cait tugged at the lapels of her blazer, grinning. "Thanks. I wasn't sure what look to go for, so I decided on this."

"Let me guess, you have your comfy jeans and boots on underneath?" Cait was definitely a comfy jeans kinda girl, but so was Harper. If it didn't feel good against her skin, it didn't come home to live in her wardrobe. That had always been a number one rule.

"Should I have worn that?" Cait wrinkled her nose. "I mean, I had to put in a little bit of effort."

"Hey, you look gorgeous whatever you're wearing. I'm just not used to seeing you looking so professional and serious. But let me say, it looks fantastic on you. Very dominating. You'll have that room of people wrapped around your little finger in no time."

"I'll bear that in mind. It beats thinking of them all naked."

"Ew. I've never understood people who give that advice out. There are very few people I would want to imagine naked."

"Oh?"

"I wouldn't worry. You're top of the list." Harper winked, chomping down on her sandwich. "You'll always be top of that list."

Cait sighed, rocking back in her office chair. "I didn't realise how much I needed you to come by today."

❄

CAIT THREW her head back laughing, almost choking on her cup of coffee as Harper snorted her own laugh. That only sent her howling again, almost tipping back on her chair. She waved a hand in front of her, silently begging Harper to stop, but that tickle remained and Cait couldn't contain it.

"I think I've ruined your makeup." Harper grimaced. "My apologies."

"You know what, I don't even care." Cait blew out a deep breath, wiping the tears from her cheeks. "This has been everything I needed today. You've definitely kept my mind off the panic I felt earlier."

Harper's face morphed into a serious expression. "You have no reason to worry about anything. You're beautiful and you're going to nail it today. They'd be lucky to go into business with you."

"It's already basically a done deal. It's just some finalising."

"And you're worried about that? Why?"

Cait shrugged. "They've asked me to put together a presentation."

"Seems a bit dramatic if things are already concrete."

Cait had to agree. She'd wondered if she read the email right a few days ago. "I know. But they've asked if I'd put one together, so I have."

"Well, you're going to be fine anyway." Harper smiled one of her sweet smiles. "Did you want me to walk you down? I don't mind…"

"I'm driving."

Harper quirked an eyebrow. "To the lake? That's not like you. You walk everywhere."

"Mm. But my choice of footwear would guarantee a broken neck before I reached the bottom of the hill."

Harper frowned.

Cait pushed her chair back from her desk, lifting her leg to expose the six-inch heels she was wearing.

"H-holy shit!" Harper's eyes widened, her mouth falling open as her eyes trailed the length of Cait's leg, landing on her thigh. "You've been sitting behind there this whole time like that?"

Okay, Cait was lost. "I have. Why?"

Harper turned her watch towards her. "What time did you say you had to leave?"

"I have two hours yet—"

A knock on the door interrupted their conversation, and Cait immediately dropped her leg. She smiled when her brother came to rest against the doorframe. His usual stance with his arms crossed as he did so. "You two sound like you're having a wonderful time up here."

"Sorry. Too loud?"

Jude shook his head. "Not at all. And all the guests are out at the minute. So, laugh away."

"Did room 6 decide to go hiking?"

Jude nodded. "I've given them the map they need. They asked me to thank you for recommending it."

"They prefer something a little more demanding. They've been coming here for years now."

"Well, they were raring to go just an hour ago. And while I'm here, I have to pop out to the supplier. We seem to be out of black pudding for breakfast tomorrow."

"Okay, well I'll be leaving around two-thirty."

Jude pushed off the doorframe. "Don't worry, I'll be back. See you, Harper."

"Bye, Jude." Harper turned back to Cait as the door swung shut, swallowing hard. "So, uh…"

"Right," Cait said, blowing out a deep breath. "You have me for another hour, and then I have to get ready to leave." Cait slid her glasses on, focusing on the screen. "But just give me a couple of seconds to print out the notes."

Harper fell silent. Cait felt her eyes burning through her, but she had no idea what had happened in the short space of time since they'd been laughing together, but Harper's sudden lack of conversation didn't sit well with Cait. She looked up, and Harper was still staring.

"I mean, you don't have to stay. If you had things to do, I understand. I have plenty to get on with here anyway."

Harper got to her feet, approached the door, and turned the lock. As she turned back, leaning against the door, she blew out a deep breath. "You've been sitting here dressed like that since I arrived, and I had no idea."

"Should you have?" Cait's confusion grew.

"Y-yeah, I should have." Harper nodded, not appearing to be quite in the room with Cait. "Because…I mean…wow. You look, just wow."

"Well, thank you." Cait smiled, getting to her feet and clearing away their lunch. It wasn't often she was complimented by other women, but when Harper did it, it fired up everything inside her. "Like I said earlier, I just wanted to make an effort, is all."

Harper stalked towards Cait, holding out a hand that Cait immediately took. She would never turn down such a gesture. Not from Harper. "You're really turning my world upside down, Cait."

"I'm not sure how to take that." Cait paused in her step, eyeing Harper suspiciously. "I thought everything was going fine this afternoon."

"You make my head spin, you make my mouth dry, and you make my skin tingle."

Cait's heart swelled at those words. "You're going to make me blush."

"And I've never met anyone quite like that before. Someone who just lights up an entire room by being in it. Someone who makes me feel like I want to stay home and snuggle all night. Deep down, it's all I've ever dreamed of, but did I ever think I'd find it? Here? No."

"But you're happy that you feel that way?"

"Happy doesn't describe how I feel about you," Harper said, pulling Cait in flush against her. "Happy means nothing when I think of you. My entire world has been consumed by you, and I wouldn't have it any other way."

Cait lifted her free hand, feathering her fingertips across Harper's cheek. Her auburn hair sat in a messy bun atop her head, her skin soft to touch. "You've really changed my life, too. I'm enjoying every moment of this with you."

"And being here with you today—dressed like this. God, I'm really struggling to keep my hands to myself."

Cait's blood travelled south with that admission. Harper found this version…attractive? Well, who knew!

"But I wouldn't ever do something to make you feel uncomfortable at work. I'm not that kind of person. So, I was wondering if I could see you tonight?"

Oh, no. Harper couldn't say things like that, things that got Cait worked up, only to backtrack. Cait perched herself on the edge of her desk, pulling Harper between her legs. "You can see me any time, you know that."

"I know, but I wasn't sure what plans you had."

"I have a while before I have to leave," Cait said, narrowing her eyes. "You know…"

Harper's eyes immediately darkened, her hands gripping the lapels of Cait's blazer. "Please, don't say things you don't mean."

Wrapping her legs around Harper's waist, her skirt riding up as Cait dug her heels into Harper's backside, Cait pulled her in close and gripped the back of Harper's neck. "I wouldn't do that to you. Knowing that you want me here and now…" Cait chewed on her lip; she really didn't know where all of this boldness had come from. "I think I'd be a fool to turn you down."

Harper slid Cait's blazer from her shoulders, her fingers making light work of the blouse tucked into Cait's pencil skirt. "The door's locked."

Cait focused on Harper's eyes. "I know."

"And you look incredible sitting on that desk."

Cait felt her skin flush as Harper's hands settled on her bare thighs. "I do?"

"You look so fucking hot." Harper's fingers disappeared up Cait's skirt, dragging her underwear down her thighs and throwing them to the floor.

Cait placed her palms flat on the desk behind her, allowing Harper to take the lead as she dragged her towards the edge of the desk. The coolness against her skin only heightened that arousal Cait felt. This sense of being a little bold was really working well for her. She could safely say that she'd never been taken on her desk.

"Harper," Cait whispered as their lips met. Her heart sped up, her pulse thundering in her ears, but Harper was all she felt. The building could burn to the ground this second and Cait would still only see the woman standing between her legs. "God, I need you to touch me."

Harper dropped to her knees, forcing Cait's skirt further up her thighs. She dragged her nails along Cait's skin, sending a shiver throughout her entire being. And when Harper's lips touched Cait's aching sex, her tongue gathering her wetness, Cait lit up with a hypersensitivity she'd never experienced before.

Separating slick folds with her thumbs, Harper wasted no time in diving in. Her lips enveloped Cait's clit, two fingers slowly pushing inside her. Cait's breath faltered, her hands gripping the edge of the desk as Harper pushed in and out. God, this woman would be the death of her.

Cait lifted her feet onto the desk, her heels digging into the wood as she opened herself up to Harper. And judging by the grin on Harper's face as she paused and looked up at her, Cait was giving her everything she wanted.

"Fuck, you taste amazing." Harper tugged at her bottom lip before she dove back in, fucking Cait at a pace that kept her on the edge. But as she curled her fingers, hitting a spot nobody had ever become acquainted with before, fresh arousal slipped out without the need for any coaxing. Harper…was a dream come true.

An overwhelming sensation had Cait's stomach rolling with anticipation, but Harper didn't let up. She angled her fingers, locked her wrist, and rubbed vigorously at Cait's G-spot. "O-oh." Cait's eyes slammed shut. "W-what the hell are you doing to me?"

"You're about to find out," Harper said, her voice dripping with desire. With those words, an unusual pressure built between Cait's legs, and then came the gush. "Fuck, yes." Harper continued her movements, moaning as wetness covered Cait's thighs. "Uh-huh. That's fucking hot."

Cait's legs trembled. Had Harper just…made her squirt? She slumped back on her elbows; her body spent. Every ounce of energy she had disappeared; Cait really needed a moment to gather herself.

With her mind racing, Cait smiled when Harper scooped her up into her arms, kissing her hair. "You with me?"

"Mm." Cait nodded slightly, nuzzling her face into the crook of Harper's neck. "You're just full of surprises, aren't you?"

"Stick with me. We're going places."

Cait smiled against Harper's ear. "The only place we're going right now…is upstairs."

Harper pulled back, meeting Cait's eyes. "Oh. We are?"

"We definitely are."

CHAPTER TWENTY-THREE

HARPER UNPLUGGED THE HOOVER FROM THE SOCKET AT THE SIDE OF the TV unit, wrapping the lead up as she shoved it back under the stairs. She'd woken this morning with one hell of a spring in her step, finishing three projects she was working on by 11 a.m. Cait was working today, Jude had personal things to see to, but Harper could live with that. Two weeks on from Harper's scene in the office, and life was flowing pretty damn well.

Cait spent most evenings with Harper at home, the B&B quiet this time of year, and Jude took care of the place at night in return for several days off through the week. It worked, and it meant everyone was happy with the arrangements in place. Harper could get on with her own business during the day, knowing she wasn't neglecting Cait in any way, and in order to give Cait a break away from work most nights, they ended up snuggling on Harper's couch, the fire lit as they enjoyed one another's company. Really, everything was perfect.

Harper may have been used to spending the evening with another woman—she'd done it for years with Callie—but Cait really wasn't Callie. In fact, they couldn't be any more opposite. While Callie used to sit across the dining table talking about work, everything that concerned her, and without asking Harper how her day had been, Cait wanted to know about Harper before she discussed her own day. And there was no such thing as eating at the dining table anymore. Instead, they'd get to the floor, pull the coffee table closer, and sit beside one another while they talked about everything and anything. When Cait arrived at night, they struggled to separate for more than five seconds.

Cait's hand often found its way to Harper's while she was cooking dinner, and Harper's arms unconsciously landed around Cait's waist every time she rinsed the dishes before they went into the dishwasher. And it worked. It was becoming second nature to them both. As Harper stood at the window, her hands shoved in her pockets, she realised that this home could be the making of her in terms of her personal life and happiness.

And even though she disliked Callie, she truly hoped she was happy with how her own life had shaped itself. Harper may hate what her ex had done to her—who wouldn't?—but she would never wish to see Callie struggling. If she allowed herself to feel that way, it would only mean that Callie still swirled around in her mind. The more time Harper spent with Cait, the quicker the memories of her old life fizzled away. Memories that she didn't wish to hold onto.

As Harper turned to finish tidying up, a familiar red car pulled up outside the house. *Oh crap!* She smiled through gritted teeth as her mum waved frantically through the car window. This really wasn't how Harper's day was supposed to go. In an ideal world, she would call her mother this evening, listen to her talk about the locals, and then promise to be in touch soon.

Instead, she found herself moving towards the door and opening it. "Hi, Mum."

"Oh, love. You look wonderful." Katherine Grey always told Harper what she thought she needed to hear, but this time around Harper actually believed her. "You've been eating more vegetables, haven't you? I told you that it would make your skin glow."

That's mind-blowing sex, Mum. Not vegetables. Harper cleared her throat, forcing her best smile. "Yep. More veg."

"If you'd just listen to your mother more often, we wouldn't need to have these discussions."

Harper opened her front door wider, inviting Kath inside. "I don't believe we had a discussion. I just sat quietly while you talked at me."

"Oh, this place looks fantastic. Really homely. I might not leave."

Harper closed the door, steeling herself as she followed her mum into the living room. "Sorry, Mum. No room for a long-term lodger."

"That's fine. You and I can top and tail."

"Because that wouldn't be weird," Harper laughed.

"Excuse me! I wiped your arse for years. If I decide to stay a while, I'm sure you can find a space for your poor old mum."

Harper's eyes widened. Had Kath really just called herself old? Something was wrong. "Mum, it's not that I'm not happy to see you, but why are you here?"

"Your dad's playing golf with thingy." Kath waved a hand. "The one with the toupee…"

"Clarke?"

Kath nodded. "That's the one. They've just bought a caravan in Wales. He invited me to lunch with the wife, but I didn't want to listen to how wonderful it is. It's a piece of tin surrounded by sheep."

"You turned down lunch?" Harper's eyebrow rose. Her mum loved to be one of those ladies who lunch.

"I'm sure it's lovely." Kath ran a finger along the mantelpiece, bringing it up to her face and inspecting Harper's cleaning. "Very impressed. It's almost as though you're keeping this place clean for a reason."

"Huh?"

Kath eyed Harper suspiciously. "Is that a new hoodie hanging over the dining chair?"

Harper glanced over her shoulder. It was Cait's. "Yeah."

"It doesn't look like your size."

"And you can tell that from looking at it from ten feet away?"

Kath quirked an eyebrow. "I have good sight. It's not really your colour either."

"Mum, if you have a question to ask, just ask it!"

"I thought you would have been home for a weekend since you arrived. Why haven't you?"

"Oh, I don't know. Because I've been moving into a new home and getting my life together? Does that appease you?"

"Mm. Not really."

Harper flopped down onto the couch, running her fingers through her hair. It was no use lying; her mum knew her better than Harper knew herself. "I'm seeing someone, okay?"

"I knew it!" Kath grinned, clapping her hands. It was a habit that Harper loathed. "And Autumn may have let it slip last weekend."

"When did you see Autumn?" Had Harper's best friend really said too much in front of Kath? It was possible; Autumn was terrible at keeping quiet. Especially around Kath.

"She was at ours. Came to borrow a pair of your shoes."

"Which shoes?" Harper frowned. "She didn't tell me she'd been to see you. And she didn't tell me she'd swiped my shoes either. She knows I don't like her going through them."

"You should have brought them with you. Which reminds me, I need you to get the last of the things out of your room. I'm turning it into a meditation suite thing."

"Oh, thanks!"

"But never mind that. Tell me all about Cait."

Harper eyed her mum. She may not know what day it is half the time, but she knew she hadn't told Kath who she was actually dating. As far as Kath was aware, Cait had helped Harper when she moved here. Nothing more. "What's Autumn told you?"

"That you're madly in love with the local B&B owner. Very romance novelly."

"Novelly?" Harper snorted. Her mother was out of her mind. "That's not even a word—" Harper cut herself off. Did it even matter if it was a word or not? What Autumn had done was not cool. "I'm not madly in love with her." *Liar!*

"But you are happy?"

Harper's entire body relaxed. She didn't have to think twice about that answer. "I'm so happy, Mum."

"And this is the same Cait who put you up when you had issues here?" Kath took a seat at the opposite end of the couch, her coat still buttoned up. "That lovely lady who came to your rescue?"

"It's the same Cait, yeah."

Kath visibly relaxed, crossing her legs and clasping her hands on her knees. "And do you think I'll happen to bump into her while I'm here?"

Harper grimaced slightly. "I don't know, Mum. She works all day and I just about manage a few hours with her in the evening. I was planning on cooking something fancy for us tonight, you know, impress her a little bit."

"Impress her? I'm not sure you've ever had to impress anyone, my love."

"Maybe not, but I want to keep her interested. We both know what happened with Callie, and I know that wasn't my fault, but perhaps if I'd tried a little harder, she wouldn't have done what she did."

"Callie was always just...Callie," Kath said, shifting closer to Harper and taking her hand. "But you seem different with Cait in your life. I know I've only been here for five minutes, but I know when you're happy. And you are. Settled, shall we say. So, maybe Callie had to do what she did in order for you to find Cait."

"It was still a really shitty thing she did to me, Mum."

"I know." Kath patted Harper's hand, offering a sympathetic smile. Her mum always knew what to say to make Harper feel better. But she didn't need that anymore. Harper was more than happy with her life. "It doesn't make my hatred for her any less, but I really do believe this happened because it was supposed to."

"Yeah?"

"Do you have any idea how terrified I was watching you drive away? You're my baby. You always will be. And watching you pack up your life to move all this way…I didn't like it. It wasn't so bad when you were supposed to move here with *her,* but knowing you'd be alone…I just wanted to drive here and stay with you."

"You know I'm okay."

"And I always did know that, but it doesn't mean I'm not allowed to worry. If anything had happened to you up here, what would I have done? The leak…you kept that from me, didn't you?"

"I just didn't want to worry you. I'm sure you understand that."

Kath nodded. "I do."

"Tell you what, I'll send Cait a message and let her know that you're here. Maybe if she has a few minutes to spare, she'll call in."

"Oh, don't be worrying her over needless things, love. I'm sure you'll introduce me to her when the time is right for you."

Harper focused on her hands. She really did want Cait and her mum to meet, but what if Cait wasn't keen on the idea? What if Harper was getting ahead of herself with all of this? Harper really didn't want to put any pressure on this relationship. Because if she lost Cait, she really would crumble and disappear.

Cait meant more than Callie ever had.

"Would you mind if I give it a little bit more time? I'm not sure if Cait is at the point of meeting parents and stuff, and I don't want to scare her off."

"I understand." Kath squeezed Harper's hand before letting go. "But I'm staying for a little while if that's okay? I've missed you a lot since you left."

"Lunch?"

"Lunch."

❄

Cait yawned as she dragged her feet up the stairs, her aching body relieved as she reached her front door. Though Harper wouldn't be greeting her, it didn't matter. She would be with her girlfriend in no time at all, providing she didn't fall asleep as she walked through the door. Cait just needed to grab her overnight bag, and then she would be on her way down the street. Harper didn't know it yet, but Cait was spending the night. That wouldn't be overly surprising, but the fact that she didn't have to rush back to the B&B for 7 a.m. would.

C: Heading to you in the next ten minutes.

Cait didn't expect a reply from Harper, she just felt better announcing her impending arrival. She did it every night, and each time, she was greeted by a waiting Harper at the door, the fire lit and ready for the evening.

But then Cait's phone pinged in her hand, the vibration shocking her slightly.

H: Could you give me a couple of hours? I have my mum here. I think she's leaving soon.

Cait frowned. Why didn't Harper want her to meet her mother? Perhaps something had happened, a family crisis of some kind.

C: Is everything okay?

H: Of course. Yeah.

C: Okay, well if you want me to come over later, just let me know. I'll settle down for the time being.

H: She's definitely leaving soon. I promise.

Cait didn't have the first idea of what that meant. Did Harper not want them to meet? Was she keeping Cait a secret? Cait really hoped that wasn't what this was.

C: She doesn't know about me, does she?

H: She does. And she can't wait for the day when she meets you.

C: No time like the present…

H: Really? You're sure you want to meet her?

C: Well, since I'm not planning on going anywhere, I would love to meet her. Should I bring anything?

H: Just yourself. See you soon x

Cait's shoulders relaxed; she hadn't known she'd been tensed up since Harper's first reply. But instead of worrying, Cait had simply asked the question she had on the tip of her tongue. The outcome being that she would now spend those extra hours with Harper. Precious time, in Cait's opinion.

Cait rushed into her bedroom, almost ripping her phone charger from the wall and shoving it into her bag. She wouldn't need pyjamas; they only ended up on the floor anyway. With that thought, Cait grinned and slung her bag over her shoulder.

Okay. Time to be sensible. This moment is huge for you. Cait didn't often discuss her past, but it was one that had never included meeting someone's parents. It wasn't really an issue for her, it had just never happened. But even if she had met numerous parents over the years, this one was still the one that mattered most.

Just be yourself. This is going to be great. Cait had to keep that in her mind. If she didn't, she would become a bumbling mess on arrival.

Satisfied that she was ready to leave, she gave herself the once over in the mirror, and left her flat. As she rushed down the stairs, offering a small smile to the couple sitting in the lounge, Cait's eyes focused on the front door. Harper was outside, her leg bent with her foot leaning against the dry-stone wall.

Cait opened the main door with a frown. "Everything okay?"

"Yeah. Just thought I'd meet you and walk down with you."

"To the next block?"

Harper shrugged. "Wanted a moment alone with you before my mum grills you for the next hour."

"She's really going to do that?" Cait swallowed. What if Harper's mum didn't like anything Cait said?

"I'm joking. Mum's laidback. Don't worry."

"Right. Okay."

They linked arms, taking a slow pace out of the driveway of

the B&B. "Mum is one of those women who is quite happy telling the world that she has a gay daughter. But she's also one of those people who silently mouths the word lesbian as though it's the biggest secret in the world."

"Ah. One of those." Cait laughed. "My mum is the same."

"Then this is going to be fine. Mum is really going to love you. And about before…" Harper paused. "It wasn't that I didn't want you to meet her, I just wasn't sure if you were ready for that."

"I'm ready for everything with you, Harper. There's not a single thing I'm wary of, okay?"

Harper turned her head, leaning in to press a kiss below Cait's ear. "Okay."

"How was your day?" Cait huddled closer to Harper, resting her head on her shoulder. "Did you get everything done?"

"I did. In record time."

"Remind me to take some business cards from you. And if you want a spot on my website, some promotion, let me know. I'm due an overhaul in a few weeks…"

"Thanks. I will."

They arrived at Harper's front door. Cait was more than ready to get inside and relax. She just hoped that would actually happen given the fact that Harper's mum was in town. But then she realised just how wonderful Harper was, and all of her fears dissolved. Cait knew without any hesitation that Mrs Grey would be just like her daughter.

"You ready?"

Cait nodded, certainty rolling through her. She straightened her back, put on her best smile, and followed Harper inside. "One hundred percent."

The living room lighting was warm, just a small lamp illuminating one corner of the space. The fire roared as it often did at night, and a woman who had a striking resemblance to Harper was standing in the brightly lit open-plan kitchen.

She smiled a wide smile, shoving her gloves into her pocket. "Hi. I'm Kath. Harper's mum."

Cait crossed the space, offering a hand. "Cait. Lovely to meet you."

Kath studied Cait, but that smile remained as she shook her hand. When Kath narrowed her eyes slightly, she looked like Harper's twin. Her hair was a shade or two darker than her daughter's, but that rare blue eye combination was definitely in the family. "I'm really sorry for sticking around this late, but we got talking, and, well, here I still am."

"Don't apologise for visiting Harper. I'm sure she's loved having you here." Harper didn't really discuss much from back home, but Cait didn't worry. If Harper's relationship with her parents was strained, she surely would have mentioned it. "Can I get you a hot drink?"

"Oh, no. Thank you." Kath tightened her scarf. "I really should make a move. But I'd love to come back soon for a visit. Maybe a day when you're both available?" Kath eyed Harper. "Would that be okay with you, love?"

"Of course, Mum. Just let me know what day you're thinking of heading up, and I'll make sure we can all spend at least a few hours together."

"Let me know the date, and I'll have Jude take care of the B&B."

"Jude?" Kath asked.

"My brother." Cait shrugged her coat off, hanging it inside the hidden closet. "And before I forget, Harper, I bumped into Fred this morning when he came to the B&B."

"Fred?" Harper looked confused. Cait had to remember she didn't know many people yet.

"The milkman. He's going to add you to his round. I've put you down for one bottle every other day for now. If you want to change it, you can."

"A milkman? How cool is that!"

"Well, you're forever going out first thing in the morning when it's freezing because you ran out. Now you won't have to."

"Thanks, babe." Harper leaned in, pressing a kiss to Cait's cheek. "That means a lot."

"Well," Kath cleared her throat. "I think I've seen all I need to see for the time being."

Cait and Harper frowned, switching from one another to Kath.

"I just...wanted to be sure that you two were happy together. And you are." Kath opened her arms and took Harper into an embrace. "I've never seen you smile like that before, love. It's beautiful." Kath pulled back, holding Harper at arm's length. "Please, can I come back and spend the day with you?"

"You're welcome here any time, Mum."

"Cait, it's been wonderful meeting you." Kath hesitated with her hand held out, but Cait shook her head, instead pulling her into a hug.

"We don't really do handshakes around here, Kath. We're all a bunch of huggers."

"Thank God!" Kath laughed. "Now, I'm going to go home and arrange a day to come and treat you both to lunch down at the lake. I'm sure you can recommend some places, Cait?"

"That I can definitely do."

"Cait is also the local tourist information centre, aren't you, babe?"

"Unofficially, yes. If you need anything, I'm your girl."

"It's really been wonderful meeting you." Kath sighed with what sounded like contentment. That meant a lot to Cait. Knowing Harper's mum approved of Cait, trusted that she would take care of Harper and Harper would take care of her in return... it was everything Cait never expected this evening. Their time alone with one another was thrilling, but Cait felt as though she'd just received approval. Life was coming together. "I'll send you a little message when I get home, love." Kath took her bag from the dining table and headed for the door. "Goodnight, ladies. Look after one another."

"We will," they said in unison, garnering a laugh from all three of them.

Cait wrapped an arm around Harper's waist, pulling her against her as they followed Kath to the door. As the cool evening air blasted them through the door, a shiver ran through Cait. But Harper sensed it, tightening her own grip on Cait's waist. "Goodnight, Kath."

"Goodnight! Don't be strangers."

CHAPTER TWENTY-FOUR

THE SIZZLE OF BACON HAD CAIT'S NOSTRILS FLARED. THIS MORNING, she was starving. With her toast buttered on one plate and Harper's eggy bread about to come out of the pan, she rested back against the counter and blew out a deep breath. She had another hour before she needed to leave for the supplier and standing in the B&B's kitchen really wasn't how she wanted to spend that time.

Tom spun around, a cheesy grin spreading on his mouth. "Bacon."

"Thanks." Cait handed the plate over, noting the suspicious look in his eyes.

"And the eggy bread? That's yours, too?"

"Yep."

Tom stopped, the pan hovering over the stove mid-air. "Why don't I believe you?"

"I've no idea, but I pay your wages, so I'd mind my own business if I were you."

Jude breezed past her, whistling. "Harper not coming down for breakfast?"

"Harper?" Tom splayed one hand across his chest, mock astonishment on his face. "Well, well, well."

"Thanks, Jude." She gritted her teeth. Could nobody leave her alone around here?

"What? What did I do?" Jude spun, genuine confusion on his face. She couldn't blame him; she hadn't exactly told her brother to keep quiet about her relationship.

"Nothing. Never mind."

"Is Miss Cait Taylor hiding a body upstairs?" Tom narrowed his eyes, smirking as he refused to plate up the eggy bread. "Because I'm fairly certain nobody who goes by the name of Harper is on the books here."

"First of all, your dramatics are wasted, Tom. It's really not a big deal. Secondly, hand over the eggy bread before you're looking for another job in the next ten seconds."

"Ooh," Tom teased. "Someone needs to run upstairs, and it's *not* for breakfast."

"FIVE! FOUR! THREE! TW—"

"Fine. Relax." Tom tossed the breakfast onto the plate, dropping the pan as he held up his hands. "Jesus. I think I need to speak to this lady of yours. She's clearly not getting rid of all that pent up…whatever it is."

Cait turned on her heel, rolling her eyes as she walked away. "Jude, make sure Tom doesn't leave until this kitchen has been scrubbed to within an inch of its life."

"Oh, come on!" Tom huffed. "I was only playing…"

"Bye, Tom. Have a lovely shift."

Cait rushed towards the stairs before someone else could stop her, taking them two at a time. She didn't make it a habit to eat from the B&B when she wasn't working; she'd learnt her lesson in the earlier days. Because they had so many regular guests, they would often interrupt Cait at the dining table, expecting her to be working. But this morning, she was all out of anything that could potentially be a sustainable breakfast.

She balanced Harper's plate against her wrist, her own bacon on toast sitting beneath it, and pushed the flat door open with her hip. Harper was snuggled up in the bucket seat in the window, her beautiful hands wrapped around a huge cup of coffee.

"Breakfast is served."

Harper got to her feet, taking her plate from Cait and not moving until she'd leaned in for a kiss. "Thanks. This looks great."

"And if there is a knock on the door," Cait paused, reaching for her ketchup, "don't answer it. It'll be Tom."

"Um…Tom?"

"The young man who has just made your breakfast. Jude went and mentioned you, so now he'll obsess about us until he's met you."

"Why would he do that?" Harper took the couch, leaving a space for Cait to snuggle in beside her.

"Because my love life is the only interesting thing that goes on in this place. Tom is lovely, but I don't have long with you this morning and I'd like to enjoy it without any interruptions."

"Understandable."

"So?" Cait took a bite of her breakfast, dripping ketchup down her chin.

Harper reached out and plucked a tissue from the side table, handing it over. "So, my mum has already sent me a text with the next six months' worth of dates she has available."

"She's great. I love that. I'm planning on calling my own mum this evening when I've finished here. She should probably know that her daughter is on cloud nine, shouldn't she?"

Harper tucked her legs beneath herself, pulling apart her eggy bread. "Will she be happy?"

"That I'm dating?"

Harper nodded; her mouth was full.

"She will. She always asks if there's someone when she calls me. I know she just wants to see me happy and not alone, so I think she's going to be all out ecstatic when I tell her."

Harper blew out a deep breath. "This is getting really serious, isn't it?"

Cait slowly chewed her food, eyeing Harper's profile. She appeared relaxed, but Cait wasn't quite sure how to take that comment.

"I didn't for one second think I'd be dating so soon after leaving Callie," Harper explained. "To be honest, I wasn't sure it would ever happen. It was the last thing on my mind as the dreaded drive here hit me back in January."

Cait had to admit that she was surprised to see Harper sitting here, too. As the clock struck midnight on New Year's Eve, she had promised herself that her personal life would improve. Cait didn't know what those improvements would produce, but to be sharing breakfast with a woman she was desperately hoping to spend forever with…no, that wasn't what she had in mind. Getting out more, maybe some extra healthy eating, picking up a book more often and making time for herself…yes, all of that.

"Cait," Harper said, twisting in her seat as she interrupted Cait's thoughts. Those full blue eyes glared back at her, soft, but Harper appeared hesitant. "Are you enjoying spending time with me?"

"I'm not sure I'd call it enjoyment," Cait paused, dropping her toast to the plate and wiping the crumbs from her hands. "I mean, of course I'm *enjoying* it, but it's more than that for me, Harper. I know things have been hard for you, and I'm not sure anybody would expect you to be sure about your future any time soon, but I really want to be a part of it. I want to *be* it."

Harper slid her plate onto the coffee table, frowning as she scooted closer to Cait. "Don't for one second think that I'm not sure about this with you. I totally am. I just want to know that you like having me around. People are different, Cait. I don't want whatever I did wrong with Callie to spill over into this relationship. The thought of not making you happy, of being here too much…I want to do this right."

Cait got to her knees on the couch, holding Harper's face as she stared down at her. "You know if Callie ever shows up here again, I'm going to shake her hand. I may even buy her a drink."

"Why?"

Cait leaned down, smiling into a kiss. It wasn't heavy or filled with passion, but a simple slow kiss packed full of gratitude. "Because if she was here with you, *I* wouldn't be."

Cait's heart swelled when Harper smiled from ear-to-ear. "You're right."

"Sometimes I am."

"I wasn't coming, you know…"

Cait's forehead creased. "What do you mean?"

"I was going to pull out of buying the house. I was going to move back in with my parents and look for something to rent on my own. I laid in bed in Mum's spare room the week before I was due to sign on the dotted line and decided I wasn't going to go through with it."

"What made you change your mind?"

Harper smiled. "I had a dream that week. I was walking with someone. Hand in hand. I couldn't see their face, I had no idea who they were, but we were laughing. Holding one another. Just…happy. Here, in The Lakes."

Cait felt a swell of emotion surge up her throat. She tried to swallow it down, but tears pricked her eyes regardless. "I really wish you wouldn't say things like that."

"Why?" Harper's thumb caught a tear as it slid down Cait's cheek.

"Because I'm feeling things I've never felt before. And as much as I want to feel them, as much as I want to be with you like this, I'm terrified, Harper."

Harper cocked her head, concern etched on her face. "Terrified of what?"

"Not making you happy. You realising that life with me is probably the most boring thing you could ever possibly commit to. I could go on, but I won't."

"Cait Taylor, you are not boring. Your life isn't boring. You make me ridiculously happy."

"I just hope you still think that of me a year down the line."

Harper lifted to her knees, wrapping her arms around Cait's waist. "Oh, I'm going to think so much more of you by then. We will probably be fighting over who loads the dishwasher correctly this time next year."

"I…don't have a dishwasher."

"I do."

Cait sighed, pulling Harper against her. This was truly the life she wanted, just her and Harper, happy and wrapped up as life fleshed itself out around them. "You do. But you won't let me do the dishes."

"Babe, I'll have to give you something to do around the house. But don't worry, it won't be anything too strenuous. You'll be coming home from working here all day. I'll even rub your feet for you."

"Coming home?" Cait quirked an eyebrow.

"You don't think I'm going to spend my life in that big old house alone, do you? Besides, it was your dream home. It makes sense to one day be a permanent fixture. If this all goes to plan anyway…"

Those words rocked Cait to the core. Could Harper truly see them living together? Was that a real possibility? Had Cait's life pieced itself together for good?

"I mean, I don't expect you to even consider it right now, I know you have this place to run. But down the line, I think it could be something beautiful, don't you?"

Cait should disagree, shouldn't she? Isn't that what society would say? That she was moving too quickly. That it would surely crash and burn if they went headfirst into this.

Society could believe what they liked; this was Cait's life. "I…do."

"And you'd only be five minutes away if you had to be on-call. It's doable, right?"

From the moment Cait met Harper, from the second she knew something was budding between them, she'd promised herself she would make it work. The B&B was her livelihood, yes, but didn't she deserve something more than late-night calls from guests? She absolutely did. So, down the line, Cait would do what was best for her. For a happiness she was beginning to imagine she couldn't live without. It wouldn't be the end of the world if she moved out of the flat, but it would be the end of *her* world if Cait couldn't hold onto Harper because of work. "It's doable. Without a doubt."

"Then I think it's time I invited my family and friends here for a drink. Just a small get-together."

"O...kay."

Harper settled back on the couch, tugging Cait between her legs. "I want everyone to know who you are. I want you to be a part of my family."

"They won't think you're moving too soon with all of this?"

"I don't really care what they think. Half of them didn't like my previous relationship, anyway."

"Because it was with a woman?" Cait asked, worried for the answer.

"Because it was with Callie. My family loves me for who I am. They always have."

Cait relaxed. The thought of having to move, dress, and get to work soon didn't please her whatsoever. "Then I would love to help you get them together. It'll be a lovely evening."

Harper sighed, wrapping her arms around Cait. "You're so beautiful."

CHAPTER TWENTY-FIVE

Cait rested against Harper's kitchen counter, smiling as her girlfriend caught up with family she hadn't seen in a while. She adored seeing Harper smiling, knowing she had played a part in making her feel that way. But what Cait loved more than anything was knowing that she would climb into bed tonight next to Harper, both of them blissful and content.

For the first time in her life, Cait felt as though she was a part of something other than just the B&B. She wouldn't change anything that had happened previous to all of this, but she did wish she'd met Harper sooner. Even just a couple of years earlier than they had. As she stood here, aged 41, Cait got the impression that she'd missed out on too much. The early morning shifts, the night calls, none of it mattered if she didn't have someone by her side. But it had never worked out…and that was just the way it fell sometimes.

Kath crossed the room, a glass of prosecco in her hand. "Harper says you made the food this evening."

"Well, we made it together." Cait straightened herself; she wouldn't slouch while she was talking to Harper's mother. It was rude.

"It's lovely. All of this," Kath said, her eyes wandering around the room. "I'm so happy Harper's settled here. I worried about her, all parents would, but after the break-up, I worried more than I knew I should have."

Cait nodded. "She knows what she wants. You should be very proud of her."

"I am. No doubt about it." As Kath sipped her prosecco, Autumn came swanning through the front door. Harper and Cait didn't know if she would make it, something about work and overtime that Autumn couldn't get out of, but Cait was happy to see her. "Oh, look. It's my second daughter. Must go and say hello."

Autumn walked towards Cait and Kath, but Cait was surprised when Autumn threw her arms around her, bypassing Harper's mum completely. "Thanks for making my best friend so happy."

"I, uh…you're welcome." Cait frowned.

"No, seriously." Autumn held Cait at arm's length, a smile beaming from ear-to-ear. "When I was here last time, I thought she'd blown it with you. You know, all that Callie stuff. But look at you both now. God, you look *so* gorgeous together."

Cait could only smile, lowering her eyes. She didn't take compliments very well, they always made her feel uneasy, but she had to agree with Autumn a tiny bit. Harper *did* look gorgeous at Cait's side.

"Kath, it's lovely to see you. What do you think of our Cait here?" Autumn cocked her head, grinning. "Isn't she fab?"

"Perfect, is what she is."

Cait's skin flushed. "Okay, I'm just going to go mingle."

As she weaved through the bodies congregating between the kitchen and the living room, she felt a hand grip her own and pull her to the side of the room. "I'm missing you."

"I'm right here. I was just letting you mingle while I minded my own business."

"Come and mingle *with* me," Harper offered her best puppy dog eyes.

Cait turned her watch towards her. "My mum should be here in the next few minutes. You go and chat, and I'll find you once she's arrived."

"Can't wait." Harper leaned in, pressing her lips against Cait's. "Really...can't wait."

"You know what I can't wait for?" Cait's lips hovered around Harper's ear. "Summer with you. Autumn with you. Winter with you. Just...everything."

Harper's eyes welled with tears. "You've been thinking about that stuff? I thought it was just me."

"Of course I have. And it's good to know that you have, too."

"It's all I ever seem to think about, Cait. Everything I want to do with you. Plans we're yet to make. Memories that I cannot wait to look back on over the years."

Cait wanted to drag Harper away from her get-together, but she really shouldn't. In an ideal world, they would be making their way up the stairs, tangled up in one another. But that would come later. For the time being, Cait simply smiled, kissed Harper, and let go of her girlfriend's hand.

"Go and be with your family and friends. I'm not going anywhere." Harper reluctantly inched away from Cait, sticking out her bottom lip for dramatic effect. Cait laughed, shooing Harper away as the doorbell rang out. "I'll get it."

As she reached for the door, Harper suddenly appeared behind Cait. "Let's do this together. I want your mum to know I mean business when it comes to her daughter."

Cait turned, capturing Harper's lips. This, tonight, meant everything to her. It may be Harper's evening, welcoming her family and friends to her new home, but Cait hadn't once felt out of place. Every person who had so far walked through the door had been welcoming. Cait pulled back, steadying herself with one hand on Harper's chest. "You mean the world to me. Don't ever forget that."

"Open the door, pretty lady. I don't like to keep potential

mother-in-laws waiting." Harper winked, taking Cait's hand. "And you mean the world to me, too."

The doorbell rang out again. This time, Cait should really answer it.

When she did, her mother stared back at her with a gentle smile. "Caitlin, I'm so sorry I'm late."

"You're not late." She pulled her mum into a hug, squeezing her tight. "I'm just glad you could make it."

"You think I'd miss this evening? Not in a million years."

"Mum, this is Harper." Cait stood to the side, their fingers still laced together. "Harper, this is my mum, Carol."

"Lovely to meet you, Mrs Taylor." Cait noted the brilliant smile Harper wore. Some may say it was fake, perhaps overly enthusiastic, but Cait knew it was real. Harper didn't have a fake bone in her body. "Come in. I'll get you something to drink."

"Call me Carol, love. We're all friends here." Cait's mum followed Harper through to the living room, introductions taking place as she did.

Cait stopped for a moment, watching the perfect life unfolding before her eyes, and sighed. As the door closed gently behind her, she side-stepped one of Harper's guests and followed her girlfriend and mum through to the kitchen. Tonight was going to be faultless.

If only Jude could be here tonight to meet Harper's family and friends. They'd lived in one another's pockets for a long time, but Cait had always felt protective towards her brother. Though they'd had some slight disagreements as the year began, she missed him being here this evening. Even Harper had made a comment about wishing he could be here when they were preparing the food this afternoon. But there was going to be all the time in the world to have Jude here for get-togethers. Cait would absolutely make sure of that. Because she had no intentions of being anywhere else.

❄

"UNCLE JERRY SAID he loves his room at the B&B." Harper sidled up beside Cait, instinctively wrapping one arm around Cait's waist. "They've decided to book again for early summer."

"Lovely," Cait said, pulling herself away from the conversation she was having with Kath and two friends of Harper's from back home. "Tell him he can have a discount."

"No. He's a bit of a dick and I'm not overly fond of him, so he can pay full price."

"I can't charge your family full price when they stay with me, Harper." Cait turned away from the group, frowning. "Can you imagine what they'd say about me during Christmas dinner?"

"They wouldn't say a damn thing about you. I'd make sure of it."

Cait lifted one hand, pressing her palm against Harper's cheek as her thumb feathered across her skin. "You're adorable, do you know that?"

"Adorable? Really?" Harper wrinkled her nose, disappointed that adorable was the first thing to come to Cait when she described Harper. "I would have preferred sexy or something similar."

"Oh, you are. Very sexy. But right now isn't the time to discuss just how much..."

Harper narrowed her eyes. "Not even a teeny bit?"

Cait took Harper by the hand, guiding her to the corner of the kitchen. "Are you trying to make me blush in front of your entire family?"

"Oh, this isn't even half of them." Harper snorted. "I don't like the rest."

"Either way, I know what you're doing..."

Harper shrugged, stepping closer to Cait. "Just trying to keep my woman on her toes."

Cait had that shy look in her eyes—the one Harper loved—but it didn't quite have the same effect as it once had. The reason being that Harper knew exactly what Cait was like in the bedroom. Blushing really was useless.

"Don't give me that 'butter wouldn't melt' look. I know what you're capable of, remember."

"Can't you just…take the recycling out or something?"

"Depends. Are you coming with me?"

Cait shook her head; she clearly knew exactly what Harper was doing. "I'm sorry, I can't. I was in the middle of a very important conversation with your mother about caravans."

"You mean you're turning me down so you can talk about tin surrounded by sheep?"

Cait barked a laugh. "Funny. She described it exactly the same way."

Harper blew out a deep breath. "Fine. I'll remember that later."

"I'm sure you won't." Cait winked, turning back to her conversation.

Harper grabbed the empty wine and prosecco bottles from the counter, taking them to the front door. Teasing Cait was supposed to be fun, but this wasn't. She only wanted a quick peck out of view of the family, maybe a little fumble upstairs while nobody was around. But no, she found herself opening the door to dispose of the recycling. How exhilarating.

Harper lifted the lid on the recycling bin, a chill running through her body. The temperature was beginning to pick up, but it was still a cold evening. Colder than Harper would have liked, anyway. She pushed the recycling down, closing the lid only to be met with a body in front of her.

"Jesus fucking Christ!" She gripped her chest, rooted to her spot. "Callie?" Harper squinted, making out Callie's features as fear spread through her. She'd never been snuck up on before. Honestly, Harper was surprised she hadn't reacted by stepping forward and punching Callie without thinking.

"Hey," Callie said quietly. "I know I wasn't invited, but I wanted to drop by anyway."

"Um, why?" Harper hadn't spoken to Callie since the last time she was here. Her arrival didn't make any sense. Then again, Callie didn't usually make sense with her decisions. Harper calmed her breathing, taking a second to realise that there wasn't a mass murderer standing in her front garden. "I mean…you have a bag with you."

"Yeah. I figured it would be okay to spend the night. Maybe we could talk. You could show me what you've done with this place." Callie looked up at the house, a small smile on her lips. "It's still as amazing as I remember."

Harper shook herself from her dismay, a laugh erupting from her throat. "You want to stay the night? Here? With me?"

"Yeah. I can take the spare room if you don't want to share. But I really would like to be here tonight."

"How did you even know about tonight?"

"I still have Jasmine and your uncle Pete on social media."

Harper bit back a scoff. "You still have my family on your profiles? That's weird."

"I got on with them. Just because we weren't together didn't mean I couldn't speak to them. To check in and say hi."

Harper pinched the bridge of her nose, baffled that this was happening. "Callie, are you okay? I mean…do you *feel* okay?"

"I feel better now that I'm here." Callie took a step forward, her smile widening. "And I know I have a lot of making up to do, but we were so good together. You know it makes sense to try again."

"N-no." Harper frowned. "You can't just show up here expecting us to try again. It doesn't work like that. I'm happy here, Callie. I'm happy here without you."

Callie quirked an eyebrow. "You're happy alone?"

"I'm not alone. I have everything and everyone I need here. And those people don't concern you. They never will."

Callie dropped her bag to the ground, reaching inside and pulling out what looked like an expensive bottle of champagne. "I got this for you. A housewarming gift. I thought we could share it."

"Are you not listening to me? You need to turn around, get in your car, and leave."

"Harper, I still love you. And I'm going to do everything I can to prove that to you," Callie paused, then blurted "Life is awful without you. I can't even do my job properly anymore. I just...I want you back, Harper. Even if you resent me for years to come, I still want you back."

"No."

Callie sighed. "Please give me another chance. One more, it's all I'm asking for."

"You don't deserve a thing from me. And I'm not sure you ever did. I'm happy, Callie. Here, with the life I have, I'm truly happy. You showing up months down the line doesn't make any difference to me whatsoever. You're out of your mind to even think that I'd consider taking you back."

"Be happy with *me*." Callie reached out her hand, but Harper pulled away. "Because we can be. We can *so* be that again."

"You know, I did sit here wondering if I could ever take you back. We've been through a lot together. I knew we'd been in a good place at one time, and I knew we'd had some great times over the years. But then I realised I wasn't really content. I thought I was, I thought that you gave me everything I needed—"

"I did. And I can again."

"But you didn't. You talked *at* me. Our life revolved around *you*. Unless it was something that got your attention, you didn't care." Harper hadn't realised she needed to say this to Callie, but as each word spilled from her mouth, she felt lighter. "How often did we sit down together and discuss our day?"

"All the time."

"No. We talked about *your* day. Not mine. Just yours."

"That's not—"

"How often did we settle down at night together and hold one another on the couch? Hand in hand. Laughing. You playing with my hair, me stroking your skin?"

"I, uh..."

"Never. You were always too busy talking with friends on the phone or updating your social media or doing anything to avoid being alone with *me*."

"Harper, that's not true. I loved you. I still do."

"But I've met someone now who does those things. She doesn't want every second of my attention so she can harp on about her day. But even if she did, I'd sit and listen because she has a beautiful voice. She has one hell of a smile. And she makes *me* smile. We share dinner together almost every night. We wake up with one another, and there's no rush. And you know when I take a bath, but she's not finished work quite in time to join me? She pops into the bathroom with a warm towel for me. Fresh clothes. She asks if I'd like a hot chocolate, she asks if I've had a good day, and she wants to talk about my job."

"Who is she?"

"She's the woman I have a feeling I'm going to spend forever with. And you coming here is not going to ruin that for me."

"Harper…"

"I should get back inside. I have guests to entertain." Harper threw her thumb over her shoulder, shaking her head. "I'm sorry you drove all the way here."

"I love you, Harper."

Harper blew out a deep breath, aware that what she was about to say would change *everything* inside of her. There was no going back after this. "Yeah, well, I love Cait. I love her like I didn't know it was possible to love. And it may only be early days, but I hope that one day, she will love me just as much. Because it's all I think about. When I wake up, when I sit down to eat, when I'm out walking around this beautiful town. I think about the moment when she tells me she loves me…and I pray that *that* day will actually arrive."

"Cait? The frumpy one from the B&B?"

Harper frowned. How dare Callie say that. "Excuse me?"

"Yeah, she looks like the real life and soul of the party." Callie snorted.

"She's the life and soul of *my* party. She's the woman responsible for the constant bliss I feel. And you know what? She's more loyal and trustworthy than *you* could ever claim to be."

"You've really downgraded, Harper. I feel bad for you."

"Oh, don't. *Don't*, for one second, feel bad. I'm living the dream here without you. So thanks for fucking Ruby behind my back. It was the best thing you ever could have done for me. I owe you."

"So that's it?"

"That's it. You're going to go home, and I'm going to go back inside to spend the rest of this beautiful evening with the woman I love."

"Wow."

As Harper turned to head back inside, leaving Callie standing on the drive, a body came from the shadow to the side of the house. Harper's eyes widened. "C-Cait?" Harper's voice was elevated, sheer panic tearing through her. Cait was never supposed to know that Callie had been here.

Cait said nothing. She simply stepped forward, tugged Harper's hand, and dragged her back into the darkness.

"Babe, what's going on?"

"Callie was here." Cait pressed her body to Harper's, pinning her against the outside wall.

Harper could make out Cait's features, but she had no idea what she'd heard. "She was. But she's leaving now."

"And you told her you love me."

"You heard that?" Harper's shoulders slumped. "I'm sorry. It shouldn't have happened like that. And she, of all people, shouldn't have been the first to hear it."

Cait leaned in, crushing her lips against Harper's. It was needy but filled with passion. It was desperate yet soft. Cait had a way of firing up Harper's body, but tonight was different. Tonight was everything and more. No holding back. No hesitation. Cait was kissing Harper as though her life depended on it.

When she pulled back, her thumb feathering across Harper's bottom lip, Cait smiled with tears in her eyes. "Did you mean it?"

"That I love you?" Harper asked, her heart rate through the roof from the most incredible kiss of her life. "Of course I meant it. And I know it's probably not what you want to hear, maybe it's far too soon for you, but I really do, Cait."

Cait leaned in again, capturing Harper's lips slowly this time. And then she smiled against Harper's mouth. "I love you, too."

Whoa! What? Harper's mouth dried, her palms clammy as she held Cait's hips against her own. "Y-you do?"

"I do."

CHAPTER TWENTY-SIX

"CHRIST, THAT WAS INTENSE." HARPER SHOOK HER HEAD AS SHE checked her puffy eyes in the bathroom mirror. Cait hiding as she spoke with Callie should have unnerved her more than it initially had, the declaration of love should have terrified her, but it didn't. It couldn't possibly. Because for the first time since she moved to the town, Harper felt complete. She didn't feel homesick or wonder what could have been if she'd stayed. No, she felt as though she was in the right place. A place she would remain in for the rest of her life…with Cait.

Harper steadied her nerves, blowing out a deep breath as she placed her hand on the door. She'd been stupid to even entertain Callie for a second, but Harper was, in some ways, glad that she'd shown up. There really was nothing else to say to one another now. Harper had given her both barrels, and that was that. But then Harper was reminded of the insult Callie had hurled towards Cait. Did she know that Cait was close by and listening? Did she just choose to insult her for no good reason?

Harper seethed. How dare *anyone* talk about Cait that way!

A knock on the door jolted Harper, her hand instantly turning the handle. "Sorry."

Cait's mum stood in front of Harper, slight concern etched on her face. "Harper, is everything okay?"

"Oh, yeah." She lowered her eyes. Carol didn't need to see how swollen and red they were.

"Then why are you up here crying while my Caitlin is downstairs with a smile beaming from ear-to-ear?"

Was she? That instantly lifted Harper's mood.

Harper loved hearing Carol call Cait by her full name. It made everything feel all the more personal.

"I was just…having a moment." Harper couldn't offer any more than that. She also didn't understand why she was hiding in the bathroom. "But I'm fine."

"Has something happened? You seem upset, lovely." Carol placed a soothing arm on Harper's shoulder. "If you needed to talk…"

"I just messed up a little while ago," Harper explained, wringing her hands in front of her. "But I think Cait is okay, so I really shouldn't worry so much."

Carol quirked an eyebrow. She looked like Cait when she did. "Messed up?"

"My ex showed up just before. I haven't seen her since early January."

"Right. Okay." Carol lowered her hand from Harper's shoulder, clearly wary of what else could possibly come from Harper's mouth. "Your ex…"

"Don't worry. I'd never do anything to hurt Cait." Harper focused fully on Carol. She had to know that Harper was a good person. "And I didn't know that Cait was listening in when we were talking…"

"Well, Caitlin seems happy enough, so I trust that you haven't upset her."

"I told my ex that I'm in love with Cait," Harper paused, failing to gauge Carol's reaction to that piece of information. "Because I am. Very in love with her."

Carol guided Harper back into the bathroom, sitting her down on the edge of the tub. "Sweetheart, I don't know what the problem is here. You love my daughter. I'd say that's wonderful."

"But Cait shouldn't have heard it like that. She means more to me than overhearing those words while I'm having a conversation with someone else. And my ex? That just makes it even worse."

"I'm sure Caitlin is perfectly fine. But she won't be if she sees how upset you are, so why don't we get you tidied up, and then you can head back downstairs. I know she'll be looking for you."

"Thanks for being so nice." Harper smiled weakly.

"Oh, I'm not just being nice. I like you, and my daughter is besotted with you."

Harper's chest ached. Cait…was everything.

"And this evening has been wonderful."

"I'm really happy you could make it. Cait was worried that you wouldn't, so it's nice to see her with a smile on her face."

"I should make more time for her. But she's always so bloody busy with that B&B. Jude is borderline useless in most things, so Cait spends her life being the best she can be."

"Jude has actually stepped up and taken on quite a role at the B&B. You'd be impressed."

"I'm glad to hear that. It's about time. I don't know how many times I've told him that his sister needs him. She can't be expected to run that place every second of the day. She needs a break."

"Don't worry; she gets one." And it was true. If Cait had been working all day, Harper welcomed her with open arms, a hot bath, and snacks. What more could anyone want after being on their feet all day? "I'll look after her, Carol."

Carol smiled, shaking her head. "God, I bet she thought it was Christmas when you walked into her life."

Harper could only shrug, aware that a blush was spreading fast across her cheeks. "Maybe. I don't know."

"I do. She called me last week to say she was dating. That call lasted an hour."

"Wow. She must have had a lot to catch up on with you."

"No, sweetheart. She *only* spoke about you."

Harper got to her feet, no longer worried about the slip-up earlier. Cait wasn't the kind of woman who held a grudge or took offence to things. Cait was just…well, Cait. "I should get back downstairs then, shouldn't I?"

"You should." Carol nodded, stepping out of the way and allowing Harper to leave the bathroom. "And Harper?"

"Yeah?" Harper turned on her heel, a beaming smile now on her face.

"Thank you."

She frowned. "For what?"

"Finding my Caitlin."

❄

CAIT BRACED herself against the dining table, belly laughing as Harper's Uncle Frank downed another shot of tequila. She hadn't realised beer pong could be so much fun, nor did she realise just the alcohol contents involved. Autumn had decided to jazz it up a bit, exchanging cider for shots. Honestly, Uncle Frank would probably hit the deck after the next one.

"Come on, Cait." Autumn wrapped an arm around Cait's waist, leaning towards her ear. "I know you're tipsy, but I need you to concentrate now. This is the end. Loser has to down whatever is left."

That thought alone had Cait's stomach rolling. No way could she mix the lot and drink it.

"I think I just remembered something I have to do…" Cait pulled away from the table, only to be dragged back by Autumn.

"Oh, no. You have the better shot out of the two of us. And I really need you to get this right."

"Autumn, I can't even see in a straight line. You've got no chance."

Autumn held up her hands, calling for a time-out. She dragged Cait away from the table, huddled as though she was about to give away the secrets of everyone in the room. "Look, I know my best friend loves you, but if I end up getting her girlfriend hammered, it won't end well for either of us."

"So, admit defeat and I don't know…accidentally knock the table until the drinks fall over. No drinks, nothing to drink. See, I'm not completely useless."

Cait didn't want to be here anymore. No, she wanted to be with Harper…

"This could all be over in the next ten seconds and then you can find your woman and do God knows what's going on in your mind."

"Fine." Cait would take her final turn, and then she was gone.

As she approached the table, Tom from the B&B walked shyly through the living room. Harper had insisted she invite Tom and Jude, but Jude had chosen to send Tom over rather than neither of them. "Thomas! Get your backside here!" Cait yelled above the noise of Harper's friends and family. "Your boss needs you!"

Tom rushed to Cait's side, frowning. "Oh, my God! Are you drunk? This is amazing."

"I'm not drunk. Don't be ridiculous. I've had what? Two—"

"Five shots." Autumn cut in holding out her hand. "And you are?"

"Cait's breakfast guy. Tom. Nice to meet you."

"Autumn. Harper's best friend and assassin when needed." She studied Tom, narrowing her eyes. "You look like you play beer pong."

"I do. Well, when my friends will actually agree to the challenge. I have been known to avoid a single shot in a game."

"Cait, go and find Harper. Do your…lesbianing. Tom can take over."

Cait's eyebrows shot up with surprise. "Lesbianing?"

"Whatever it is you two get up to when nobody is around." Autumn rolled her eyes, shooing Cait away. "Harper went upstairs a while ago."

"She did?"

Autumn nodded, turning her back and clearly done with this

conversation. Cait's mind wandered to Harper and her whereabouts, her eyes taking in the room with no sign of her girlfriend. As Cait moved through the group who had congregated around the fireplace, Harper appeared with Cait's mum beside her.

"Oh, no. What's going on?" Cait muttered, putting her best fake smile on. "Everything okay with you two?"

"Sure, babe. I was just chatting with your mum."

"Um…where?"

"Well, I was in the bathroom. We bumped into one another as I was coming out."

Cait narrowed her eyes. "Really?"

"Caitlin, I think we should wind this party down now. I'm sure you and Harper would like a few hours together."

Cait could really get on board with that. She eyed Harper, lifting a brow. "What do you think?"

"I think I like the sound of that," Harper said, stepping forward and taking Cait's hand. "I wanted to talk to you, if that's okay?"

"Let's get everyone out of here."

❄

CAIT CLEARED AWAY the last of the glasses on the kitchen counter, putting the dishwasher on its final cycle of the night. Anything remaining could be tackled in the morning; right now, she wanted to settle down with Harper. Autumn had gone back to the B&B with Harper's relatives, and Cait's mum had headed home as the last of the gang made their way up the hill.

The quietness was a stark contrast to just thirty minutes ago when everyone was still here, but Cait had truly enjoyed herself. If she pushed the fact that Harper wanted to talk to the back of her mind, the rest of this night would surely be just as wonderful.

Cait glanced over her shoulder. Harper was clearing away the living room. The couches were back in their usual position, the coffee table had been brought back down from upstairs, and with a quick hoover of the carpet, it was hard to believe anyone else had been here.

"Need a hand in there, babe?" Harper called out, her back to Cait.

"No, I'm done. I'll be in now. Did you want coffee?"

Harper turned as Cait dried her hands on a tea towel. "I'd love coffee if you're making some."

"It's ready." Cait quickly poured two cups and moved into the living room. The distance between them was too great for her liking; she wanted to be closer. "Sit down for five. The rest can wait until the morning."

"You're right." Harper blew out a breath, flopping onto the couch. "God, I'm shattered now."

They got comfortable beside one another, the silence in the room broken by the crackle of the fire. "You said you wanted to talk to me?"

Cait gripped her coffee cup tighter, wondering what the hell Harper could possibly have to say. As far as Cait was concerned, there was nothing to talk about. The evening had been a success, words had been spoken unexpectedly, but overall Cait had felt good. Really good, actually.

"About before…" Harper paused, lifting her coffee cup and sipping.

Cait waited for a response, but nothing came. Harper just stared off into the fire.

"Look," Cait started, "I know everything was said in the heat of the moment. Callie was there, you didn't expect it, and it's really okay that it was said as some kind of defence mechanism. It doesn't change how I feel *or* what I said, but I really don't want you to tell me something so important if you don't mean it. I can live with this how it is until you *do* mean it. If that day ever arrives."

Harper's forehead creased as she turned to face Cait. "I did mean it. I meant every word of it."

"Har—"

"No, Cait." Harper gripped Cait's hand, moving closer as she took Cait's coffee from her. "I *did* mean it. I love you."

Cait's belly swirled with a million and one emotions. "Then why the hesitation?"

"I just…I really hate how you heard it. And I can't take it back for a do-over, but I want you to know that I'm so sorry you heard those words while I was arguing with her. It was *never* supposed to be that way."

"Really, it's okay."

"Not to me it isn't." Harper clenched her jaw, visibly angry about what she had done. But Cait meant it when she told Harper it didn't matter. What mattered to Cait was whether Harper was still repeating those words a year down the line. Maybe ten. "She always has to ruin everything. And those things she said about you…God, I wanted to kill her."

"Those things she said about me were said out of jealousy, we all know that." Cait rolled her eyes. "I may be some things, but frumpy is not one of them. And if Callie wants to try her hand at insulting me again, I'll show her just who I am."

"Oh yeah?" Harper grinned, her eyes darkening.

"Get your mind out of the gutter!"

"You're not frumpy. And I haven't downgraded." Harper cupped Cait's face with both hands, her soft smile lulling Cait into a world of her own. "You've made me so happy, Cait. Don't ever change."

"This is me. And I love that you love me." Cait leaned in, taking Harper's bottom lip between her teeth. "Thank you for noticing me. For giving me a chance. Just…for everything."

"I don't ever want to be anywhere else, okay?"

"I don't want you to be anywhere else."

Harper caressed Cait's cheek. "I'm so ready for this with you."

"I've been waiting for you my whole life."

EPILOGUE

"Right, I'm leaving," Cait grabbed her holdall, turning back and throwing a wave over her shoulder. Jude was finalising the new breakfast menu in the office, the sun beaming through the window. "Are you sure you don't need me to do anything before I go?"

"Just go before I change my mind and take back the offer of a week away from here."

"I'll only be down the road if you need me anyway."

"Exactly. So, let your baby go, and have some fun."

Her baby. Cait's Rest.

It had been exactly that over the years, the love she'd put into this place did make it feel like her child, but lately, she couldn't wait to get away for the evening. She couldn't recall the last time she slept in her own bed or ate alone, but that was exactly what she'd hoped for going into this with Harper. She wanted someone who didn't want to see her leave in the morning. She wanted someone who was excited to see her walking through the door at night. What she wanted, she had. And then some.

"You'll look after it, won't you?"

"Do I look stupid enough to let this place go down the pan? And have to face you because of it?"

"Don't ask questions that you won't like the answer to." Cait gave Jude a knowing look, smirking as his eyes widened. "Relax, brother. I'm joking."

"Sometimes I wonder. That girlfriend of yours has led you astray."

Cait smiled, her heart fluttering at the mere thought of Harper. "I'm headed off, okay?"

"Have a lovely week off, Cait. Say hi to Harper for me, won't you?"

"I will. Call me if you need me."

Without another word, Cait was trudging down the stairs with her holdall, almost skipping out of the door. Harper was waiting, so she should really move herself.

Cait glanced back at the B&B momentarily, exhaling a slow breath as all tension fell from her shoulders. She wouldn't think about the place this week; she had much more pressing stuff on her mind.

Harper. Harper was the *only* thing on her mind.

As Cait approached the house, the sound of heavy music thumped through the doors and windows. She caught a glimpse of Harper in the kitchen, but Cait preferred to be inside. She took the key Harper had given her over a month ago and slid it into the lock. The familiar sound of Meatloaf's *I'd do anything for love (but I won't do that)* played out, and as Cait closed the door and moved into the living room, Harper appeared in the kitchen, head-banging and playing air guitar with a spatula. Cait knew she should let Harper know that she'd arrived, but she couldn't. She had to watch on, delighted by just how happy Harper looked this afternoon. Truly, Cait was mesmerised.

Harper spun as the music slowed, and the incredible vocals of Lorraine Crosby started to fill the air. Phew, the sound of that woman would always send a shiver down Cait's spine. Harper caught Cait's eyes, holding out a hand and beckoning Cait closer.

Cait dropped her bag to the floor, her eyes never leaving Harper's. As they met in the middle of the room, hand in hand, Cait offered Harper a full smile. "Missed you today."

Harper leaned in, kissing Cait. "I've missed you, too."

"And I was quite enjoying you playing air guitar."

"You know you shouldn't sneak in and watch people, don't you?"

As a particular lyric played out, Cait laughed. "Maybe you should do as she says…"

"What's that?" Harper narrowed her eyes, a sexy squint presenting itself. "Hose you down with holy water?"

"Uh-huh."

"It's not blessed, but the shower could do the trick."

Cait tugged Harper's hand, guiding her back towards the stairs. "The shower works for me."

Within moments, Cait found herself at the top of Harper's staircase, her skin cool as she stood in nothing but her underwear. Their clothes lay scattered up the stairs and across the landing, Harper's chest heaving as she watched Cait with a hunger in her eyes. "You know, I could get used to this."

"Mm. Me too," Cait said, grabbing Harper by her bra straps, their bodies colliding. "But I'm not sure I'll ever get used to this body. God."

"Oh, keep talking." Harper backed Cait up against the wall beside the bathroom door, pressing against her as her thigh slid between Cait's legs.

"It's your skin," Cait whispered against Harper's lips. "Soft. Smooth. Delicious."

"I did tell you my skin tasted pretty good…"

Cait gripped the back of Harper's neck, pulling her into a searing kiss. Her lips burned, her entire body tingled, and in all honesty, she wasn't entirely sure they would make it to the shower. The plush carpet beneath her feet seemed much more appealing right now. Cait pressed her forehead to Harper's. "I need you now, Harper. Right now."

Harper grinned. "Take whatever you want, babe."

Cait sunk to her knees, dragging Harper down with her. She swiftly unhooked Harper's bra, throwing it to the floor, Cait's own following immediately after. As she forced Harper down onto her back, straddling a strong thigh as she did, Cait dragged her nails up the inside of Harper's thigh. "I need to touch you." Cait dipped her head. "All over." Sucking Harper's nipple into her mouth, Cait smiled when Harper gasped. "Every inch of you."

"I'm all yours…" Harper arched her back, encouraging Cait to take her to the heights of ecstasy as she clung to the back of her head. "Fuck. Always."

"Mm. What I love to hear." Cait gathered Harper's wetness on her fingertips, rolling them over her clit before teasing her entrance. "God, you're so wet."

Cait trailed her tongue up Harper's chest, kissing her jaw. She was truly in awe of Harper and how free she felt with her body. Nobody had ever been so adventurous or spontaneous before. But Harper…she was a revelation. "I-inside," Harper moaned. "Please, I need you inside me."

Cait obliged, sinking deep into Harper with two fingers. Nothing about this moment was slow. No, it was pure want. That urge to make Harper scream. Because when she did, it was music to Cait's ears. Their bodies moulded, and Cait sank deeper, curling her fingers. "Mm. I could spend all night like this with you."

"F-fuck." Harper grasped at the carpet, failed, and instead held Cait against her. "Yes."

Sensing that Harper was ready to come, Cait suddenly slipped out of her, spreading her legs and sitting low on her hips. Harper's wetness was enough to send Cait over the edge, sex on sex almost too much to take. Harper's hands trailed down Cait's sides, resting on her hips as she guided Cait back and forth. "Oh, Jesus." Cait instinctively grabbed at her own breasts, squeezing as she threw her head back. Heaven. That's what this was. When they were like this, Cait didn't know any other world.

"Cait," Harper spoke breathlessly.

Harper lifted her hips, pulling Cait down and meeting one another, thrust after thrust. Cait rocked harder, every nerve ending firing up. "Baby, I-I…"

"Fuck, yes." Harper gripped Cait's hips harder, her trimmed fingernails causing Cait to hiss. But it only added to the incredible pleasure she felt coursing through her. "Babe, I'm so close…"

With those words, Cait's orgasm ripped through her, the intensity overwhelming. There were moments in her life that she'd enjoyed, some she'd loved, but Harper was doing everything in her power to overwrite all Cait had ever known.

Harper shuddered, her hips rolling as her chest heaved. Instead of finding the words to describe just how she felt, Cait lay against Harper, turning her face into the crook of her neck. Her fingertips stroked at Harper's skin, Cait's pulse thrumming in her ears. "Let's stay here forever."

Harper held Cait close, nothing but love surging through them. "Let's do exactly that."

❄

IT MADE sense to be here, down at the lake, hand-in-hand. Harper would never forget that evening when she joined Cait, sharing a Belgian waffle and hot chocolate as they spoke about their dream relationships. Harper would admit that she'd had a soft spot for Cait from the moment she'd arrived, perhaps in her subconscious it had always been there, but she couldn't have possibly dreamed that this would be her future, standing at the lake and watching the world go by. She'd never demanded much from life, Harper was pretty easy going in that sense, but she wanted so much with Cait. As they lay with one another every morning, Harper couldn't imagine being anywhere else. Cait…made sense.

She looked down over the railing at the rocky shoreline, colourful gravel visible through the clear water. It was a busy day on the lake today, the height of summer bringing in flocks of crowds. Every accent from all over the country could be heard, and Harper loved it. She loved the diversity that The Lakes lured in. The beauty of it meant that it was the ideal place if you wanted to get away. Cait was brave taking a week off from the B&B considering they were fully booked for the next three months, but Tom had taken a more hands on approach, becoming Jude's wingman when Cait wanted a day off.

Everything around them just worked. Harper knew Cait had repeatedly kicked herself for refusing to live her life over the last several years, but it had all been worth it. They both knew that. Regrets were a waste of time; Cait couldn't change them.

The roar of a boat motor caught Harper's attention, a smile settling on her mouth as another lake cruise docked in front of them. She hadn't quite built up the courage to try another boat yet, but today was the day. It had to be. Harper had promised herself she would try while she had Cait to herself for an entire week, so here they were, about to pay for and enjoy a lake cruise.

Cait's hand settled on Harper's lower back. "Everything okay with you?"

"Mm. You wore me out back at mine this morning."

"I'm sorry. I couldn't keep my hands off you."

Harper turned her head, capturing Cait's lips slowly. "Don't ever be sorry. You're amazing."

"So, did you want to maybe find a place to stop and have something to eat?" Cait asked, her eyes bright and inviting. "I'm not sure what plans we have."

"Actually, I was hoping you'd join me on a lake cruise and then we'll head back to mine and get ready for this evening."

"Y-you want to go on a lake cruise?"

Harper wrapped her arms around Cait's waist. "Will you promise to hold my hand?"

"I'll *always* be here holding your hand."

"Then I'd really like to spend part of our day date shitting my pants while I spend some time with you."

"Harper…"

"No." Harper silenced Cait with a kiss. God, she could spend forever kissing this woman. "I want to do this, okay?"

"Okay."

"And then this evening, I'm taking you to that Mediterranean I was supposed to take you to many months ago."

Cait grinned, a look of true appreciation on her face. "Yeah?"

"Mmhmm. Anything for my one and only." Harper squeezed Cait one final time before reluctantly letting her go. If she could just hold onto this body until the end of eternity, life would be incredible.

"I love you."

Harper brushed a curl from Cait's face, her skin as soft as it ever was. "I love you, too."

SIGN UP TO WIN!

Sign up to my mailing list to be the first to hear about new releases, and to be in with a chance of winning books!

WWW.MELISSATEREZEAUTHOR.COM

DID YOU ENJOY IT?

Thank you for purchasing Breaking Routine.

I hope you enjoyed it. Please consider leaving a review on your preferred site. As an independent author, reviews help to promote our work. One line or two really does make the difference.

Thank you, truly.

Love,
Melissa x

ABOUT THE AUTHOR

Oh, hi! It's nice to see you!

I'm Melissa Tereze, author of The Arrangement, and other bestsellers. Born, raised, and living in Liverpool, UK, I spend my time writing angsty romance about complex, real-life, women who love women. My heart lies within the age-gap trope, but you'll also find a wide range of different characters and stories to sink your teeth into.

SOCIAL MEDIA

You can contact me through my social media or my website. I'm mostly active on Twitter.

❄

Twitter: @MelissaTereze
Facebook: www.facebook.com/MelissaC.Author
Instagram: @melissatereze_author
Find out more at: www.melissaterezeauthor.com
Contact: info@melissaterezeauthor.com

ALSO BY MELISSA TEREZE

Another Love Series

The Arrangement (Book One)

The Call (Book Two)

The Ashforth Series

Playing For Her Heart (Book One)

Holding Her Heart (Book Two)

Other Novels

Mrs Middleton

In Her Arms

Before You Go

Forever Yours

The Heat of Summer

Forget Me Not

More Than A Feeling

Where We Belong: Love Returns

Naked

Co-writes

Teach Me

Titles under L.M Croft (Erotica)

Pieces of Me